The Plays of Georgia Douglas Johnson

The Plays of Georgia Douglas Johnson

FROM THE NEW NEGRO RENAISSANCE TO THE CIVIL RIGHTS MOVEMENT

Edited and with an Introduction by

Judith L. Stephens

UNIVERSITY OF ILLINOIS PRESS

URBANA AND CHICAGO

Manufactured in the United States of America
∞ This book is printed on acid-free paper.
1 2 3 4 5 C P 5 4 3 2 1

Library of Congress Cataloging-in-Publication Data
Johnson, Georgia Douglas Camp, 1886–1966.
The plays of Georgia Douglas Johnson from the new Negro
renaissance to the civil rights movement / Georgia Douglas Johnson ;
edited and with an introduction by Judith L. Stephens.
p. cm.
Includes bibliographical references.
ISBN-13: 978-0-252-03092-5 (cloth : alk. paper)
ISBN-10: 0–252–03092–3 (cloth : alk. paper)
ISBN-13: 978-0-252-07333-5 (pbk. : alk. paper)
ISBN-10: 0-252-07333-9 (pbk. : alk. paper)
1. African Americans—Drama.
2. Civil rights movements—Drama.
I. Stephens, Judith L. (Judith Louise), 1943–
II. Title.
PS3519.0253A6 2005
812'.52—dc22 2005011095

In memory of my aunt,

Anna Louise Morris (1913–2004)

. . . best known to the family's younger generation as "Weezie."

Contents

Acknowledgments

Support for this volume came from many sources but I want to acknowledge especially the invaluable assistance of librarians and archivists: Joellen ElBashir, Moorland-Spingarn Research Center at Howard University; Karen L. Jefferson and Cathy Lynn Mundale, Atlanta University Center, Robert Woodruff Library; James V. Hatch and Camille Billops, Hatch-Billops Collection, New York City; Anthony Bogucki and Stephanie Poxon, Library of Congress; Diana Lachatanere and the librarians at the New York Public Library's Schomburg Center for Research in Black Culture; librarians and staff at the Beinecke Rare Book and Manuscript Library, Yale University; and Ann Snyder and Roseanne Chesakis at Penn State Schuylkill Campus. My gratitude to friends and colleagues Kathy Perkins, Winona Fletcher, William Mahar, Barbara Lewis, Eileen Smith, Koritha Mitchell, Ethel Pitts Walker, Lundeana Thomas, Vernell Lillie, David Krasner, Sandra Richards, Glenda Dickerson, Helen Hendy, Kelli Eberlein, Anita Vickers, Steve Littell, Marge Gaughan, Diane Evans, and members of the Black Theatre Network (BTN). Thanks to the Research Council of Penn State University's Capital College and to Provost and Dean Madlyn Haynes for granting me a sabbatical for fall semester of 2001 to carry out research for this project, as well as to Karen Correll for typing many of the plays. Thanks also to Julian Bond for his encouragement. Finally I acknowledge, with gratitude, the support of my family: Stephen E. and Nora Lea Garay; Mary Jane Stephens; Stephen R. and Suzie Garay; and their sons, Andrew and Jason.

A Note on Terminology

In matters of style, I have chosen to use the terms *Black* and *African American* interchangeably. I have capitalized *Black* and *White* when they appear as nouns, but not as adjectives. *Negro, Afro-American,* and *African American* appear when quoted or when appropriate to the period under discussion.

The Plays of Georgia Douglas Johnson

Introduction

Georgia Douglas Johnson (1877?–1966) was one of the earliest African American women playwrights and, with twenty-eight plays, one of the most prolific of her era.[1] From her home in Washington, D.C., she contributed to the artistic productivity of the Harlem, or "New Negro," Renaissance, as well as to early twentieth-century African American drama and the corresponding national black theatre movement. Although she was a multitalented artist, writing poems, plays, short stories, and music, most critical attention has focused on her poetry and her reputation as the "lady poet" of the New Negro Renaissance.[2] Examining Johnson's contributions as a playwright and generating a profile of her life in the theatre not only supplements the work of previous scholars, but also contributes to a fuller understanding of her place in cultural history and provides insight into her rich and complex dramatic vision.[3]

This volume is the first to focus on Johnson as a playwright and to include all of her extant plays. Only a few of her plays were published in her lifetime and, while some production records exist, documentation for the staging of many dramas is difficult to find, since they were mainly produced in schools, churches, lodges, YWCAs, and other amateur venues of the New Negro theatre.[4] Published here in their most complete form, Johnson's plays will be of interest to students and scholars of theatre, African American studies, women's studies, and cultural studies. Indeed, Johnson's plays will appeal to anyone interested in the cultural history of the United States, since they comprise one of the earliest and most diverse collections of dramas by an African American woman. Although other African American women such as Pauline Hopkins, Katherine Davis Chapman Tillman, Angelina Weld Grimké, Mary P. Burrill, and Alice Dunbar-Nelson wrote plays before Johnson, none were as prolific, as widely produced, nor as practiced in the dramatist's craft.

Johnson is a key figure in theatre history and her plays are landmark contributions to both African American theatre and American theatre in general. She wrote for community-based, nonprofit venues that offered alternatives to a predominantly white, male, and New York City–centered theatre; she was a pioneer in the national movement known as the New Negro theatre of the 1920s and 1930s; and she is the most prolific playwright in the American "lynching-drama" tradition.[5]

The twelve one-acts collected here represent Johnson's dramatic oeuvre and reflect both her productivity and versatility as an early twentieth-century black playwright. In this introduction, the plays are examined as a body of work initiated within the distinct historical, cultural, and critical contexts of the New Negro era and continued at least until the mid-1950s. The plays are discussed in relation to the generic categories Johnson created for them and, when information is available, in relation to their conditions of production and reception.

The Plays: Sources

Johnson's typescripts for ten of the plays are in collections housed in academic or public institutions. Typescripts of *Safe*, *A Sunday Morning in the South* (black church version), *A Sunday Morning in the South* (white church version), *Blue-Eyed Black Boy*, *William and Ellen Craft*, and *Frederick Douglass* are all in the script files of the Federal Theatre Project at the Library of Congress. Both versions of *A Sunday Morning in the South* are published together for the first time here, along with the musical scores Johnson arranged for them. *Paupaulekejo* is in the Georgia Douglas Johnson Papers at the Moorland-Spingarn Research Center at Howard University, and scripts for both *Starting Point* and *Paupaulekejo* are in the James Weldon Johnson Collection in the Beinecke Rare Book and Manuscript Library at Yale University. Typescripts of *A Bill To Be Passed* and *And Yet They Paused*, previously categorized as lost, were recovered by this author in 1999 in the National Association for the Advancement of Colored People (NAACP) Papers at the Library of Congress and are published here for the first time. *A Bill To Be Passed* and *And Yet They Paused* are essentially the same play, but with significant differences, especially the addition of a skit, *Kill That Bill*, attached to *A Bill To Be Passed* and written, not by Johnson, but by Robert E. Williams of the NAACP chapter in Cleveland,

Ohio. The typescripts have been edited here for consistency of format and obvious spelling errors. The play *Plumes* (1927) is reprinted with permission from publisher Samuel French. *Blue Blood*, published in 1926 by Appleton-Century as a single play (Johnson retained the copyright), is reprinted from the copy in Johnson's papers at Howard University's Moorland-Spingarn Research Center.[6] Johnson's radio play, *Brotherhood*, is lost but the music "Brotherhood Marching Song" (1945), written to accompany the play, is published here for the first time.

The collection is representative of Johnson's work as a playwright in that it reflects her preference for the one-act form; on the other hand, these twelve plays are less than half of her total dramatic output. In fact, according to her self-compiled "Catalogue of Writings" (copies at Moorland-Spingarn and the Library of Congress), Johnson wrote twenty-eight plays, most of them one-acts, that she arranged into four categories: "Radio Plays," "Primitive Life Plays," "Plays of Average Negro Life," and "Lynching Plays." Unfortunately, most of these works are lost. The transcript of an interview with Owen Dodson, former Howard University theatre professor and a friend of Johnson's, indicates that many of her unpublished manuscripts were discarded from her home following her funeral in 1966. Dodson remembers he "clearly saw manuscripts going into the garbage" and thinking, "a lifetime to the sanitation department!"[7]

Fortunately, in November 1992 (twenty-six years after Johnson's death), Karen L. Jefferson and Joellen ElBashir, both from Howard University's Moorland-Spingarn Research Center, were presented with the opportunity to rescue many of Johnson's papers that remained in her former home at 1461 S Street NW, Washington, D.C., before it was to be renovated and sold. According to ElBashir, curator at Moorland-Spingarn, four or five hours were spent collecting papers that eventually filled seven boxes.[8] Among the many papers that were retrieved were a typescript of Johnson's play *Paupaulekejo,* a copy of her Catalogue of Writings, miscellaneous pages from earlier versions of the Catalogue, and correspondence with major Harlem Renaissance figures such as Langston Hughes, Alain Locke, Jean Toomer, Jessie Redmon Fauset, and Zora Neale Hurston, as well as with 1921 Pulitzer Prize–winning playwright Zona Gale. Additional correspondence, relevant to Johnson's plays and dramatic productivity, is in collections at Atlanta University's Robert Woodruff Library, Yale University's Beinecke Library, and the New York Public Library's Schomburg

Center for Research in Black Culture. Most of Johnson's dramas are lost, but from her Catalogue, her extant plays, and her correspondence, it is possible to glean an outline of her contributions to the theatre and of her playwriting career.

Johnson as Playwright

Johnson's correspondence reveals her long career as a playwright who consistently sought feedback on her plays and struggled to see them published and produced. In reviewing and assessing Johnson's career as a dramatist, it is important to remember that she began writing plays during the 1920s, an era in which a black female playwright was an anomaly and when the groundbreaking theatrical successes of Lorraine Hansberry and Alice Childress were still decades away. As theatre historian Kathy Perkins points out, "the voice of the black woman playwright was slow to emerge because of racial and sexual barriers," and when Johnson's plays first appeared, "blacks were just learning the art of playwriting."[9]

As an African American woman playwright, Johnson was a pioneer. She was a member of the group of black women who wrote before 1950 and who became visible for their achievements in community theatre and through the one-act playwriting contests sponsored by the journals *Opportunity* and *The Crisis.*[10] Among this group of pioneering playwrights were Mary P. Burrill, Alice Dunbar-Nelson, Angelina Weld Grimké, Marita Bonner, Eulalie Spence, May Miller, and Zora Neale Hurston. In fact, Johnson, Harlem playwright Eulalie Spence, and Howard University student Thelma Duncan were the only black women included among the twenty playwrights whose work was published in Alain Locke's groundbreaking 1927 anthology *Plays of Negro Life: A Source-Book of Native American Drama.* While Johnson is a constituent member of this pioneering sisterhood, she also stands apart from the group due to her lifelong dedication to writing plays and seeking outlets for their publication or production. Johnson's career as a playwright extends from the decades of the Harlem/New Negro Renaissance to the mid-twentieth century's civil rights movement.[11]

As early as 1925 Johnson wrote to Howard University professor Alain Locke requesting his opinion of her recently completed *Blue Blood*, which she felt confident enough to describe as "a mighty good play."[12] In 1926 she submitted *Blue Blood* to the one-act play contest for dramas on black life, sponsored by the Urban League's journal *Opportunity*, and won honorable mention; in 1927 her play *Plumes* was awarded the competition's first prize. Between 1935 and 1939 Johnson submitted at least five plays to the Work Project Administration's (WPA) Federal Theatre Project; in 1937 she informed her friend and Harlem Renaissance art patron Harold Jackman that four of her plays were with a Broadway producer who "writes me very favorably." In 1936 she sent several of her plays on lynching to NAACP leader Walter White, and in 1938 she contributed her playwriting skills to the organization's national antilynching campaign. By 1943 she had submitted an entire "book of plays" for "appraisal with a view to publication" to the Wendell Malliet publishing company in New York.[13] Further correspondence with Harold Jackman reveals that Johnson continued to seek advice on publishing her book of plays in 1952, and as late as 1955 Johnson wrote to her friend Langston Hughes, thanking him for encouraging the "Phyllys [sic] Wheatly" YWCA to request one of her plays for production.[14] Johnson's letter to Hughes, written the same year that Alice Childress's *Trouble in Mind* opened at the Greenwich Mews Theatre in New York, marks a period of transition in which the pioneering, community-centered one-act dramas, written by the black women playwrights of the Harlem/New Negro Renaissance, were eclipsed by the work of critically and commercially successful dramatists of the 1950s civil rights era such as Childress and Lorraine Hansberry. While Johnson was grateful for a YWCA production in 1955, Childress's play would win an Obie award for best original off-Broadway play, and Hansberry's *Raisin in the Sun* (1959) was only a few years away from its revolutionary Broadway debut.[15] Johnson's playwriting career provides an important link in the history of black women playwrights; from the 1920s to the 1950s, she persevered in her craft and carried the "little theatre" spirit of the New Negro Renaissance to the brink of the civil rights movement.

By the time she tried her hand at playwriting, Johnson had already established her reputation as a poet with two published volumes, *Heart of a Woman and Other Poems* (1918) and *Bronze: A Book of Verse* (1922).[16] Johnson began her career as a playwright through the encouragement of friends, such as Pulitzer Prize–winning playwright Zona Gale (*Miss Lulu Bett,* 1921). By the time Johnson sent her play *Blue Blood* to Alain Locke in 1925 she had already received a supportive response from Gale.[17] Later, Johnson would dedicate her third volume of poetry to Gale, "whose appreciation, encouragement and helpful criticism have so heartened me."[18] In addition to Gale's influence, the friendship Johnson developed with black women playwrights such as Mary P. Burrill, Angelina Weld Grimké, and Alice Dunbar-Nelson (who had all seen their plays published and/or produced) was most likely another factor in her decision to write plays, as was the opportunity for publication and recognition provided by the *Crisis* and *Opportunity* one-act play contests. The fact that her early plays, *Blue Blood* and *Plumes*, garnered public praise undoubtedly provided further encouragement for Johnson and perhaps, at the same time, prompted fellow playwright Willis Richardson to observe, "Georgia Johnson was a poet [until] she saw that people paid more attention to plays than poems."[19] Johnson's own words from a July 1927 *Opportunity* interview suggest her career as a playwright was also driven by personal creative instincts: "I write because I love to write. . . . I was persuaded to try it [drama] and found it a living avenue and yet—the thing left most unfinished, less exploited, first relinquished, is still the nearest my heart and most dear."[20]

Johnson's long career as a playwright shows she did not "relinquish" her dramatic endeavors but continued to work in the genre for financial possibilities as well as artistic reasons. Johnson's practical, business-oriented approach to dramatic writing is reflected in her 1951 letter to Langston Hughes inviting him to collaborate with her on a play or pageant to be used by the Elks Grand Lodge. In soliciting Hughes's collaboration, Johnson writes, "I'm sure you can understand the *business* of it."[21] Although Hughes, citing previous commitments, turned down Johnson's offer to collaborate, he wrote, "I can see where it might be profitable . . . as hard as things theatrical are to get on, everything that helps toward a living production should be done" and added, "I'm sure you can write it your self."[22] Financial stability was a major concern for Johnson, especially after the 1925 death of her husband. As early as 1927 Johnson spoke of her "struggle to live beyond the reach of the Wolf's fingers."[23]

Shortly before her death Johnson finalized her Catalogue of Writings, which includes a synopsis for each of her twenty-eight plays, most of them unpublished.[24] Noting the emphasis Johnson placed on her dramas in the Catalogue, scholar Gloria T. Hull observed, "were it not for the peculiarities of the genre and the vagaries of literary fortune, she [Johnson] could have just as easily come down through history known predominantly as a playwright rather than a poet."[25] Johnson's Catalogue includes summaries of her books as well as lists of her short stories, songs, and organizations of affiliation, but the largest portion (five pages out of a total of eighteen) is devoted to the categorization and synopsis of her twenty-eight plays.

Johnson's Creative Environment: Washington, D.C., the New Negro Renaissance, and the Little Theatre Movement

Georgia Douglas Johnson (née Camp) was born of racially mixed parents in Atlanta, Georgia, attended the public schools of that city, and was a member of Atlanta University's Normal School class of 1893.[26] Johnson subsequently taught school in Marietta, Georgia, and later in Atlanta. In 1902 she resigned her teaching position to pursue her interest in music and attended the Oberlin Conservatory of Music in Ohio. Years later Johnson would write, "Long years ago when the world was new for me, I dreamed of being a composer—wrote songs, many of them."[27] Johnson wrote music from 1898 until 1959, and she incorporated music into several of her plays. *A Sunday Morning in the South*, *A Bill To Be Passed*, *And Yet They Paused*, *Starting Point*, and *Brotherhood* all include the sounds of hymns, spirituals, marches, or the blues, while *Paupaulekejo,* one of the era's earliest plays set in Africa, calls for the sounds of "jungle music."

After studying at Oberlin, Johnson returned to Atlanta, where she served briefly in the public school system as assistant principal. In 1903 she married Henry Lincoln Johnson, an Atlanta attorney, and in 1910 moved to Washington, D.C., with her husband and two young sons, Henry Lincoln Jr. (1906–1990) and Peter Douglas Johnson (1907–1957). Johnson lived in Washington until her death at Freedmen's Hospital in 1966.[28]

When Georgia Douglas Johnson moved to Washington, the city was already recognized as a black cultural capital, known especially for its college-educated elite society. Civic leader Mary Church Terrell, local NAACP president Archibald Grimké, and Howard University Professor Kelly Miller were a few of the eminent Washingtonians who worked to encourage racial pride and self-help in the black community, while they simultaneously battled segregation and discriminatory laws. Recalling the city's many forms of covert racism, as well as the segregated train cars running between the nation's capital and southern states, playwright and theatre historian Loften Mitchell described Washington prior to the 1950s as "a citadel of jimcrow."[29]

Despite the capital city's white hostility, Johnson exhibited an ambition, pride, and resiliency that were undoubtedly sustained by what music scholar Mark Tucker has termed "the black consciousness of Washington D.C." Tucker credits the city's large number of black professionals, especially doctors and lawyers, and institutions such as Howard University and M Street High School (later known as Dunbar High) for Washington's reputation as "a place that fired black ambition, fostered black pride, and honored black achievement."[30] Theatre historian Winona Fletcher noted that Johnson was both artist and activist, "a participant and leader in most of the groups and organizations in the Washington area committed to concerns of women and minorities," and scholar Gloria T. Hull characterized Johnson's move to the nation's capital as a "turning point" that "sharpened the pace of her life" and "provided opportunity for broadening contacts."[31]

As an educated woman with a strong interest in the arts and culture, Johnson benefited from living in a black community that fostered a drive to excel as well as a resilient optimism. Scholars who have examined Johnson's life have frequently commented on her "undaunted optimism" even in the face of her many rejections on grant applications that, if successful, would have allowed her time to focus more fully on her writing. In 1950 Johnson wrote to Harold Jackman, "You would be surprised to know how many foundations I have tried, and more surprised to learn that each one said 'no' but *most* surprised to learn that I still have high hopes—am looking with my heart's bright eyes to the bright tomorrow!"[32]

Johnson's life in Washington, D.C., spanned decades of racial discrimination as well as social change: years of segregation in government offices and the barring of Negroes from city restaurants, barber shops, theatres, and hotels; the founding of the local branch of the NAACP in 1912; the 1919 race riot; a 1925 Ku Klux Klan parade on Monument grounds; the 1939 Marian Anderson concert at the Lincoln Memorial; the 1954 integration of the city's public schools; and the 1963 funeral procession of assassinated president John F. Kennedy.[33] Throughout these changing social conditions and historic events, Georgia Douglas Johnson doggedly pursued her crafts as a playwright, poet, and composer.

Johnson's involvement in theatre, coupled with her interest in interracial efforts, served to help dismantle previously impenetrable racial barriers in Washington. In her 1929 letter to Mr. George E. Haynes, secretary of the Harmon Foundation, Johnson thanked him for his work in organizing a National Interracial Conference, and reported she had recently attended "a tea at Stoneleigh Court [one of the most exclusive and luxurious apartment complexes in the Washington area] to talk about putting on plays in Washington." "This was," Johnson adds, referring to the interracial nature of the meeting, "a primal move for this group."[34]

Breaking down racial barriers through accomplishments in art and literature and asserting pride in black identity were complementary philosophies of the Harlem/New Negro Renaissance. The flowering of art and literature generated by the Harlem Renaissance coincided with the little theatre movement, a nationwide movement to create community-centered, amateur (not-for-profit) theatres where plays (mostly one-acts) could be inexpensively produced. During the same time period, roughly the early decades of the twentieth century, American playwrights were attempting to forge a "native drama" by drawing on the folk life, customs, and speech patterns common to a particular people, culture, or region. Like many playwrights who wrote for community (little theatre) venues across the nation, Johnson attempted to capture the idioms, patterns, and rhythms of speech common to black families living in a particular location, time period, or community.

While a few early twentieth-century white playwrights such as Ridgely Torrence (*Three Plays for A Negro Theatre,* 1914); Eugene O'Neill (*The Emperor Jones,* 1920); and Paul Green (*No 'Count Boy,* 1924) wrote about black life, many of their portrayals of black people were degrading, or at best unconvincing, because they reproduced the old, negative stereotypes such as the lazy buffoon or razor-toting criminal (for men), or the caretaking mammy or over-sexualized floozy (for women). Ralph Matthews, theatre columnist for the (Baltimore) *Afro American,* reasoned that a "Negro theatre" could hardly be classified as such if the productions for the most part were from the pens of white playwrights. "Through their productions," wrote Matthews, "seeps an unconscious strain of Ofay psychology that presents the Negro not as he sees himself but as he is seen through the condescending eyes of the detached observer."[35] Similarly, race leader and historian Carter G. Woodson acknowledged contemporary white playwrights who were attempting to portray black life on the American stage but cautioned, "They see that the thing is possible, and they are trying to do it; but at best they misunderstand the Negro because they cannot think black."[36]

Heated discussion surrounding the portrayal of black characters was equaled by debates on the use of dialect. Plays of the Negro little theatre occupy a unique position in the literary heritage of the Harlem Renaissance, since they offer an aural language, words intended primarily for the voices of black performers. James Weldon Johnson contended that Opal Cooper's delivery of the dream speech in the New York production of Ridgely Torrence's *Rider of Dreams* was the "finest representation" of the intonation practiced by the "old time Negro preachers"; this comment suggests the challenges stage dialogue presented to both playwrights and performers.[37] In 1924 New Negro playwright Willis Richardson wrote, "Every phase and condition of life may be depicted [in Negro drama]. . . .The lives and problems of the educated with their perfect language and manners may be shown as well as the lives and problems of the less fortunate who still use the dialect . . . .We have learned the English language but the dialect of the slave days is still the Mother tongue of the American Negro."[38] Theatre scholar Leslie Catherine Saunders credits Richardson for making an important connection between his dialect-speaking characters and his middle-class audiences, but she cites Georgia Douglas Johnson as one of the few playwrights who reproduced more accurately "the vivid imagery and rhythms characteristic of black speech."[39] Saunders asserts, "one of the most novel aspects of the serious Negro theatre was its use of dialect for sentiments other than comic [as seen in minstrelsy]—its demonstration that dialect could be eloquent."[40]

The dialogue in Georgia Douglas Johnson's plays, including her use of dialect, attests to her sensitivity to the spoken word and her skill in reproducing human speech that is an integral part of her characters. In the black church version of *A Sunday Morning in the South,* Sue Griggs asks her seven-year-old grandson, Bossie, where the food on his breakfast plate has disappeared to, and he responds by smiling, rubbing his stomach, and saying, "It's gone down the red lane struttin'."[41] In *William and Ellen Craft* (set in "slavery time") the character of Mandy, an elderly slave, warns: "Dey caught Jack and Sophie last night and whupped 'em till dey tole all about de secret plans and meetin' places."[42] In *Starting Point*, set in Charleston, South Carolina, in the 1930s, hard-working Henry Robinson complies with his wife's plea to rest his weary feet by responding: "You're mighty right—my feet seem like they don't belong to me a'tall, they're that tired—Let me get my slippers."[43] The dialogue in Johnson's plays (some of which may be too easily dismissed as "outmoded dialect" by contemporary readers) was carefully crafted to reflect the variety of ages, education levels, and social classes of her characters as well as the time period and regional black communities in which they live.

The ideas of the little theatre movement, the Harlem/New Negro Renaissance, and the search for a "native" American theatre were conjoining influences on Johnson's construction of dialogue, characters, and settings. As a prolific playwright of the New Negro era, Johnson participated in, and was undoubtedly energized by, ongoing debates concerning the nature and goals of a "real" Negro theatre, the use of dialect, the portrayal of black characters, and the role of white playwrights in the Negro little theatre movement.

Since the white-dominated American theatre of the 1920s and 1930s did not welcome either black artists or audiences, leaders in the African American community took it upon themselves to create the necessary opportunities for black artists. Theatre historian Addell Austin (Anderson) has summed up the situation succinctly: "Blacks believed that their own writers could portray themselves more realistically. What was needed were vehicles to promote these writers and their works."[44]

One of the most dynamic and versatile black leaders was writer and visionary W. E. B. Du Bois, who, as editor of the NAACP's magazine *The Crisis*, launched a literary contest for black playwrights that offered cash prizes and publication for the best one-act plays that dealt with black history or experience. Du Bois also founded the Krigwa Players Little Negro Theatre to produce a "real Negro theatre" that would address itself to the black community. In the words of Du Bois, the theatre would be "About us, By us, For us, and Near us."[45] While mandating that the emphasis would be on promoting plays written by black playwrights and intended for black audiences, Du Bois added that artists of all races would be welcome as would "all beautiful ideas." Charles S. Johnson, editor of the Urban League's journal, *Opportunity*, also offered cash prizes and publication for the best black-authored one-act plays dealing with black experience.

In addition to W. E. B. Du Bois and Charles S. Johnson, Alain Locke and Montgomery Gregory were also important as cultural leaders who created opportunities for black theatre artists. As professors at Howard University, they established the Howard Players and the Department of Dramatic Arts as a professional training ground for actors, directors, and designers. While overseeing the Howard productions, Locke and Gregory edited *Plays of Negro Life: A Source-Book of Native American Drama* (1927), the earliest anthology of plays focusing on black life. While all of these leading figures were dedicated to promoting black playwrights and the development of black drama, important philosophical differences existed. Discussions of black theatre in the Harlem/New Negro Renaissance invariably address the differing theories of black drama held by Locke and Du Bois. Essentially, Du Bois favored "propaganda plays" that revealed the racial prejudice and violence encountered by black Americans, while Locke promoted "folk drama" that focused on black themes and characters but without emphasizing racial oppression.[46] Many playwrights of the period, including Johnson, combined strands of both types in a single work. Of course, other types of plays were written, such as plays addressing the historical themes of slavery or African heritage, but the Locke/Du Bois debate (folk drama versus protest drama) produced much of the theatre theory in the New Negro era.

The one-act play contests, theoretical debates, and little theatre movement contributed to the formation of amateur theatres in black communities throughout the nation. The Harlem Experimental Theatre, the Krigwa Players (with units in Harlem, Baltimore, Washington, D.C., and Denver), the Cube Theatre (Chicago), the Howard Players, and various Negro units of the Federal Theatre Project were only a few of the newly formed play-producing organizations in the 1920s and 1930s. Theatre scholar James V. Hatch has described the proliferation of plays, dramatic theories, and production venues in the Harlem/New Negro Renaissance as "a theatre that could speak to and for African Americans." "During those years," Hatch continues, "black playwrights injected very serious business into amateur theatre with drama that embraced more than entertainment."[47]

Into the highly creative atmosphere of a developing New Negro drama, black women playwrights such as Johnson brought their own approaches to creating self-defined images, resisting stereotypes, and responding to new opportunities to reach a wider public. Nellie McKay has recognized the Harlem/New Negro Renaissance as a special time in the evolution of black women playwrights because they produced a drama that is both woman-centered and racially conscious while they struggled to find a place for themselves in a burgeoning theatre tradition.[48] As Kathy Perkins has pointed out, women outnumbered men in submitting plays to the one-act play contests and most of the award winners were women.[49]

The era's black women playwrights, such as Johnson, Zora Neale Hurston, Alice Dunbar-Nelson, Mary P. Burrill, May Miller, and Angelina Weld Grimké, were, to a certain extent, considered privileged women in their day because they were college educated and possessed a cultural awareness that was rare among the masses of black people. Fully conscious that they were writing at a time when the majority of black women, whether rural or urban, earned meager wages by working in some type of domestic service, these playwrights wrote about all classes of black people in an attempt to create authentic portraits of black life. These women were not professional playwrights in that they did not make their living from writing but supported themselves with other full-time jobs. Many were teachers, a few (such as Johnson) were government workers, others worked at a variety of jobs, but all were aware that opportunities for black women playwrights in the white-dominated professional American theatre were non-existent.[50] These playwrights wrote for the love and challenge of writing, for their communities, and for recognition as artists.

When Johnson's husband died in 1925, she worked at various day jobs to support herself and her two sons; in a letter to Alain Locke, Johnson noted that, except for Sundays, she worked from 8:00 A.M. to 6:30 P.M.[51] For several years she was employed as a Commissioner of Conciliation in the Department of Labor, but while she spent her days earning a living, she managed to find time to write poetry, drama, music, and short stories from her home in Washington. During the 1920s and 1930s, her home became a gathering place for writers and artists and, of special interest to this study, pioneering playwrights, directors, and theorists of the New Negro theatre. The leadership Johnson provided in building a community of black artists and intellectuals in Washington is an accomplishment that equals and complements her own contributions as a playwright, poet, and composer.

Johnson's "Saturday Nighters" and the New Negro Theatre

Shortly after moving to Washington, Johnson began to hold gatherings of artists and writers in her home at 1461 S Street NW. These informal Saturday-night gatherings, attended by friends and artists who called themselves the "Saturday Nighters," are sometimes referred to as Johnson's "S Street Salon."[52] These gatherings in Johnson's home are memorialized in works such as Langston Hughes's autobiography *The Big Sea;*[53] histories of the Harlem/New Negro Renaissance such as David Levering Lewis's *When Harlem Was in Vogue;*[54] and most recently in Elizabeth's McHenry's *Forgotten Readers: Recovering the Lost History of African American Literary Societies* (2002). While Lewis characterizes the literary gatherings in Johnson's home as "a freewheeling jumble of the gifted, famous, and odd," McHenry more fully examines the "safe and supportive" atmosphere of Johnson's home as a place "where Harlem Renaissance writers struggled with their literary work and where that work found its first audience."[55] Part of the attraction of Johnson's Saturday-night gatherings was their informal nature: Langston Hughes remembered Johnson's home as a place where artists would come to "eat Mrs. Johnson's cake and drink her wine and talk poetry and books and plays," and Johnson's good friend, poet and playwright May Miller, commented, "everything Georgia Douglas did was informal. . . . Maybe ten people would attend at a time. . . . It was a drop in place. . . . And she just made everybody at home."[56]

Johnson's home became a hub of activity in the New Negro Renaissance, and the gatherings included major Renaissance writers such as Langston Hughes, Jean Toomer, Jessie Redmon Fauset, and Zora Neale Hurston. Of even greater importance to this study, most of the primary figures of early twentieth-century black theatre congregated in Johnson's home. Dramatists whose work is now recognized as definitive of black theatre in the New Negro era such as Angelina Weld Grimké (*Rachel*, 1916), Willis Richardson (*The Chip Woman's Fortune*, 1923), Mary P. Burrill (*Aftermath*, 1919, and *They That Sit in Darkness,* 1919), Alice Dunbar-Nelson (*Mine Eyes Have Seen*, 1918), May Miller (*Graven Images*, 1929), Zora Neale Hurston (*Color Struck*, 1925), and Marita Bonner (*The Purple Flower*, 1928) attended Johnson's soirees.[57] In addition to these playwrights, leading black theatre theorists Alain Locke and W. E. B. Du Bois , as well as Howard University theatre director and historian Montgomery Gregory attended the gatherings.[58] Johnson's home became one of the major sites outside of New York where the leading dramatists, directors, theorists, and theatre historians of the New Negro era would meet and exchange ideas on a regular basis.

Since Johnson's salon was a place where artists would share their work and experiment with new ideas, many of the era's landmark publications were conceived in her home. According to playwright Willis Richardson, "Every Saturday night we used to meet at nine o'clock and stay until two or three in the morning, discussing things like writing . . . some would read their poems and they would discuss them."[59] Georgia Douglas Johnson's house was the site where writer and artist Richard Bruce Nugent first met Langston Hughes and where they later discussed ideas that subsequently led to the publication of the provocative and experimental *Fire!!* (1926).[60] This was a journal of art and literature devoted to younger Negro artists; only one issue was printed. Johnson's house also provided a setting where the charismatic Jean Toomer read from his greatest work, *Cane* (1922).[61] Reflecting Toomer's southern and racially mixed ancestry, *Cane* is a literary work that expresses African American life and culture through poetry, prose, and drama.

Within this nurturing and creative environment, plays were undoubtedly read and discussed. It is not unlikely that scenes from dramas by Johnson, Grimké, Richardson, Burrill, and others were read and critiqued by the playwrights as well as by other artists who were gathered in Johnson's home for the evening. In fact, it was at one of these Saturday-night gatherings that playwright Willis Richardson and race leader and historian Carter G. Woodson began discussing "the stage as a means for teaching black students," which led to the publication of Richardson's 1930 anthology *Plays and Pageants from the Life of the Negro*. Richardson's collection was intended primarily for use in the schools and, according to scholar Christine Gray, was "the first anthology to contain only plays written by African Americans."[62]

Johnson's salon was also the setting where playwright May Miller was persuaded, by Woodson, to collaborate with Richardson on their landmark anthology *Negro History in Thirteen Plays* (1935).[63] In addition to several of their own plays, Richardson and Miller's anthology included two dramas by Georgia Douglas Johnson and a play by black theatre pioneer Randolph

Edmonds, another salon attendee. The anthology was introduced by Woodson as a collection representing "the vision of the Negro in the new day" and as "another step of the Negro toward the emancipation of his mind from the slavery of the inferiority complex."[64] This drama anthology and Richardson's, both sparked by the creative and supportive atmosphere of Johnson's salon, were among the first of their kind and are recognized by theatre scholars and historians as cutting-edge publications of the New Negro era.

Johnson's influence on the New Negro Renaissance, both as a writer and as a cultural sponsor, is reflected in the comments of younger writers. Critic Cedric Dover credited Johnson with being the first writer to instill pride in peoples of mixed-race origin: "We found in her the blood and bone we needed to fight the evangelists of colored inferiority and their converts within our own groups."[65] In his Harlem Renaissance memoir, Glenn Carrington compared Johnson's importance to that of Alain Locke when he wrote, "If Dr. Alain Locke was godfather to the younger writers and artists, Mrs. Johnson was certainly their godmother."[66]

Studies of the New Negro Renaissance have overlooked the importance of Johnson's influence, possibly because she practiced an informal brand of community building that was closely tied to her home as a site of artistic activity. While Professor Alain Locke's intellectual leadership in the Harlem Renaissance is universally acknowledged, Georgia Douglas Johnson's role as community builder has been marginalized by the title "hostess." Gloria T. Hull has suggested "cultural sponsor" as a more appropriate term for recognizing Johnson's contributions in building and sustaining the era's artistic community, and Elizabeth McHenry's recent study *Forgotten Readers* provides a detailed account of Johnson's leadership role.

Johnson's salon was not racially exclusive nor were invitations limited to writers and artists. According to David Levering Lewis, white poets such as Edna St. Vincent Millay, Vachel Lindsay, and Rebecca West were known to have attended the gatherings.[67] Johnson would also invite incarcerated men with whom she had corresponded, once they were released. Johnson may have met and corresponded with the prisoners through the encouragement of her close friend Glenn Carrington, one of the earliest black parole officers.[68]

At times, meetings at Johnson's house were decidedly political in nature.

When A. Philip Randolph and Chandler Owen were working to unionize sleeping-car porters, Johnson's home provided them with a platform. After Randolph became president of the Brotherhood of Sleeping Car Porters (organized in 1925), he wrote to Johnson expressing his gratitude for "the time when you got a few friends together at your home to meet Chandler Owen and myself who were outlawed and recognized as ungodly radicals. You were among the very few who were willing to even listen to us and did it despite our criticism of your splendid husband and Judge Terrell."[69]

Known as a person with a big heart, Johnson took in and cared for out-of-luck artists as well as stray cats and dogs; she also organized a correspondence club "for lonely people all over the world." Johnson named her home "Half-Way House" because she saw herself as "halfway between everybody and everything and trying to bring them together" and also because she wanted to make her home "a place where anyone who would fight halfway to survive could do so."[70] "Half-Way House" appears in capital letters under Johnson's name on the title page of her Catalogue of Writings and on pages of her personal stationery.

In later years, Johnson's S Street salon served as an inspiration for her own writing. In the completed version of her Catalogue, Johnson recorded the title "The Literary Salon" and described it as "a book," on the literary gatherings in her home, "that began under the Taft administration and continued into the years indefinitely."[71] But unbound pages from earlier versions of her Catalogue at Moorland-Spingarn Center suggest that Johnson was, at least at some point in time, working to shape her memories of the Saturday Nighters into a stage performance. On a single page, where she had listed the titles of her published plays, Johnson wrote: "PERSONS AS THEY APPEAR ON THE STAGE OF THE SALON (SILHOUETTED)" and listed the following individuals:

Toomer, Jean
Locke, Alain Leroy . . . Rhodes Scholar
Wm. Stanley Braithwaite . . . Anthologist
W. E. B. Du Bois. . . World Scholar
Grimkee [sic], Angelina
Jackson, Mae Howard . . . Sculptor
Hughes, Langston . . .
Dodson, Owen[72]

This entry from an early version of Johnson's Catalogue suggests she was experimenting with the idea of a dramatization that would capture some of the events and personalities of her literary salon. It's possible that Johnson's initial idea was to present each salon figure individually in silhouette, delivering a monologue, or perhaps several characters would appear together, moving on and off the stage at different times, engaging in discussion and debate, or reading from their work. Whatever type of dramatization Johnson had in mind, the mix of personalities and events from the Saturday Nighters could provide today's directors with material and inspiration for a uniquely creative and historical performance. At the time, Johnson was persistent, although unsuccessful, in her efforts to tell the story of her literary salon. Her correspondence reveals that as late as 1964, two years before her death, she was still trying to publish her "literary salon book."[73]

As a center for artistic gatherings and, at times, political activity in Washington, Johnson's home played a major role in establishing the New Negro Renaissance community. It is clear that Johnson's informal salon was a place in which literary works were read and plans for important collaborations were made. Hull has suggested that Johnson's role as a cultural sponsor was all the more important because she played it away from Harlem, thus providing an impetus for the intercity connections that helped to make the movement a truly national one. Salon attendees characterized Johnson as a "catalyst" and "magnet," always noting her ability to bring people together.[74] Considering her own contributions in drama, poetry, and music, as well as the artistic activity nurtured and generated by her Saturday-night gatherings, Johnson's former home at 1461 S Street NW (currently a private residence) deserves recognition and preservation as a historic site and cultural landmark.

The Plays—Genres and Themes

Johnson was an innovative and activist playwright speaking to the issues of her time and creating socially conscious dramas that explored the effects of racial injustice on families and communities. At times she courageously addressed topics most other playwrights avoided. Plays such as *Blue-Eyed Black Boy* and *Blue Blood* address the issue of miscegenation and interrogate the formation of racial identity in America by exposing the historical relationship between race and violence. Her unprecedented and unflinching focus on the brutality of lynching, beginning with *A Sunday Morning in the South* (c. 1925) and culminating in *A Bill To Be Passed* (1938), reflects her overriding concern with racial violence as well as her involvement in the NAACP's national antilynching campaign and the Writers League Against Lynching.

While Johnson was bold in choosing to create plays dealing with racially charged subject matter, she also wrote plays that were lighthearted and intended as pure entertainment. For example, her synopsis of her (lost) play *Holiday* indicates a mix of humor and romance:

> Plain sister remains at home while attractive ones take holiday. Eligible visitor meets girl as she prepares for solitary lunch in home alone, falls in love with her. When sisters return, they are chagrined by her wonderful fiancée. Cinderella type.[75]

Johnson's plays are notable for their variety of themes and characters. Her originality and versatility as a playwright are reflected in the dramatic genres she created to organize and preserve a record of her productivity. In her Catalogue of Writings Johnson arranged the titles and plot summaries of her twenty-eight dramas under the categories of "Primitive Life Plays," "Historical Plays," "Plays of Average Negro Life," "Lynching Plays," and "Radio Plays."

Primitive Life Plays

Both *Blue Blood* and *Plumes*, listed in the Catalogue as Primitive Life Plays, are Johnson's most frequently published and produced dramas. Johnson eagerly took advantage of the unprecedented opportunities for black playwrights offered by the one-act play contests sponsored by the journals *Opportunity* and *Crisis*. She submitted *Blue Blood* to the 1926 *Opportunity* contest and won honorable mention; in the 1927 contest, she won first prize with *Plumes*. *Blue Blood* treats the subject of white men's sexual exploitation of black women as two black mothers discover that their children, who are about to be married, have the same white father, while *Plumes* concerns a black southern mother's struggle with poverty and the approaching death of her young daughter. By featuring middle-aged black southern women as central characters and locating the action in their kitchens, *Blue Blood* and *Plumes* established a female-centered precedent for most of Johnson's later plays and placed a generally ignored population on the American stage.

Both of Johnson's award-winning dramas were produced and published in the New Negro little theatre venues. *Blue Blood* was produced in 1927 by pioneering black theatre groups such as W. E. B. Du Bois's Krigwa (Crisis Guild of Writers and Artists) Players at the 135th Street branch of the New York Public Library and, later, by Gough McDaniels's Krigwa group in Baltimore, as well as by the Howard Players in 1933.[76] *Blue Blood* was published as an individual play by Appleton-Century and also included in Frank Shay's *Fifty More Contemporary One-Act Plays* (1928), a collection intended for use by little theatre groups throughout the nation. Johnson and Willis Richardson supplied Shay's collection with the only two plays written specifically for black little theatre groups. After the list of characters in *Blue Blood*, a line in italics reads: "These characters are Negroes."

Plumes, published in 1927 by *Opportunity* and in 1928 by Samuel French, appeared in Alain Locke's groundbreaking collection *Plays of Negro Life* (1927) and in V. F. Calverton's *The Anthology of American Literature* (1929). A 1927 New York *Amsterdam News* review praised the play as "real Negro literature," since it was written by a Negro author, had a Negro theme, and was intended for a Negro audience.[77] Years later, in 1951, Langston Hughes wrote to Johnson that *Plumes* "is one of the best little plays I've ever seen."[78]

In addition to receiving the first-place award in the *Opportunity* contest and appearing in groundbreaking collections, *Plumes* was produced by the Harlem Experimental Theatre (1928–1931). According to Regina Andrews, one of the theatre's founders, the Harlem Experimental Theatre followed in the footsteps of Du Bois's Krigwa Players and sought to produce plays in Harlem, "where the black playwright's audience lived."[79] Meeting in the apartment Regina Andrews shared with Ethel Ray Nance (assistant to *Opportunity* editor Charles S. Johnson) and in the135th Street library, Harlem artists, writers, and community leaders envisioned and organized a theatre that furnished opportunities for aspiring Negro actors, directors, and designers and provided a laboratory for the Negro playwright. *Plumes* was also produced in 1927 by the "little" Cube Theatre in Chicago and by student and community organizations such as the Students Literary Guild at the Central YMCA in Brooklyn.[80]

As two of Johnson's earliest plays, *Blue Blood* and *Plumes* were major contributions to the development of black theatre in the New Negro era. Their significance is evident by their presence in major publications and on programs of landmark theatres. Locke's *Plays of Negro Life*, Du Bois's Krigwa Players, the journal *Opportunity*, the Howard Players, the Harlem Experimental Theatre, the Cube Theatre in Chicago, and various YWCAs were all vital venues in the New Negro little theatre movement. The high visibility of Johnson's *Blue Blood* and *Plumes* provided the movement with a focus on the struggles of black southern women. Due to its vivid examination of race, class, and gender, as well as its appearance in Locke's *Plays of Negro Life*, *Plumes* is the play most frequently chosen by contemporary editors to represent Johnson's work.[81]

Red Shoes and *Well Diggers* are two lost plays included in Johnson's Primitive Life Plays category. According to Johnson's summary, *Red Shoes* was written for actress Rose McClendon and portrays a mother who buys a pair of "precious" red shoes for her baby's burial only to have them stolen and sold for whiskey by the father. When the father steals the shoes back again, he is arrested and taken to jail but wins the forgiveness of his wife.[82] In her correspondence, Johnson wrote the title as "Red Slippers" and described the drama as "a one-act play with a touch of tragedy and pathos."[83] *Well Diggers* concerns two black lawyers in the South who hold conflicting views of trial ethics; one wins a case defending a well digger by flattering the judge "at the expense of Negro character," while the other's disapproval ends their partnership.[84] Unlike *Plumes* and *Blue Blood*, both of these plays remain obscure, and documentation of neither play's production has been found.

Exactly what Johnson meant by the phrase "Primitive Life Plays" is unclear. During the 1920s, the Cult of Primitivism, or the demand for the "primitive" or "exotic" by Anglo-American patrons, promoted a bifurcated and stereotyped image of the Negro. Blacks were seen either as innocent, naive, and an uncorrupted remnant of preindustrial life or as illiterate, superstitious savages. Primitivism, as David Krasner points out, "allowed for the reduction of black culture to either inferiority or idealization; primitives may be child like and violent but they may also be 'noble savages.'"[85]

A review of Johnson's extant plays and plot summaries in this category suggests she is not using the term "primitive" to refer to black people or culture in the condescending sense meaning "irrational, uncivilized and not-yet modern."[86] Nor does it appear she meant plays that focus only on the lives of poor, rural, southern Blacks. A trait notably shared by the four plays is that they each reveal how all classes of black Americans, attorneys as well as washerwomen, continued to struggle with repercussions from institutionalized slavery such as severe poverty (*Plumes* and *Red Shoes*), the progeny of white men's sexual exploitation of black women (*Blue Blood*), and the pervasiveness of negative black stereotypes in both black and white communities (*Well Diggers*). The texts and plot summaries of the four plays listed under the Primitive Life category suggest Johnson's own interpretation of the term "primitive" was not the pervasive modernist interpretation that viewed black people as either innocent and "unspoiled by European decadence" or as uncivilized and unrestrained. Instead, Johnson's Primitive Life plays serve to shift the focus away from black *people* as "primitive," toward a consideration of the uncivilized (primitive) institution of slavery, its far-reaching effects, and of how post-emancipation African Americans must deal daily with its consequences.

Johnson's independence in devising dramatic categories suggests she developed her own views on the theatre and maintained a clear sense of the contribution made by her plays. Unlike Locke and Du Bois, Johnson theorized theatre through decades of writing plays and seeking out venues for their production. She did not use the now familiar descriptions "folk plays" or "protest/propaganda plays" to categorize her dramas. Although *Plumes* is subtitled "A Folk Tragedy" in Locke's *Plays of Negro Life*, Johnson didn't use that subtitle. She does not apply the phrases "folk tragedy" or "folk drama" to the play in her Catalogue, and when *Plumes* was first published in *Opportunity* it was subtitled simply "A One-Act Play."[87] Since Locke favored the term "folk drama," it is possible that, as editor of the collection, he attached the descriptive phrase "folk tragedy" to Johnson's drama (an award-winning play), to promote his theory of black theatre. Whether he did this with or without Johnson's approval must be left to conjecture.[88]

Historical Plays

Johnson's Historical plays focus on antebellum black heroes and heroines and were possibly produced in the Washington, D.C., schools. Both *William and Ellen Craft* and *Frederick Douglass* are easily produced plays with a single setting. *William and Ellen Craft* depicts a tension-filled escape from slavery by a young couple willing to risk their lives for freedom, while *Frederick Douglass* portrays the famed abolitionist's love interest and his sudden dash for freedom disguised as a sailor. Both escapes are made via a northbound train and are assisted by friends who remain behind in the slave community. According to Johnson's Catalogue, an alternate, nonextant version of *Frederick Douglass* included a second scene depicting a white church in Boston, where the abolitionist speeches of a subsequently free Douglass and of William Lloyd Garrison are overheard and reported by a black group standing outside the church's window. (Creating a situation in which onstage characters report an ongoing but unseen or offstage event was a technique Johnson frequently employed.)

In dramatizing the events leading up to each escape, Johnson displays her mastery of building suspense through intrigue, disguise, sound effects, and close attention to the details of character and situation. *William and Ellen Craft* includes a scene in which Ellen must disguise herself as a white man, "young Marse [master] Charles," as part of the escape plan:

> ELLEN: But how kin I be like young Marse? I'm all shakin' now.
> WILLIAM (soothing her): All you got to do is walk. You don't have to talk, you don't have to do a thing but just walk along bigity like a white man. See here. (Shows her how to walk.) Try it.
> ELLEN (Tries to walk like him.): Dis way?
> WILLIAM: You doin fine![89]

This scene recalls earlier (antebellum) "entertainments" by slaves whose performances often mocked the arrogance, habits, or demeanor of the white master or plantation owner.[90] As a playwright, Johnson knew the value of entertaining her audience while also educating about the courage of slaves who attempted an escape to freedom. While Johnson's plays are model history lessons taught in an engaging and memorable way, Claudia Tate notes they serve an additional valuable function by focusing on "intimate moments in the lives of these runaway slaves that were effaced in abolitionist documents."[91]

In a 1972 interview, playwright and poet May Miller, a close friend of Johnson's, stressed the importance of men such as Carter G. Woodson and Randolph Edmonds (both Saturday Nighters) as innovators in the effort to dramatize black history.[92] Woodson felt that many school students were not taught sufficiently about black history and were thus unaware of the great black heroes and heroines of the past. Willis Richardson and May Miller's *Negro History in Thirteen Plays* (1935) was one of the earliest attempts to fill this educational void. In addition to Johnson's *Frederick Douglass* and *William and Ellen Craft*, the anthology included plays on other heroic figures such as Crispus Attucks, Nat Turner, Harriett Tubman, and Sojourner Truth. Vague references to productions of Johnson's Historical Plays exist: for example, in a letter to Harold Jackman, Johnson wrote, "Tomorrow they are putting on *William and Ellen Craft* here in Washington. I don't know if you have seen it."[93]

Between 1935 and 1938, Johnson submitted *Frederick Douglass* and *William and Ellen Craft* to the Federal Theatre Project (FTP) but neither was produced. Since the FTP was envisioned during the Depression era by WPA director Harry Hopkins as a "free, adult, uncensored theatre national in scope and regional in emphasis," scholar Winona Fletcher reasoned that Johnson was "encouraged by expectations that the FTP would be a haven for fledgling playwrights, that experimental productions not likely to get produced elsewhere would be mounted, that plays of social protest would be welcomed, and that serious dramatic efforts would be judged on their merits."[94]

In three FTP reader reports, *William and Ellen Craft* is critiqued as "a fair dramatic story of the desperation of the slave," "a competent dramatic script," and "recommended for production, following revisions."[95] While one reader saw the play appealing to "The Negro Youth Theatre," another felt it was "fine" for amateur or little theatre groups, while a third recommended it as suitable for "showboat production."

Frederick Douglass was recommended for production by three FTP readers but rejected by three others. One reviewer recommending production saw the play as "an interesting drama based upon the life of an early American," and as "excellent material for Negro dramatic groups."[96] The two other readers recommending production cautioned, "It would probably appeal to high-school children if presented by them—especially to colored students. It would have small interest for any other group, unless for a colored audience" and "This piece is worthy of production in the Negro little theatres. It is not worthy of production in a theatre such as the Negro group at the Lafayette Theatre [a professional acting company in Harlem], but I will recommend it for production in the little theatres." Readers rejecting the play for FTP production criticized it as "devoid of understanding and warmth," and for having "no characterization, no emotional appeal." One reader dismissed it as "not a finished play but merely the statement of a potentially dramatic incident which the author has apparently been artistically unable to develop. Her helplessness with her material is clearly indicated by the fact that she found nothing in her treatment for purposes of dramatic development. Therefore, we have no action in the play until the swift crisis at the last moment." These mixed reviews may be one reason neither *William and Ellen Craft* nor *Frederick Douglass* was produced by the FTP.

Securing new production opportunities for her plays was apparently an endless task for Johnson. In 1937 she wrote to Jackman, "Harold, do you have any contacts with the WPA Theatre Project? If so, can you get them interested in putting on my play Frederick Douglass? It is already approved and accepted by the New York Theatre Project board. Only awaits presentation."[97]

Johnson also submitted three of her lynching dramas (discussed below) to FTP, but they fared no better than her historical plays. Winona Fletcher's article "From Genteel Poet to Revolutionary Playwright: Georgia Douglas Johnson" examines the FTP's reception of Johnson's lynching dramas and reveals how racist attitudes and myths surrounding the occurrence of lynching in society became barriers to their production.[98] Comments on *Blue-Eyed Black Boy*, for example, ranged from "a very well constructed playlet," to "a pointless piece of melodrama without significance."[99] One reader of *Safe* resented that the play "proceeded from an absurdity—that they lynch Negro boys Down South for defending themselves from thieves [when] in fact, the crime that produces lynchers is vastly fouler."[100] Even though statistics refuted the myth that black men were raping white women, this myth persisted as the most commonly used "reason" for lynching. Perhaps the most negative response pertained to Johnson's Primitive Life play *Blue Blood*, prompting one reader to write, "This work is so bad that it is almost a caricature."[101] While David Krasner has pointed out that some readers recorded favorable responses to Johnson's plays,[102] clearly the Federal Theatre Project did not offer the new production opportunities Johnson had hoped for.

Plays of Average Negro Life

The category containing the greatest number of plays in Johnson's Catalogue is "Plays of Average Negro Life," and three additional plays appropriate to this category are listed separately as "Stories of Average Negro Life." Unfortunately, only two plays, *Starting Point* and *Paupaulekejo*, first published in Claudia Tate's volume, are extant, but the themes, plots, and characters of the remaining plays can be surmised from the synopses Johnson provided.

Plays in this category deal with a wide variety of topics such as romance, interracial friendships, postwar stories, living with physical disabilities, and "passing." Some plays are clearly intended to be entertaining and humorous, such as *Miss Bliss*, which concerns mistaken racial identity:

> MISS BLISS—(Being colored) young white man when about to propose to beautiful girl acquaints his father with fact, who tells him he has colored blood. Thereupon, he regretfully tells the girl's mother the state of affairs, when she in turn, tells him a like story. Both are amused and pleased. Wedding planned.[103]

Another play, *Heritage*, probably intended for production in schools, encourages young people to value the inheritance of character over wealth:

> HERITAGE—Young high school boy tells his mother regretfully that he has no heritage of wealth as the other boys do and is disconsolate. When final tests are made in scholarship, character, etc. it is found that he who had no wealth had a heritage greater than any resulting from his father's splendid life.[104]

Johnson probably drew on the complexities of her personal experience as a light-complexioned black woman working in government service to write *Little Blue Pigeon*:

> LITTLE BLUE PIGEON—Government Service Background. All of section lost jobs at Christmas time and dark members of group powder and dress up in their own fine clothes. Young mulatto mother, making it possible for her to "pass" in another unit and being able to take care of her baby—she being a newcomer in Washington and a stranger.[105] [My own interpretation of Johnson's fragmented summary is that as a Christmas "gift" the dark-skinned members of the group help the young mulatto

mother "pass" (undetected) for white, so that she keeps her job and is able to care for her baby.]

In a 1930 newspaper article, Johnson observed that dramas of the past had "portrayed the Negro furthest down" and, in a pointed critique that could apply to some of her early plays, questioned the continued use of "dialect" as well as the repeated use of the kitchen setting that "kept thoughts tethered around its drab center."[106] Johnson encouraged contemporary playwrights to create dramas that told the stories, aspirations, and heartbreaks of "our great middle class." Continuing in the same article, Johnson warned young writers to "avoid crossing the race line," at least "until the time is ripe for that," and cautioned, "those that touch too vitally upon the issues that are as yet raw had best wait their time." Johnson may have been speaking from experience here, since her plays on lynching, certainly a "raw" issue of race relations in the 1920s and 1930s, were never published in her lifetime, although she had submitted them to Samuel French, publisher of *Plumes*.

Starting Point portrays a working-class family's struggle for a better life. Aging black parents in the South saved their money from the father's job (working for a white employer as a messenger) so that their son, Tom, could go to college. Despite their high hopes for their son's success, Tom quits school, becomes involved with the illegal "numbers racket," and returns home with his new wife, a blues singer. It is only through the honesty and persistence of the young wife that the truth about the son's life is finally told. Tom recovers his self-respect but finds himself at a new "starting point" in life as he agrees to take over his father's job as messenger.

In a letter to Harold Jackman, Johnson indicated that the ending was intended to be not in any way victorious, but ironic: "The third scene ends with the boy going to take his failing father's job. That is, sitting at the white man's door taking orders—THE STARTING POINT."[107]

Starting Point is notable for representing a modern urban black family and for the character of Belle, one of the earliest portrayals of the female blues singer in American drama. As Tom begins to fabricate a story (in order to avoid telling his parents the truth about why he is not finishing college), the sound of Belle's song interrupts his speech:

TOM: Well, you see Mother—(Belle's voice is heard in a popular blues song off stage. All three lift their heads with varying expressions. Father and Mother taken aback look askance at each other because of the type of song and rowdy music.)

TOM: (proudly) That girl's a wow! She sure can sing. Knocked 'em dead in Washington! (Continues his broken speech) Well, as I was saying. It's like this. . . .[108]

Since Johnson does not specify the song Belle sings, the director or actress is free to choose which "popular blues song," with "rowdy music," will be included in the production. The lyrics in songs such as Gertrude "Ma" Rainey's "Big Boy Blues," or her "Hear Me Talkin' to You," or Bessie Smith's "Golden Rule Blues" would compliment the play's plot, but the choice would also depend on the capabilities of the actress as a singer. Belle is a complex character since she is, as Johnson explained in the same letter to Jackman, "a low class wife" which "added to the heartbreak of the parents." "But," Johnson continues, "the wife in sympathy with the parents, forces him [Tom] to accede to his father's wishes."

Upon finishing the third scene of *Starting Point* in 1938, Johnson wrote to Langston Hughes, "I feel that the play is done much better than any other of mine, more dramatic, and I want you to read it over." Johnson refers to Belle as "a cabaret girl" and sees her as "the pivotal point" of the play because she "causes the boy to cease rebelling and accept his father's proposition, which is to take his place as messenger at the bank."[109] Although, upon first reading, Belle may seem to be a secondary character, she is actually a pivotal figure both in Johnson's play and in American drama since she is one of the earliest portrayals of the female blues singer.

Deborah McDowell notes the daring nature of the black female blues singers such as Bessie Smith and Gertrude "Ma" Rainey, who sang openly and seductively about sex and female desire, and Angela Davis locates black women's blues as a site where "a feminist impulse intersects with a working class consciousness." In contrast to the club movement of black middle-class women who focused on defending black women's moral integrity and sexual purity, Davis suggests that "women's blues provided a cultural space for community building among working-class black women" and that, furthermore, it was "a space in which the coercions of bourgeois notions of sexual purity and 'true womanhood' were absent."[110]

The sound of the blues is not only musical but also cultural, and signifies a particular cultural perspective that grew out of the social conditions of black Americans as they entered and dealt with the modern era. In his

1928 essay "The Negro Artist and the Racial Mountain," Langston Hughes criticized the "Nordicized Negro intelligentsia" and encouraged them to "catch a glimmer of their own beauty" through art that was an inherent expression of Negro life: "Let the blare of Negro jazz bands and the bellowing voice of Bessie Smith singing the blues penetrate the closed ears of the colored near-intellectuals until they listen and perhaps understand."[111] If, as Cheryl Wall argues, the literary figure of the blues woman first appeared in Langston Hughes's 1930 novel *Not Without Laughter,* then Georgia Douglas Johnson is certainly among the earliest playwrights to portray the female blues singer (in 1938) as a dramatic character. Johnson's Belle is a harbinger of the contemporary theatre's gutsy blues-singing women such as Gertrude Rainey in August Wilson's *Ma Rainey's Black Bottom* (1984) and Billie Holiday in Aishah Rahman's *Lady Day: A Musical Tragedy* (1972), or in Lanie Robertson's *Lady Day at Emerson's Bar & Grill* (1986).

Paupaulekejo, one of two plays by Johnson with an African setting (the other is *Jungle Love*), reflects an interest in the African continent that grew out of the ferment of the New Negro movement. W. E. B. Du Bois's spectacular pageant *Star of Ethiopia* (1913) paid tribute to Africa for its "gifts to civilization," and Alain Locke's essay "The Negro and the American Stage" expressed doubt that "a complete development of Negro dramatic art" could occur "without some significant artistic reexpression of African life and the tradition associated with it."[112] "African life and tradition," Locke maintained, "offer a wonderfully new field and province for dramatic treatment. Here both the Negro actor and dramatist can move freely in a world of elemental beauty, with the all the decorative elements that a poetic emotional temperament could wish." Since both Du Bois and Locke (one of the few Harlem Renaissance artists and intellectuals to actually visit Africa) frequently attended the literary gatherings in Johnson's home, African culture and influences were undoubtedly among the topics of discussion, and Johnson was thus probably inspired to try her hand at creating plays with African characters and settings. In her November 1926 "Ebony Flute" column in *Opportunity*, cultural critic Gwendolyn Bennett noted that Johnson's "African play" was in rehearsal at Washington's President Theatre.[113] Since Johnson did not provide dates for her plays in her Catalogue, Bennett's column helps to locate *Paupaulekejo* among the earliest Harlem Renaissance plays to be set in Africa.

In her attempt to create the impression of an "authentic" African setting, Johnson called for "jungle music," dancing, warriors, witch doctors, and tom-toms. Theatre historian and scholar James V. Hatch points out that playwrights responded to Locke's proposal to draw on "ancestral sources" by writing plays which "express an Africa researched more in the imagination than in the village."[114] New Negro Renaissance plays with African themes invariably display jungle settings, "jungle music," dancing, and tom-toms, all of which Michael Feith has called "emblematic symbols . . . signifiers of the African landscape."[115]

According to Arthur Davis and Michael Peplow, the vast majority of African Americans were not deeply interested in Africa either as homeland or literary subject prior to the 1920s, and Harlem Renaissance poets were among the first to use Africa as a subject. However, Hatch dates African American theatre's "conscious alliance" with Africa from 1820, the founding of the African Company, the first professional black acting company in America.[116]

While *Paupaulekejo* has remained obscure, other plays from the period provide a perspective of Johnson's drama as part of a group effort to foster an African presence in the New Negro theatre. Both Thelma Duncan's *The Dance of Death: An African Play* (1923) and Richard Bruce Nugent's *Sahdji: An African Ballet* (c. 1927) were published in Locke's *Plays of Negro Life*, and May Miller's *Graven Images* (set in Egypt) won honorable mention in the 1929 *Opportunity* contest. These plays can be seen as among the early tentative steps by African American playwrights toward an exploration of African-based expressive strategies—a fruitful line of contemporary performance scholarship as reflected in *Black Theatre: Ritual Performance in the African Diaspora,* edited by Paul Carter Harrison, Victor Leo Walker II, and Gus Edwards.

Despite the "emblematic" African characters, setting, and props, *Paupaulekejo* concerns the historical American preoccupation with miscegenation. Claudia Tate's astute analysis emphasizes Johnson's innovative approach to the subject: "This is a miscegenation play set in Africa. Rather than relying on the often forced sexual pairing of white men and black women, which was the staple of American miscegenation stories, Johnson reverses the racial and sexual identities of the couple and depicts a story of probable miscegenation by consent."[117]

Paupaulekejo, a tale of interracial love (consensual miscegenation) and tragic death, contrasts "African" characters and culture with English Christian missionaries and biblical teachings. The play takes an ironic look at Christianity through a plot constructed to determine whether an all-encompassing "Christian love," as taught by the missionaries, is capable of transcending strictly enforced racial and sexual boundaries between black men and white women. *Paupaulekejo*, set in Africa and addressing what was considered taboo subject matter in America, is exemplary of what David Krasner has recognized as a great paradox of the New Negro era. "The period," Krasner observes, "was a complex interplay of forces in which black artists were influenced by the search for new forms and values in American culture and at the same time were also committed to a unique search for their own culture and artistic expression."[118] *Paupaulekejo* portrays English and African characters, but because of its focus on miscegenation and insurmountable racial barriers, Johnson saw no incongruity in placing the drama in her Stories of Average Negro Life category.

Paupaulekejo was written under the name "John Tremaine," one of the various pseudonyms Johnson sometimes used. Tate notes Johnson had written two short stories under the nom de plume John Tremaine and suggests that its use signals sexual content that Johnson evidently thought needed to be "masked with masculine authority."[119] But Johnson is clearly named as the playwright in Gwendolyn Bennett's column; Johnson's play *Plumes* lacks sexual content and yet she chose to submit this early drama to the *Opportunity* contest under the name "John Temple." Johnson's correspondence suggests she may have thought her work on many subjects would be more readily accepted if it were submitted under a male name, or she simply may have enjoyed playing an identity game through the use of pseudonyms. In 1938 she wrote to a friend, "You see Paul Tremain is one of my pseudonyms. I used it on the stories. I rewrote them you know and feel kind of a pride in their reception. I only changed the form of expression etc. not the content."[120]

The American preoccupation with race, and Johnson's own mixed-race ancestry, probably provided the impetus for her several plays addressing the miscegenation theme. *Jungle Love* is another "forbidden" romance story, set in Africa and dealing with the love between an aide of the victorious Burmese king and a daughter of the conquered king.[121] *One Cross Enough* concerns a "light colored girl in Germany" and her young Jewish admirer who proposes to her. She refuses his proposal when "she considers his cross of being a Jew is quite sufficient without adding to it her own cross of color."[122]

Other plays summarized under the Plays of Average Negro Life category are not specifically concerned with race but follow the plot development of romance-melodramas, postwar stories, and overcoming physical disabilities. Despite what today would be considered anachronistic and insensitive terminology, Johnson's synopsis for *Scapegoat* suggests she may have been one of the earliest black playwrights to treat the topic of individuals who are physically challenged:

> SCAPEGOAT:—One-act play with Government background, heroic action of cripple in the Unit.[123]

Only two plays in the Average Life category are set in the distant past: *Money Wagon* shows the "pluck and courage" of an old Negro slave woman, while *Jungle Love* (mentioned above) makes the point that "England and Spain were using bows and arrows and Burmese had guns and gunpowder."[124] Johnson's Plays of Average Negro Life are broad in scope and deal with the daily struggles, defeats, and triumphs of black people throughout history, but they focus predominantly on modern life. Their significance lies in the fact that many were written during an era when most white theatre audiences were exposed only to what drama critic Ralph Matthews called "extremities of Negro life" through commercially successful plays such as Eugene O'Neill's *The Emperor Jones* (1920), Paul Green's *In Abraham's Bosom* (1926), and Dorothy and DuBose Heyward's *Porgy* (1927).[125] While Johnson did write plays offering the heightened allure (and distance) of jungle settings and interracial (i.e. forbidden) love themes, her Plays of Average Negro Life overwhelmingly reflect the infinite variety of daily struggles and achievements.

With their broad range of characters and themes, Johnson's Plays of Average Negro Life are her contributions to a theatre envisioned as early as 1919 by salon attendee Willis Richardson as "a Negro drama that draws on the rich material of ordinary Negro life" and "shows the soul of a people; and the soul of this people is surely worth showing."[126]

Lynching Plays

Johnson is the central figure in the lynching-drama tradition, a dramatic genre formed by the responses of playwrights to the racial violence of lynching. She was the first playwright to name and develop a category of drama that drew attention specifically to the injustice of lynching and its effects on families. The six dramas she categorized as her Lynching Plays and referred to in her correspondence as her "plays on lynching" reveal her dedication to both the antilynching struggle and the artistic development of the genre in the New Negro era. Although other playwrights of the period, both black and white, wrote lynching dramas, Johnson contributed more plays to the genre than any other playwright in history.[127]

Johnson's six plays on lynching are: *A Sunday Morning in the South: A One-Act Play in Two Scenes* (white church version, c. 1925); *A Sunday Morning in the South: A One-Act Play in One Scene* (black church version, c. 1925); *Safe: A Play on Lynching* (c. 1929); *Blue-Eyed Black Boy* (c. 1930); *And Yet They Paused* (1938); and *A Bill To Be Passed* (1938).[128] None of Johnson's lynching dramas were published during her lifetime. *A Sunday Morning in the South* (black church version), the first to be published, appeared in James V. Hatch and Ted Shine's collection *Black Theatre U.S.A.* in 1974, eight years after Johnson's death. Johnson's outrage against lynching and her artistic vision for a theatre of social protest compelled her to work in the genre for over a decade. James V. Hatch places lynching dramas in the protest tradition initiated by antislavery plays: "The antilynch dramas, comparable only in passionate appeal to antislavery plays became the second form of American protest drama."[129]

Admittedly, many New Negro artists addressed the brutality and violence of lynching in their poetry, fiction, music, and drama. Billie Holiday's rendition of *Strange Fruit* (1939) is probably the most recognized single artistic work addressing the legacy of lynching.[130] But Johnson's six plays constitute an entire body of work that spans a decade. By sheer volume, Johnson's contributions to the lynching-drama tradition reflect the sustained influence of the antilynching struggle on the art and literature of the New Negro Renaissance.

As a single-authored body of work, Johnson's dramas are historically and artistically significant for their multiple portrayals of a black family confronting the lynching of one of its members. Judging from volumes such as Ida B. Wells's *On Lynchings: Southern Horrors, A Red Record, and Mob Rule in New Orleans* (1892, 1969), Ralph Ginsburg's *100 Years of Lynchings* (1976), and photography collections such as James Allen's *Without Sanctuary* (2002), graphic photos and detailed newspaper accounts documenting the brutality and violence of lynching were readily available to the public throughout the 1920s and 1930s. Certainly not as common were dramatic portrayals of black families confronting the lynching of a family or community member. Johnson's dramas aimed to fill this significant void in public consciousness by focusing not on the gruesome and violent nature of lynching, but on the reactions and resistance of the black family and community. *A Sunday Morning in the South*, *Safe*, and *Blue-Eyed Black Boy* are all set in southern homes and depict families resisting the injustice and brutality of lynching. The families are portrayed in various configurations such as a grandmother and grandsons in *A Sunday Morning in the South*; as mother, daughter, and son-in-law in *Safe*; and as mother, daughter, and daughter's fiancé in *Blue-Eyed Black Boy.*

Within each of these domestic settings a middle-aged or elderly woman is head of the household. Johnson's plays reflect the fact that black men were the primary targets of lynching but, by focusing on the actions of women characters, they express what Gloria T. Hull has called the "unique horror" black women faced in regards to lynching.[131] In each play the black family circle is expanded to include characters portrayed as friends and neighbors, who try to help the immediate family by serving as aides or messengers. These secondary characters are also invariably women: "Tildy" Brown and Liza Twiggs in *A Sunday Morning in the South*, Hannah Wiggins in *Safe*, and Hester Grant in *Blue-Eyed Black Boy*, all of whom play supporting but important roles in Johnson's extended families.

In her analysis of black women portrayed in lynching dramas, scholar Trudier Harris notes the "decrepit" nature of these female heads of families and suggests that their failing bodies, indicated by sore or injured feet, advanced age, or a weak heart, become "a metaphor for American racism" and reflect "how sick their society really is." While Harris acknowledges that playwrights such as Johnson were daring in their treatment of lynching, she also points to ways in which their portrayal of elderly black women as ailing and "ineffectual" can be interpreted as "a sympathetic response to the continuing destruction of the black male body." [132]

While it is true that Johnson's elderly female heads of households are aging and ailing as individuals, it is important to locate these characters within the context of their communities. Johnson's communal sensibility, or what Elizabeth McHenry has called her "clear vision of the importance of community to the creative artist," was vital to the success of the literary gatherings regularly held in Johnson's home.[133] Although the literary community Johnson created in her home resulted in a safe and supportive environment for New Negro artists, the concept of communal sensibility is also useful for contextualizing the individual characters she created for her lynching dramas. All of Johnson's elderly black women characters join with other members of their extended families to plan and carry out whatever resistance to lynching they can. In fact, major characters such as Sue Jones in *A Sunday Morning in the South* and Pauline Waters in *Blue-Eyed Black Boy* direct the resistance efforts while more able-bodied family members follow their commands.

The elderly black women portrayed in Johnson's lynching dramas may be "decrepit" in body, but their ailing bodies serve to emphasize both the necessity for collective action and the strong spirit of resistance that, historically, has been responsible for the survival of the African American community. These elderly women may or may not be effective in stopping the lynching, but they are represented as honored elders and valuable members in the community. They contribute in significant ways to the collective memory of the group and, through their aging bodies, they reinscribe the defiant spirit of the Harlem/New Negro Renaissance that was expressed most memorably in Claude McKay's poem "If we must die": "We'll face the murderous, cowardly pack, Pressed to the wall, dying, but fighting back!"[134]

In Johnson's later lynching dramas *And Yet They Paused* and *A Bill To Be Passed*, the extended black family is represented by the "Brothers" and "Sisters" comprising a Mississippi church congregation and by three black men (a reporter, a church elder, and a church delegate) who are presented as a multivoiced unit as they stand together outside the chambers of the United States Congress, listening and reacting to the ongoing debate on the antilynching bill. In Johnson's lynching dramas, the black family confronting a lynching served as her collective protagonist and sustained her creativity in the genre.

As an artist and activist, Johnson contributed her playwriting skills to the service of the antilynching movement, a historical struggle that began in the nineteenth century and continued during the New Negro era under the leadership of the NAACP. In 1936 Johnson sent to Walter White, executive secretary of the NAACP, several of her lynching plays for possible production by the organization's Youth Council. White eventually returned the plays, citing the council's concern that "they all ended in defeat" and "gave one the feeling that the situation was hopeless despite all the courage which was shown by the Negro characters."[135] Johnson replied that she understood the point the board was making, but that she was hesitant to rewrite the plays since "it is true that in life things do not end usually ideally" and that "they [the plays] would lose their greatest dramatic moment . . . and a play depends so largely on this."

Johnson's response to White reveals her artistic integrity as a playwright and her dedication to her own vision of theatre as social protest. Although the NAACP Youth Council apparently preferred to produce lynching dramas with more positive outcomes, Johnson would not change the content of her plays simply to appease those who controlled the production apparatus. As theatre scholar Harry Elam has noted, "the politics of representation concern not only understanding the power inherent in the visible representations of African Americans but also recognizing the mechanisms of production, which dictate the dissemination of these images."[136]

Johnson's determination to portray the grim realities of lynching clashed, in this instance, with the NAACP's goals to provide a more hopeful message: that lynching can be defeated and that change is possible. By refusing to give her antilynching plays "satisfying" endings in which a lynching is defeated, Johnson was leading her audience to confront the reality of lynching by employing the current style of theatrical "realism" in which a social problem is portrayed and left unresolved.[137] As Krasner has noted, "Johnson's realism negotiates the area between actual history and the stage. The frame that theatre provides brought to audiences a vision of the normalcy of black life and shows lynching's wrenching effect upon it."[138] While Johnson's realistic representation of lynching and its effect on black families did not serve the immediate purposes of the NAACP Youth Council, White, in an apparent gesture of appeasement, agreed to call attention to the plays through "our press service and the *Crisis* and people who might inquire about plays dealing with lynching."[139]

Johnson's 1936 correspondence with Walter White established her identity with the NAACP as an activist playwright in the antilynching cause, and in January 1938 the organization called on Johnson to write a skit on lynching for their 1938 campaign. Johnson responded by writing *And Yet They Paused* and *A Bill To Be Passed.* Published here for the first time, *And Yet They Paused* and *A Bill To Be Passed* are two separate but very similar scripts with different titles and different endings. Both portray the foot-dragging and filibustering that were responsible for the United States Congress's failure to pass a federal antilynching bill. In both versions Johnson boldly indicts the United States Congress for its complicity in mob violence and portrays the urgent need for antilynching legislation by juxtaposing scenes of unending political wrangling in Washington, D.C., with events surrounding a brutal lynching in Mississippi.

Written first, *And Yet They Paused* ends while the antilynching bill remains under debate in the House of Representatives. *A Bill To Be Passed* concludes with a victorious passage in the House and a passionate vow to fight on for passage in the Senate. Johnson was unenthusiastic but agreeable to the NAACP's suggestion that an additional skit or epilogue was needed at the end of *A Bill To Be Passed* "portraying the results of the fight in the Senate this year and ending with some challenge as to the need of redoubling efforts to pass the bill." Johnson responded, "if you care to add it, do so" and suggested "Mr. White or anyone can write the data needed to cite the action on the bill to date" (see note 135).

In the interest of increasing her play's usefulness to the NAACP, Johnson went as far as providing the short speech, or "preamble," delivered by the character ENVOY, that serves as a transition into the skit *Kill That Bill* written by Robert E. Williams of the Cleveland NAACP chapter. *Kill That Bill* is less performance-oriented than Johnson's play; it is more narrative in form, reproduces the specific facts and arguments presented during the southern senators' filibuster against the Wagner-Van Nuys antilynching bill, and includes a Commentator, who speaks directly to the audience, as well as a character who represents NAACP executive secretary Walter White. *A Bill to Be Passed* and *Kill That Bill*, capable of being produced separately or together, constitute a unique fusion of art and politics. They reflect the range of styles and techniques that antilynching playwrights employed and they provide a perspective on how the scripts were subject to negotiation in order to serve changing political needs.

The NAACP was apparently considering Johnson's play for a radio skit, but when it reached the desk of the branch coordinator, E. Frederick

Morrow, he judged it to be "rather superficial" and "hurriedly done" and, in an internal memo, expressed serious concerns regarding the representation of African Americans: "It seems to me that an organization of our type must be very careful in the kind of propaganda it spreads by radio or press. It seems to me that we can find a more effective way of presenting our subject than by resorting to so many of the features presumed to be characteristic of our group. I am referring, of course to broken and bad English; helplessly calling upon the Lord when disaster overtakes us; referring to our inability to hold meetings on time and over-emphasizing spirituals. Many Negroes would resent our participation in dramatics of this type. They would feel that since we are looked upon as a beacon light to our group, that we should at times show the public a phase of culture that so many people do not believe we have. I am sure that the subject of lynching can be attacked from another angle."[140]

Morrow's internal NAACP memo reveals how Johnson's plays contributed to both public and private discourse concerning the representation of African Americans. Even as contributions to the generally unified antilynching struggle, Johnson's plays were part of an ongoing dialogue and debate on race and representation. Morrow's memo provides an example of how the reception of Johnson's plays was contingent upon changing and, at times, conflicting ideologies of how African Americans should be portrayed. For Morrow at least, Johnson's play did not sufficiently meet an artistic standard or, in his own words, a "phase of culture" that was necessary in order to gain respect from the wider (white? middle-class?) public.

The recovery of the typescripts of *And Yet They Paused* and *A Bill To Be Passed*, as well as accompanying correspondence, provides insight into the issues Johnson faced as an artist activist. *And Yet They Paused* and *A Bill To Be Passed* also serve as a reminder that the New Negro Renaissance was not only an artistic movement but also a political struggle for social and legal change.

In addition to her work with the NAACP, Johnson was a member of the Writers League Against Lynching, an organization composed of writers, editors, and publishers who joined together to protest lynching and work for the passage of a federal antilynching bill. In the League's numerous letters and telegrams Johnson was listed as a sponsor, along with other leading New Negro figures such as Countee Cullen, E. Franklin Frazier,

Jessie Redmon Fauset, James Weldon Johnson, Alain Locke, Alfred Knopf, and Carl Van Vechten.[141] Johnson's lynching dramas reflect her role as an outspoken critic of racial violence as well as her vision of theatre as a tool for social change. She was an activist playwright and, perhaps, more directly involved in the politics of the antilynching struggle than any other artist of the New Negro era.

Radio Plays

Brotherhood, Johnson's only radio play, is described in her Catalogue as "four episodes touching upon Intolerance with a Brotherhood Marching Song as a theme—which is heard here and there throughout the play." According to Johnson's Catalogue, the YWCA was considering the play for production. While the play script has not been located, Johnson's "Brotherhood Marching Song" (1945), written to accompany the play, is published here for the first time.[142]

The song begins, "Let us march down the world way together, wherever you are, hello!" and calls for human equality and harmony, ideals shared by both the New Negro Renaissance and the civil rights movement. Johnson's correspondence suggests she may have turned her radio play into a script for television. In 1955 she wrote to Langston Hughes asking him for help with getting her script of *Brotherhood* produced as a television show. Johnson explained that the script, written eight years previously, had been "favorably commented on" by the YMCA in New York. Hughes replied that he had no contacts to suggest and that he "has never cared much" for either film or television.[143] Johnson's letter reveals she persisted in seeking out new performance opportunities for her plays. Her motivation to write for theatre audiences was sparked by the one-act play contests sponsored by the journals *Crisis* and *Opportunity* in the 1920s, as well as by the innovative technology of television in the 1950s.

Johnson suggested that the "Brotherhood Marching Song" would be "effectively sung to the sound of marching feet." Sound is a vital component in most of Johnson's plays and, perhaps because she was a composer, she frequently drew on the power of black music to help her express what spoken dialogue could not. Her incorporation of spirituals, hymns, marches, "jungle music," or the blues into her dramatic texts serves to create a sound capable of expressing the contradictions of African American

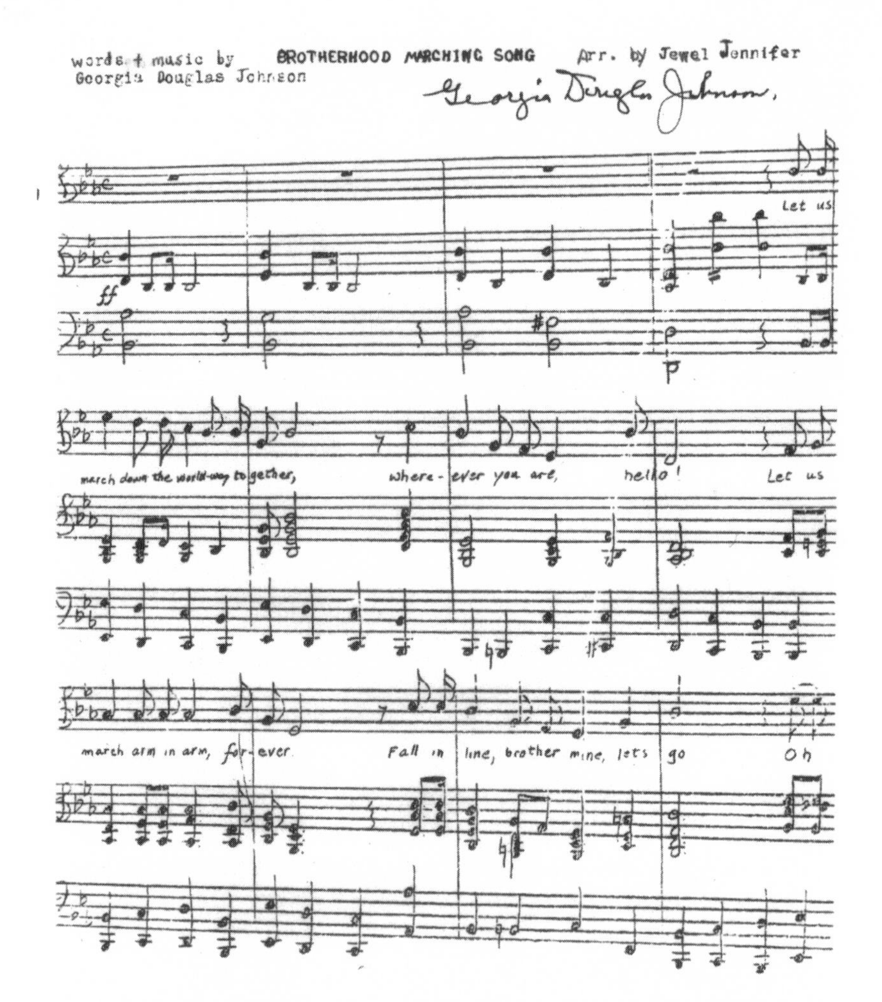

"Brotherhood Marching Song," music and lyrics by Georgia Douglas Johnson, copyright Georgia Douglas Johnson, 1945. Written to accompany *Brotherhood,* Johnson's radio play. Reprinted by permission of Glenn Carrington Papers, Manuscripts, Archives, and Rare Books Division, Schomburg Center for Research in Black Culture, the New York Public Library, Astor, Lenox, and Tilden Foundations.

come, come, come, my brother
Let's unite for the common good,
oh,
come, let us know one another,
and march onward in brother-hood

Let us march down the world-way together, wherever you are, hello!
Let us march arm-in-arm forever, Fall in line friend of mine, let's go!
O come, come, come my brother, Let's unite for the common good,
O come let us know one another, and march onward in BROTHERHOOD !

2nd verse

Let us march, march, march on together, wherever you are , hello!
Arm-in-arm let us march on forever, Fall in line brother mine, let's go!
Lift a song, lift a song my brother, Join in for the common good,
Let us step, step, step on together, To the march song of BROTHERHOOD!

Effective with sound of marching feet- Use for Brotherhood Day June 30th.
extra copies 10cts. G.B.J. Box 6455 Washington D.C.

life, or what music scholar Samuel Floyd describes as "both the struggles and the fulfillments of living in a land and an environment that was both hostile and promising, binding and free."[144]

Music is only one device Johnson employs in her propensity to focus attention on events that are occurring but remain unseen offstage. Johnson's dramas reveal her creativity in engaging the audience's imagination and evoking a sense of locale and action that is palpable but not visible. She frequently relies on sound effects or creates characters whose dialogue is vividly descriptive of events taking place offstage. The sights and sounds of an offstage funeral procession (*Plumes*), lynch mobs (*Safe*, *Blue-Eyed Black Boy*), and northbound trains (*William and Ellen Craft* and *Frederick Douglass*) permeate Johnson's plays and serve to create a sense of the larger world (hostile and/or promising) outside her localized stage settings. Johnson's most intricate evocation of unseen events occurs in *And Yet They Paused* and *A Bill To Be Passed*, in which an unseen (but vividly described) lynching in Mississippi is juxtaposed with an unseen (but overheard) antilynching legislation debate in the United States Congress. Johnson's creativity in focusing on unseen events, her incorporation of music, and her wide variety of themes, characters, and settings are indicative of her individual playwriting style.

Johnson's own categories of Primitive Life Plays, Historical Plays, Plays of Average Negro Life, and Lynching Plays shift the discussion of New Negro theatre away from the familiar Locke/Du Bois (folk drama versus propaganda play) debate. Johnson's plays call for a new, less binary perspective on the mix of themes, characters, issues, and techniques black playwrights brought to the theatre during the Harlem/New Negro Renaissance. Considered in conjunction with her Catalogue and her correspondence, Johnson's genres also reveal her persistence in writing plays and seeking production venues far beyond the historical and cultural boundaries of the New Negro Renaissance.

Conclusion

Unlike Alain Locke or W. E. B. Du Bois, Johnson never championed one type of theatre over another. Her vision of theatre, both as an art form and as a social tool, embraced many types of drama and is revealed most clearly through the wide variety of plays she wrote and themes she addressed.

Some of her plays address contemporary social issues such as poverty, miscegenation, or parent-child relationships; others were written to educate audiences about black history, or to protest the racial violence of lynching; still others offered, in Johnson's own words, "simple entertainment."[145] As a playwright, Johnson was interested in reaching a variety of audiences and seeing her plays produced in different venues: from the little theatres of the New Negro movement, to the stages of the Federal Theatre Project and antilynching rallies, to (hoped-for) productions on Broadway and television. Johnson's vision of theatre was expansive and she refused to accept limits on where she might find an audience for her plays.

Johnson's dramas contributed to both a public and private dialogue on race throughout the 1920s and 1930s. While the 1927 drama critic of *Amsterdam News* had praised the award-winning *Plumes* as "real Negro literature," a 1936 FTP reader expressed reservations concerning *Safe*, since it portrayed "the absurdity" that "they lynch Negro boys Down South for defending themselves from thieves," and an internal 1938 NAACP memo warned that Johnson's characters in *And Yet They Paused* perpetuate stereotypes that progressive organizations (such as the NAACP) should avoid supporting. Diverse and sometimes conflicting racial ideologies, both public and private, were highly influential as conditions of reception for Johnson's plays.

Georgia Douglas Johnson's Catalogue of Writings, extant plays, and correspondence document her life as a prolific, courageous, innovative, and activist playwright. She made significant contributions to the canon of plays that represent the New Negro little theatre movement, and she was among the earliest playwrights to create dramatic characters representing rural black southern women, the "African" (in an "African" setting), the female blues singer, and the physically challenged. As an artist activist of her era, she contributed her playwriting skills to the antilynching movement, and she remains today the most prolific playwright of lynching drama, a genre that continues to develop on the American stage. Johnson helped to build and sustain a community of black artists in Washington, D.C., and regular Saturday-night gatherings in her home provided the impetus for several groundbreaking collaborations and publications of the New Negro theatre.

An examination of Johnson's playwriting career suggests she was a versatile and independent dramatist. Her plays on lynching, especially in connection with themes of miscegenation and white men's exploitation of black women, are the work of a bold and courageous artist. This view of Johnson contrasts with the perspective offered by scholars who focus on her poetry. Elizabeth McHenry characterizes Johnson as "reluctant to substantively address the racial situation or her experiences as a black woman in her writing, preferring instead to rely on and recycle older formulas of genteel feminine expression."[146] Similarly, Claudia Tate concludes that Johnson, unlike the more "audacious" Zora Neale Hurston, accepted the minor role assigned to her as the "lady poet" of the New Negro Renaissance. "This was the only uncontested position available to her," Tate continues, "and she chose a non-oppositional stance for herself."[147] Clearly, Johnson's expansive and assertive identity as a playwright complicates her circumscribed and highly gendered identity as a poet.

Focusing on her less recognized career as a dramatist provides additional insight into Johnson's life, her contributions to black theatre, the Harlem/New Negro Renaissance, and women's cultural history. The careers of May Miller and Eulalie Spence, two other prolific dramatists of the New Negro Renaissance era, await similar examination.

Historically, Johnson's career provides a link between the pioneering group of black women who contributed to the *Opportunity* and *Crisis* one-act play contests, and the groundbreaking commercial success of Alice Childress and Lorraine Hansberry. Recent scholarship in Black Studies and Feminist Studies has generated new interest in Johnson's plays. While Marta Effinger cites Johnson's work as "an innovative precursor to black feminist discourses," Jasmin Lambert examines ways in which the play *Blue Blood* directly confronts "the perils of American mulatto identity," and Megan Sullivan analyzes the language in Johnson's plays as discourse that "reveals both the ways in which women challenge hegemonic definitions of culture and rely on the solidarity of female friendships."[148]

Although Johnson received more recognition as a poet than as a dramatist, this study has shown that she dedicated a lifetime to writing plays and seeking outlets for their publication or production. The value Johnson placed on her work as a dramatist can be seen in the decades over which she practiced her craft and in her gesture to preserve, through her Catalogue, a record of her plays, both published and unpublished. If produced on the stage today, these dramas would still touch our emotions. A study of Johnson's music may provide yet another perspective and, ultimately, a fuller understanding of this multitalented artist.

NOTES

1. Georgia Douglas Camp was born in Atlanta, Georgia, to George and Laura Douglas Camp on September 10, but her year of birth is uncertain; years as diverse as 1877, 1880, 1886, and 1887 are cited in various sources. Her 1966 obituaries in the *Washington Post* and the *Afro-American* state her age at death as eighty-six, thus corroborating the 1880 date, but Claudia Tate's biography of Johnson and the "Biographical Sketch" written in 1994 by Legesse Tessema for Johnson's papers at Howard University's Moorland-Spingarn Research Center state that she was born in 1877. Johnson completed her studies at Atlanta University's Normal School in 1893. A biographical sketch of Johnson at the Schomburg Center written by a close friend, Glenn Carrington, states her year of birth as 1886, while Johnson's 1929 application seeking a grant from the Harmon Foundation reports 1887 as her year of birth. As recently as 2000, a headstone with the engraved date of 1877 was placed on Johnson's previously unmarked grave in Lincoln Cemetery, Suitland, Maryland, immediately outside Washington, D.C. The headstone was the result of a group effort by contemporary scholars who hold Johnson and her work in high regard. Biographical information on Johnson's life is derived from Johnson's papers at Moorland-Spingarn Research Center, Howard University; Johnson's biographical file at Atlanta University's Robert Woodruff Library, Archives Department; Claudia Tate's introduction to *Selected Works of Georgia Douglas Johnson* (New York: G. K. Hall, 1997); Gloria T. Hull's *Color, Sex and Poetry: Three Women Writers of the Harlem Renaissance* (Bloomington: Indiana University Press, 1987); Winona Fletcher, "Georgia Douglas Johnson," in *Notable Women in the American Theatre: A Biographical Dictionary*, ed. Alice M. Robinson, Vera Mowry Roberts, and Milly S. Barranger (New York: Greenwood, 1989), 473–77; Winona Fletcher, "Georgia Douglas Johnson," vol. 51 of *Dictionary of Literary Biography: Afro-American Writers from the Harlem Renaissance to 1940*, ed. Trudier Harris and Thadious M. Davis (Detroit: Gale Group, 1987), 153–64; Jocelyn Hazlewood Donlon, "Georgia Douglas Johnson," in *Black Women in America: An Historical Encyclopedia*, ed. Darlene Clark Hine (Brooklyn, NY: Carlson, 1993), 640–42; and Marta Effinger, "Georgia Douglas Johnson," vol. 249 of *Dictionary of Literary Biography: Twentieth Century American Dramatists*, ed. Christopher Wheatley (Detroit: Gale Group, 2001), 180–88.

2. The terms "New Negro Renaissance," "New Negro movement," and "Harlem Renaissance" are often used interchangeably and refer to the flowering of art and literature by African Americans in the 1920s and 1930s. Although the Harlem Renaissance is so named because of the great number of black artists who flocked into the Harlem district of New York City, making it the black cultural capital of the world, significant artistic activity was also occurring in cities such as Washington, D.C., Chicago, and Boston. Just as the movement cannot be limited to one location, neither is it easily reducible to exact dates, but it is generally conceded that an unprecedented surge in activity among African American artists began around

World War I and extended into the decade of the 1930s. The "New Negro" artist, celebrated in Alain Locke's classic anthology *The New Negro* (1925), asserted a renewed racial consciousness and pride.

3. Both Tate's and Hull's volumes consider Johnson's work in all genres but focus predominantly on her poetry. Additional plays, music, and correspondence have been recovered since the publication of Tate's 1997 volume, which includes eight plays but provides scant information on Johnson's contributions to the theatre and her career as a playwright. Drama collections such as Kathy Perkins's *Black Female Playwrights: An Anthology of Plays before 1950* (Bloomington: Indiana University Press, 1989) and Elizabeth Brown-Guillory's *Wines in the Wilderness: Plays by African American Women from the Harlem Renaissance to the Present* (New York: Praeger, 1990) are valuable for positioning Johnson alongside her "sister" playwrights and bringing attention to the variety of themes and issues black women brought to the stage, but the breadth of each volume permitted the inclusion of only a few of Johnson's plays. Winona L. Fletcher's essay, "From Genteel Poet to Revolutionary Playwright: Georgia Douglas Johnson," ed. Beverly Byers-Pevitts, special issue, *The Theatre Annual* 40 (1985): 41–64, establishes the foundation for understanding ways in which Johnson's plays differ from her poetry. Some of the more recent publications that focus on specific aspects of Johnson's lynching dramas are Kathy Perkins and Judith Stephens's *Strange Fruit: Plays on Lynching by American Women* (Bloomington: Indiana University Press, 1998) and Trudier Harris, "Before the Strength, the Pain: Portraits of Elderly Black Women in Early Twentieth-Century Anti-Lynching Plays," in *Black Women Playwrights: Visions on the American Stage,* ed. Carol Marsh-Lockett (New York: Garland, 1999), 25–42. Megan Sullivan's "Folk Plays, Home Girls and Back Talk: Georgia Douglas Johnson and Women of the Harlem Renaissance," *CLA Journal* 38, no. 4 (June 1995): 404–19, provides a feminist or "female-centered" analysis of Johnson's *Plumes* and *A Sunday Morning in the South.* In *A Beautiful Pageant: African American Theatre, Drama, and Performance in the Harlem Renaissance, 1910–1927* (New York: Palgrave, 2001), David Krasner discusses Johnson's *Plumes* and *A Sunday Morning in the South* in relation to the philosophies of Alain Locke. Elizabeth McHenry's *Forgotten Readers: Recovering the Lost History of African American Literary Societies* (Durham, NC: Duke University Press, 2002) examines Johnson's leadership in the formation of the "Saturday Nighters" and the literary discussions they held in Johnson's Washington, D.C., home during the 1920s and 1930s.

4. Jeanne-Marie Miller writes that productions of Johnson's plays "out of necessity, were confined, in the main, to the stages of the then-segregated black churches, secondary schools, institutions of higher education, and community theatres." See Miller, "Georgia Douglas Johnson and May Miller: Forgotten Playwrights of the Harlem Renaissance," *CLA Journal* 33, no. 4 (June 1990): 363. See also Doris E. Abramson, "Angelina Weld Grimké, Mary Burrill, Georgia Douglas Johnson, and Marita O. Bonner: An Analysis of Their Plays," *Sage* 2, no. 1 (Spring 1985): 9–13.

5. In *Strange Fruit,* Perkins and Stephens define a "lynching drama" as "a play

in which the threat or occurrence of a lynching, past or present, has major impact on the dramatic action" (3). Other studies by Stephens examine lynching drama as a unique genre and locate the first reference to lynching in American drama in William Wells Brown's *The Escape; or, A Leap For Freedom* (1858). See, for example, Stephens, "Lynching, American Theatre, and the Preservation of a Tradition," *Journal of American Drama and Theatre* 1, no. 1 (Winter 1997): 54–65, and "Lynching Dramas and Women: History and Critical Context" in *Strange Fruit*, 1–13. Lynching drama developed as a genre in the early twentieth century when playwrights moved beyond brief references to lynching and focused on specific incidents. Plays such as Thomas Dixon's *The Clansman* (1906), Edward Sheldon's *The Nigger* (1909), Ridgely Torrence's *Granny Maumee* (1914), Angelina Weld Grimké's *Rachel* (1916), Mary P. Burrill's *Aftermath* (1919), Tracy Mygatt's *The Noose* (1919), Georgia Douglas Johnson's *A Sunday Morning in the South* (c. 1925), and Joseph Mitchell's *Son Boy* (1928) are only a few of the early contributions to the genre. The lynching-drama tradition includes close to one hundred (currently known) plays and continues to expand with contemporary plays such as Toni Morrison's *Dreaming Emmett* (1985), Cedric Turner's *'Dat Great Long Time* (1990), Sandra Seaton's *The Bridge Party* (1989), Michon Boston's *Iola's Letter* (1994), Yvonne Singh's *Lynch P*in* (2002), William Parker's *The Awakening* (2003), and the collaborative production at Chicago's Neo-Futurarium, *Emmett Project* (2003).

6. Typescripts from the Federal Theatre Project are all in "Play Scripts," the Federal Theatre Project Collection, Music Division, Library of Congress. *Safe* and *Blue-Eyed Black Boy* are in box 758 and box 599, respectively. Both versions of *A Sunday Morning in the South* are in box 779. *Frederick Douglass* is in box 651 and *William and Ellen Craft* (titled "Ellen and William Craft") is in box 638. Scripts for *Paupaulekejo* and *Blue Blood* are in Johnson's papers in the Manuscript Division, Moorland-Spingarn Research Center, Howard University, box 162–2, file 29 and 6 respectively. Typescripts for *And Yet They Paused* and *A Bill To Be Passed* are in the file "Anti-Lynching Bill Play, 1936–1938," NAACP Papers, box C-299, Manuscript Reading Room, Library of Congress. A search of copyright records, correspondence, and discussions with scholars who are familiar with Johnson's work have led to the conclusion that, with the exception of *Plumes*, copyrights for Johnson's plays have expired.

7. Transcript of Owen Dodson interview, Owen Dodson File: "Georgia Douglas Johnson," p. 4, Hatch-Billops Collection, New York, New York.

8. Joellen ElBashir, curator, Moorland-Spingarn Research Center, Howard University, personal interview with author, June 27, 2000.

9. Perkins, *Black Female Playwrights*, 2, 16.

10. *Opportunity: Journal of Negro Life*, founded in 1924, was edited by Charles S. Johnson and published by the Urban League, while *The Crisis*, founded in 1910, was edited by W. E. B. Du Bois and published by the NAACP. Both magazines were vital outlets for the work of black playwrights, as well as other artists, of the New Negro era. See Addell Austin, "Pioneering Black Authored Dramas, 1924–1927"

(Ph.D. dissertation, Michigan State University, 1986), and Austin, "The *Opportunity* and *Crisis* Literary Contests, 1924–1927," *CLA Journal* 32 (1988): 235–346; and more recently, Jennifer Burton's introduction to *Zora Neale Hurston, Eulalie Spence, Marita Bonner, and Others: The Prize Plays and Other One-Acts Published in Periodicals* (New York: G. K. Hall, 1996).

11. See Judith L. Stephens, "The Harlem Renaissance and the New Negro Movement," in *The Cambridge Companion to American Women Playwrights,* ed. Brenda Murphy (New York: Cambridge University Press, 1999), 98–117. For a recent and thorough overview of theatre and performance in the New Negro era see James V. Hatch, "The Harlem Renaissance," in *A History of African American Theatre,* ed. Errol G. Hill and James V. Hatch (New York: Cambridge University Press, 2003), 214–54.

12. Georgia Douglas Johnson (hereafter referred to as GDJ) to Alain Locke, March 1925, box 164–40, file 35, Alain Locke Papers, Moorland-Spingarn Research Center, Howard University.

13. GDJ to Harold Jackman, 19 March 1937, Georgia Douglas Johnson Correspondence with Harold Jackman, 1936–1942, James Weldon Johnson Collection, Yale Collection of American Literature, Beinecke Rare Book and Manuscript Library, Yale University. Wendell Malliet, president, Wendell Malliet and Co., to GDJ, 23 August 1943, and letter from Richard Lowe, director of public relations, Wendell Malliet and Co., 29 July 1943, box 162–1, file 40, Georgia Douglas Johnson Papers, Manuscript Division, Moorland-Spingarn Research Center, Howard University.

14. GDJ to Harold Jackman, 2 December 1952, box 19, folder 20, Countee Cullen/Harold Jackman Memorial Collection, Atlanta University Center, Robert Woodruff Library, Archives Department. GDJ to Langston Hughes, 8 January 1955, box 19, folder 10, Countee Cullen/Harold Jackman Memorial Collection.

15. In recording the history of African American women playwrights, scholars have paid scant attention to the years between the end of the Harlem/New Negro Renaissance (roughly the late 1930s) and the commercial and critical success of writers such as Alice Childress, Lorraine Hansberry, and Adrienne Kennedy (during the 1950s). Johnson's playwriting career bridges this gap. For a recent discussion of Childress, Hansberry, and Kennedy and their work, see Margaret B. Wilkerson's essay "From Harlem to Broadway: African American Women Playwrights at Mid-Century" in Murphy, *The Cambridge Companion*, 134–52. For a recent analysis of Hansberry's classic play, see Margaret B. Wilkerson, "Political Radicalism and Artistic Innovation in the Works of Lorraine Hansberry," in *African American Performance and Theatre History: A Critical Reader*, ed. Harry J. Elam Jr. and David Krasner (New York: Oxford University Press, 2001), 40–55. For a firsthand account of the challenges of bringing *A Raisin in the Sun* to production, see *You Can't Do That on Broadway: A Raisin in the Sun and Other Theatrical Improbabilities* by producer Philip Rose (New York: Proscenium, 2001).

16. Johnson's later books of verse were *An Autumn Love Cycle* (1928) and *Share My World* (1962). Claudia Tate's volume includes most of Johnson's poetry. John-

son's poems have been variously described as "genteel" (polite, refined, sedate, conventional verse), "modern feminist realism" (voicing the "yearning of woman for candid self expression"), and "modern romantic" (stressing the human mind's ability to "create new realities"). See Fletcher in Harris and Davis, *Dictionary of Literary Biography*,153; Alain Locke, foreword to *An Autumn Love Cycle* in Tate's *Selected Works*, 194–95; and Ronald Primeau, "Frank Horne and the Second Echelon Poets of the Harlem Renaissance," in *The Harlem Renaissance Remembered*, ed. Arna Bontemps (New York: Dodd, Mead, 1972), 265. Recent work by black feminist critics has encouraged recognition of Johnson's formally diverse, musically inspired, multilayered, and sometimes subtly subversive poetic voice. See Tate, *Selected Works*, li, and Erlene Stetson's "Rediscovering the Harlem Renaissance: Georgia Douglas Johnson: 'The New Negro' Poet," *Obsidian: Black Literature in Review* 5 (Spring/Summer 1979): 26–34.

17. GDJ to Alain Locke, March 1925, box 164–40, folder 35, Alain Locke Papers.

18. GDJ, *Autumn Love Cycle*, in Tate, *Selected Works*, 185.

19. See Christine Gray, *Willis Richardson: Forgotten Pioneer of African American Drama* (Westport, CT: Greenwood, 1999), 31 n. 16.

20. GDJ interview, *Opportunity* (July 1927): 204.

21. GDJ to Langston Hughes, 1 July 1951, box 83, Langston Hughes Correspondence with Georgia Douglas Johnson, James Weldon Johnson Collection.

22. Langston Hughes's response to GDJ, 6 July 1951, box 83, Langston Hughes Correspondence with Georgia Douglas Johnson, James Weldon Johnson Collection.

23. GDJ interview, *Opportunity* (July 1927): 204.

24. Copies of Johnson's Catalogue are in the Moorland-Spingarn Research Center and at the Library of Congress. A note on the back of the copy of Johnson's Catalogue at the Library of Congress reads "Gift of the Author, 1965."

25. Hull, 168.

26. According to Claudia Tate, Johnson's mother was black and Native American while her father was of both black and white ancestry (*Selected Works*, xxviii). Hull states that Johnson was "a black person with considerable white blood in her ancestry" (*Color, Sex and Poetry*, 155). Hull cites 1893 as the year Johnson entered the Normal School at Atlanta University, while Tate notes 1893 as the year Johnson completed her studies. The "Alumni News" in the *Atlanta Bulletin*, July 1963, lists Johnson as a member of the class of 1893 (Biographical File: Georgia Douglas Johnson, Atlanta University Center, Robert Woodruff Library, Archives Department). Johnson attended Atlanta University's commencement on May 31, 1965, and received an honorary degree as a Doctor of Literature (Atlanta University 1965 Commencement Program, Atlanta University Center).

27. Johnson quoted in "The Contest Spotlight," *Opportunity* (July 1927): 204.

28. Johnson's obituary, published in the *Afro-American* (national edition), May 28, 1966, 18, and in the *Washington Post*, May 6, 1966, C-13. Both obituaries are in the vertical file on Johnson at the Schomburg Center for Research in Black Culture,

New York Public Library. Around 1912, Henry "Link" Johnson Sr. was appointed to a four-year term as recorder of deeds for the District of Columbia by President Taft. Although the presidential appointment of her husband as recorder of deeds firmly established the Johnsons' status among the Negro elite of the city, Georgia Douglas Johnson would never lead the life of a "lady of leisure," nor was she part of the extremely color-conscious upper class of Negro Washingtonians, characterized by Langston Hughes in his autobiography as "snobbish and unbearable" (*The Big Sea*, 206). Throughout their lives, both Georgia Douglas Johnson and her husband were politically active and committed to working for social change. They were both faithful members of the Republican Party, "the party of Lincoln." Henry Johnson Sr. served as Republican national committeeman from Georgia and, in 1916, wrote *The Negro Under Wilson*, a pamphlet issued by the Republican National Committee. This document criticized the Woodrow Wilson administration and the Democratic Party for racial discrimination in government appointments that, in turn, legitimized jim crow practices throughout the city. Georgia Douglas Johnson served as secretary for the Republican Club of Washington, D.C., and was a member of the Virginia White Speel Republican Club. After his death, Henry Johnson Sr. was remembered as "one who not only bore the burden in the heat of the day for the Republican Party" but who also "gave the last full measure of devotion," while Georgia Douglas Johnson was described as one who has "gone unswervingly down the line for the G.O.P." William Henry Huff to Mrs. Samuel Fountain, 1943, box 162–2, folder 15, Georgia Douglas Johnson Papers. (Huff was apparently trying to help Johnson secure support to publish her biography of her husband).

29. Loften Mitchell, *Black Drama: The Story of the American Negro in the Theatre* (New York: Hawthorn, 1967), 11.

30. Mark Tucker, "The Renaissance Education of Duke Ellington," in *Black Music in the Harlem Renaissance: A Collection of Essays,* ed. Samuel Floyd (Knoxville: University of Tennessee Press, 1990), 112. In his discussion of Washington, D.C., David Krasner notes, "There were segregation and poverty, especially in areas known as the 'alley'; but within the black community, there was a commitment to education and self-respect" (*Beautiful Pageant,* 133–35).

31. See Winona Fletcher, "Georgia Douglas Johnson," in *Notable Women,* 473; and Hull, *Color, Sex and Poetry*, 156. Johnson's Catalogue lists her affiliation with numerous clubs and organizations.

32. GDJ to Harold Jackman, 2 March 1950, box 19, folder 20, Countee Cullen/Harold Jackman Memorial Collection.

33. See Constance Green's *Washington: Capital City, 1879–1950,* vol. 2 (Princeton, NJ: Princeton University Press, 1963).

34. GDJ to Mr. [George E.] Haynes, 6 February 1929, Harmon Foundation Records, Manuscript Reading Room, Library of Congress. See also "Stoneleigh Court" in James M. Goode, *Best Addresses* (Washington, DC: Smithsonian Institution Press, 1988), 50–54.

35. Ralph Matthews, "The Negro Theatre—A Dodo Bird," in *Negro,* ed. Nancy Cunard and Hugh Ford (New York: Frederick Ungar , 1970), 194; first published in 1934 by Nancy Cunard (London: Wishart). Johnson began writing plays in the 1920s, a decade Leslie Catherine Saunders characterizes as a period when "elevating the figure of the Negro beyond that of a buffoon constituted a victory." Leslie Catherine Saunders, *The Development of Black Theatre in America: From Shadows to Selves* (Baton Rouge: Louisiana State University Press, 1988), 7.

36. Carter G. Woodson, introduction to *Negro History in Thirteen Plays,* ed. Willis Richardson and May Miller (Washington, DC: Associated, 1935), iii.

37. James Weldon Johnson, preface to *God's Trombones: Seven Negro Sermons in Verse* (New York: Viking Press, 1927), 10. Torrence's *Rider of Dreams,* with the dream speech beginning "I wuz layin' groanin', 'O Lawd, how long,' an' I heah a voice say, 'Git up an' come a-runnin,'" is published in Alain Locke and Montgomery Gregory's *Plays of Negro Life: A Source-Book of Native American Drama* (New York: Harper and Brothers, 1927; Westport,CT: Negro Universities Press, 1976), 34. The quote is from the 1976 Negro Universities Press edition. A few years later, in his introduction to Sterling Brown's poems in *Southern Road,* Johnson locates Brown's work as emerging "just after the Negro poets had generally discarded conventionalized dialect, with its minstrel traditions of Negro life" and praises Brown for adopting as his medium "the common racy, living speech of the Negro in certain phases of *real* life." See James Weldon Johnson, introduction to *Southern Road: Poems by Sterling A. Brown* (New York: Harcourt, Brace, 1932; New York: Beacon, 1970), xxxvi. The citation is from the 1970 Beacon Press edition.

38. "Propaganda in the Theatre," *The Messenger* 6 (November 1924): 354.

39. Saunders, *Development of Black Theatre*, 33.

40. Ibid., 32.

41. *A Sunday Morning in the South*, p. 141.

42. *William and Ellen Craft*, p. 96.

43. *Starting Point*, p. 118.

44. Austin, *CLA Journal*, 32:235.

45. "Krigwa" stands for the Crisis Guild of Writers and Artists. See W. E. B. Du Bois, "Krigwa Players Little Negro Theatre: The Story of a Little Theatre Movement" (1926), reprinted in *Lost Plays of the Harlem Renaissance, 1920–1940*, ed. James V. Hatch and Leo Hamalian (Detroit: Wayne State University Press, 1996), 446–52.

46. The folk drama versus protest drama configuration conflates some of the philosophical views shared by Locke and Du Bois. See David Krasner's discussion of their theories in *Beautiful Pageant,* 146–50. Also see Samuel A. Hay's analysis of the Locke/Du Bois debate in *African American Theatre: An Historical and Critical Analysis* (New York: Cambridge University Press, 1994).

47. Hatch and Hamalian, *Lost Plays*, 18. By the 1920s black musical theatre was already successful, with Broadway productions such as *In Dahomey* by Paul Laurence Dunbar, Will Marion Cook, and Jesse Shipp (1902); *Bandanna Land* by

Jesse Shipp and Alex Rogers, with music by Will Marion Cook and Bert Williams (1908); and *Shuffle Along* by Eubie Blake and Noble Sissle (1921). For a perspective of 1890s "plantation shows" as cultural production in which African American performers mobilized themselves "to create potential touchstones for African American identification and empowerment," see Barbara L. Webb, "Authentic Possibilities: Plantation Performance of the 1890s," *Theatre Journal* 56 (2004): 63–82.

48. Nellie McKay, "What Were They Saying?: Black Women Playwrights of the Harlem Renaissance," in *The Harlem Renaissance Re-examined*, ed. Victor A. Kramer (New York: AMS, 1987), 129–46.

49. Perkins, *Black Female Playwrights*, 5.

50. According to Marta Effinger and others, Johnson also taught in the Washington, D.C., schools. See Marta Effinger, "Georgia Douglas Johnson," in *Dictionary of Literary Biography.* It should be noted here that, of those members of the New Negro Renaissance who wrote plays or were critics, the men were commonly college professors (Du Bois, Locke, Gregory, Edmonds) while the women were predominantly high-school teachers (Burrill, Bonner, Johnson, Miller, and others). Biases against women extended into the idea that women could be high-school teachers, but that college-level teaching was reserved for men. The one exception to this norm was Zora Neale Hurston, who taught at several colleges.

51. GDJ to Alain Locke, March 29 (no year), box 164–40, Alain Locke Papers.

52. See Gwendolyn Bennett, "Ebony Flute," *Opportunity: Journal of Negro Life* (October 1926): 322; (November 1926): 356–58. In her Catalogue Johnson referred to the gatherings as "literary gatherings" and as her "literary salon" (4).

53. Langston Hughes, *The Big Sea* (New York: Hill and Wang, 1993).

54. David Levering Lewis, *When Harlem Was in Vogue* (New York: Penguin, 1997).

55. Lewis, *When Harlem*, 127; McHenry, *Forgotten Readers*, 275.

56. Hughes, *Big Sea*, 216; Miller in Perkins and Stephens, *Strange Fruit*, 175.

57. Most of these plays are published in James V. Hatch and Ted Shine, eds., *Black Theatre USA: Plays by African Americans,* rev. ed. (New York: Free Press, 1996). Richardson's *The Chip Woman's Fortune* is in James V. Hatch and Leo Hamalian, eds., *The Roots of African American Drama: An Anthology of Early Plays, 1858–1938* (Detroit: Wayne State University Press, 1991), 164–85.

58. Alain Locke, "Steps Toward the Negro Theatre," *The Crisis* (December 1922): 66–68; W. E. B. DuBois, "Krigwa Players Little Negro Theatre," *The Crisis* (June 1926), reprinted in *Lost Plays*, 446–452; Montgomery Gregory, "A Chronology of the Negro Theatre," in *Plays of Negro Life*, 409–422.

59. Willis Richardson, taped interview with Larry Garvin, 24 July 1974, Hatch-Billops Collection; quoted by Christine Gray in *Willis Richardson*, 19.

60. Richard Bruce Nugent, videorecorded interview with Jean Blackwell Hutson, 14 April 1982, Schomburg Center for Research in Black Culture, New York Public Library. Nugent quoted in *Gay Rebel of the Harlem Renaissance: Selections from*

the Work of Richard Bruce Nugent, ed. Thomas H. Wirth (Durham, NC: Duke University Press, 2002), 5.

61. Richard Bruce Nugent, videorecorded interview with Jean Blackwell Hutson. Darwin Turner characterizes *Cane* as both "a harbinger" of the New Negro Renaissance and an "illumination of significant psychological and moral concerns of the 1920s." See Darwin T. Turner, introduction to *Cane* (New York: Liveright, 1975), xvi.

62. Christine Gray, introduction, *Plays and Pageants from the Life of the Negro*, ed. Willis Richardson (Jackson: University Press of Mississippi, 1993), xx, xxiv.

63. See Perkins interview with May Miller in *Strange Fruit*, 175. Christine Gray quotes from Richardson's unpublished notes, in which he alleges that May Miller's name appears on the cover of the anthology as coeditor at the insistence of her father, Kelly Miller, dean at Howard University. Richardson implies he did all the work in compiling the anthology and writes, "I didn't mind her name [Miller's] being on the cover, and so that's how the book happens to be by both of us." See Gray, *Willis Richardson*, 102 n. 1. Corroboration of Richardson's allegation has not been found.

64. Carter G. Woodson, introduction to *Negro History in Thirteen Plays*, ed. Willis Richardson and May Miller (Washington, DC: Associated, 1935), 5.

65. Cedric Dover, "The Importance of Georgia Douglas Johnson," *The Crisis* (December 1952): 635.

66. Glenn Carrington, "The Harlem Renaissance: A Personal Memoir," *Freedomways* 3, no. 3 (Summer 1963): 309.

67. Lewis, *When Harlem*, 127.

68. Richard Bruce Nugent videorecorded interview with Jean Blackwell Hutson.

69. A. Philip Randolph (international president, Brotherhood of Sleeping Car Porters) to GDJ, 18 December 1944, box 162–2, file 5, Georgia Douglas Johnson Papers.

70. Owen Dodson interview in the Hatch-Billops Collection, and Johnson's obituary in the *Afro-American,* May 28, 1966.

71. GDJ, Catalogue of Writings, 4.

72. Box 162–2, file 17, Georgia Douglas Johnson Papers.

73. GDJ to Glenn Carrington, 4 January 1964, box 6, Georgia Douglas Johnson folder, Glenn Carrington Papers, Schomburg Center for Research in Black Culture, New York Public Library.

74. Glenn Carrington wrote to Johnson on May 7, 1955, "You have no idea how often I recount to friends the many happy days and evenings I spent basking in the deep spirituality of Halfway House, with its limitless hospitality and warmth." Box 6, Georgia Douglas Johnson folder, Glenn Carrington Papers.

75. GDJ, Catalogue, 8.

76. Samuel Hay cites a production of *Blue Blood* by the Gough D. McDaniels Baltimore Krigwa Group (1929–1933) in *African American Theatre*, 175. Both the

New York and Howard University productions are cited by Kathy Perkins in *Black Female Playwrights*, 22.

77. "Negro Drama? Why Not?" *Amsterdam News*, November 23, 1927. Clipping File, Georgia Douglas Johnson, Schomburg Center for Research in Black Culture, New York Public Library.

78. Langston Hughes to GDJ, 6 July 1951, box 83, Langston Hughes Correspondence with Georgia Douglas Johnson, James Weldon Johnson Collection.

79. The Harlem Experimental Theatre's production of *Plumes* is noted under 'Achievements' in "Programme, Harlem Experimental Theatre, 1928–1931," Schomburg Center for Research in Black Culture. Regina Andrews quoted in Mitchell, *Black Drama*, 69.

80. The Cube Theatre performance is recorded in Kitty Chapelle's unpublished manuscript, "Negro Culture in Chicago," 1937, n.p., box 47, Illinois Writers Project/Negro in Illinois Papers, Vivian G. Harsh Research Collection of Afro-American History and Literature, Chicago Public Library. According to Chapelle, *Plumes* was offered on a bill with Eugene O'Neill's *The Dreamy Kid* and Paul Green's *No 'Count Boy* in February 1927; the program concluded with a "curtain speech" by Alain Locke. Johnson notes the Cube Theatre production of *Plumes* in her Catalogue along with the plot summary of the play and, again, under the section "Special Citations." Johnson was obviously pleased to have her play presented with dramas by Eugene O'Neill and Paul Green "as a trio". The program for the February 28, 1928, performance of *Plumes* by the Students' Literary Guild of Central YMCA in Brooklyn is in the Georgia Douglas Johnson file, Hatch-Billops Collection.

81. *Plumes* appears in collections such as Rachel France's *A Century of Plays by American Women* (1979), Kathy Perkins's *Black Female Playwrights* (1989), and Judith Barlow's *Plays by American Women: 1900–1930* (1985), as well as in Tate's 1997 volume *Selected Works of Georgia Douglas Johnson*. .

82. GDJ, Catalogue, 8.

83. GDJ to Jackman, no date, Georgia Douglas Johnson Correspondence with Harold Jackman, 1936–1942, James Weldon Johnson Collection.

84. GDJ, Catalogue, 8.

85. David Krasner, "Black Salome: Exoticism, Dance and Racial Myths," in Elam and Krasner, *African American Performance*, 195.

86. Sieglinde Lemke, *Primitivist Modernism: Black Culture and the Origins of Transatlantic Modernism* (New York: Oxford University Press), 5. Lemke discusses the multiple meanings of the term "primitivism" and explores the role of interracial ("Black" and "White") exchanges in the creation of transatlantic modernism.

87. Georgia Douglas Johnson, *Plumes: A One-Act Play*, *Opportunity* (July 1927): 200–201, 217, 218.

88. See *Plumes: A Folk Tragedy* in Locke's *Plays of Negro Life*. Locke apparently made some decisions on individual pieces without consulting contributors to his edited volumes. Richard Bruce Nugent tells of Locke requesting a drawing (by Nugent) for inclusion in *The New Negro*, but when the volume appeared Nugent's

contributed story, *Sahdji,* was accompanied by an illustration by Aaron Douglas. Nugent remembers, "I didn't draw again for a year. Because I couldn't draw if Locke did that. He wanted the drawing, but then when I wrote the story, the story was good, but the drawing wasn't, so he got Aaron to do the drawing. It was just very traumatic." (Nugent quoted in Wirth, *Gay Rebel*, 3). In her Catalogue, Johnson provided twenty-eight plot summaries, but she didn't use the term "folk drama" to refer to or describe any of her plays. Johnson curried Locke's friendship and solicited his opinion on her work. Locke wrote the foreword to Johnson's third volume of verse, *An Autumn Love Cycle;* however, in the introduction to her book Claudia Tate points to Locke's language that suggests that "the collection's ingenuity lies in its candor, naivety, and unsophistication" (liii). Correspondence shows that as early as 1916, Johnson invited Locke and Montgomery Gregory to her home, and as late as 1947 she wrote to Locke that she was studying French and intended to visit Paris. "No you can't get away from me even there," Johnson wrote, "I am Fate." GDJ to Alain Locke, 23 May 1947, box 164–40, folder 35, Alain Locke Papers.

89. *William and Ellen Craft* script, p. 8, box 638, Federal Theatre Project Collection.

90. According to Babatunde Lawal, "Slaves secretly gathered on the plantation to mimic the mannerisms of their masters. The need for secrecy led them to develop rhetorical strategies akin to the African tradition of using esoteric sounds, words and gestures to relate information accessible only to the initiated." Lawal notes that this phenomenon (known as "signifying") has "since become a distinctive feature of African American literature and theatre" (51). See Lawal, "The African Heritage of African American Art and Performance," in *Black Theatre: Ritual Performance in the African Diaspora,* ed. Paul Carter Harrison, Victor Leo Walker II, and Gus Edwards (Philadelphia: Temple University Press, 2002), 39–56.

91. Tate, *Selected Works*, lix.

92. May Miller interview with Cassandra Willis, 4 March 1972, Hatch-Billops Collection.

93. GDJ to Harold Jackman, 4 August 1938, box 19, folder 20, Countee Cullen/Harold Jackman Memorial Collection.

94. The Federal Theatre Project, founded in 1935, was "designed to reemploy theatre workers on public relief . . . and to bring a theatre which would be national in scope and regional in emphasis to thousands in the United States who have never before seen live theatrical performances." From the Chronology in *The Federal Theatre Project Collection: A Register of the Library of Congress*, Music Division, Library of Congress; Fletcher, "From Genteel Poet," 52, 62.

95. All FTP critical responses to *William and Ellen Craft* (also known as *Ellen and William Craft)* are from the Reader Files of the Federal Theatre Project, box 185, Ellen and William Craft file, Music Division, Library of Congress.

96. All FTP critical responses to *Frederick Douglass* are from the Reader Files of the Federal Theatre Project, box 198, Frederick Douglass File.

97. GDJ to Harold Jackman, 17 March 1937, Georgia Douglas Johnson Correspondence, James Weldon Johnson Collection.

98. Fletcher, "From Genteel Poet," 41–64.

99. Reader Files of the Federal Theatre Project, *Blue-Eyed Black Boy*, box 151.

100. Reader Files of the Federal Theatre Project, *Safe*, box 301.

101. Reader Files of the Federal Theatre Project, *Blue Blood*, box 151.

102. Krasner, *Beautiful Pageant*, 157.

103. GDJ, Catalogue, 10.

104. Ibid., 11.

105. Ibid., 9.

106. GDJ, "Book Chat," *Norfolk T and E*, 4 October 1930, Clipping File, Georgia Douglas Johnson. Schomberg Center.

107. GDJ to Harold Jackman, 4 August 1938, box 19, folder 20, Countee Cullen/Harold Jackman Memorial Collection.

108. *Starting Point*, 118.

109. GDJ to Langston Hughes, 30 May 1938, box 83, Georgia Douglas Johnson Correspondence, James Weldon Johnson Collection.

110. Deborah E. McDowell, *"The Changing Same": Black Women's Literature, Criticism, and Theory* (Bloomington: Indiana University Press, 1995), 80; and Angela Y. Davis, *Blues Legacies and Black Feminism: Gertrude "Ma" Rainey, Bessie Smith, and Billie Holiday* (New York: Pantheon, 1998), 44.

111. Langston Hughes, "The Negro Artist and the Racial Mountain" (1926), reprinted in Hatch and Hamalian, *Lost Plays*, 412.

112. Alain Locke, "The Negro and the American Stage," *Theatre Arts* (February 1926): 119.

113. Both Gwendolyn Bennett and Thomas Wirth write that Richard Bruce Nugent collaborated with Johnson in writing *Paupaulekejo* (Bennett spells it "Popoplikahu") and that it was performed in Washington (the President Theatre) in 1926, but no mention of this artistic collaboration appears in Johnson's Catalogue or papers. See Wirth, *Gay Rebel*, 3, and Bennett, "Ebony Flute," *Opportunity* (November 1926): 357.

114. James V. Hatch, "Some African Influences on the Afro-American Theatre," in *The Theatre of Black Americans: Collections of Critical Essays*, ed. Errol Hill (New York: Applause, 1987), 16.

115. Michael Feith, "The Syncopated African: Constructions of Origins in the Harlem Renaissance (Literature, Music, Visual Arts)," in *Temples for Tomorrow: Looking Back at the Harlem Renaissance*, ed. Genevieve Fabre and Michael Feith (Bloomington: Indiana University Press, 2001), 58.

116. Arthur P. Davis and Michael W. Peplow, eds., *The New Negro Renaissance: An Anthology* (New York: Holt, Rinehart and Winston, 1975), 202; and Hatch, "Some African Influences," 14.

117. Tate, *Selected Works*, lix.

118. Krasner, *Beautiful Pageant*, 4.

119. Tate, *Selected Works*, lix.

120. GDJ to Harold Jackman, 4 August 1938, box 19, folder 20, Countee Cullen/Harold Jackman Memorial Collection.

121. GDJ, Catalogue, 9.

122. Ibid.

123. Ibid.

124. Ibid., 10.

125. See Matthews in *Negro*, 194. *Porgy* was later converted into the opera *Porgy and Bess* (1935). In a 1970 historical review, theatre scholar Randolph Edmonds reviewed all three white-authored plays and acknowledged their contributions to African American theatre, but he judged *Porgy* to be "only incidentally realistic" and saw *In Abraham's Bosom* as "hopeless and depressing." Of *The Emperor Jones* Edmonds wrote, "If every playwright must write at least one really bad play, this one can be said to be O'Neill's." Randolph Edmonds, "Black Drama in the American Theatre: 1700–1970," in *The American Theatre: A Sum of Its Parts* (New York: Samuel French, 1971), 378–425.

126. Willis Richardson, "The Hope of A Negro Drama" (1919), in Hatch and Hamalian, *Lost Plays,* 438.

127. Lynching dramas reflect the brutal history of lynching (mob murder) in the United States and focus especially on the violence occurring after 1865, when lynching became a racial phenomenon carried out and supported by white supremacists as a way to keep intact the racial hierarchy imposed by slavery. According to statistics from the Tuskegee Institute, 4,734 lynchings occurred between 1882 and 1968; of that total, 1,297 were white victims while 3,446 were black. See Robert Zangrando, *The NAACP Crusade Against Lynching, 1909–1950* (Philadelphia: TempleUniversity Press, 1980). James Allen's recent publication and exhibits of his photography collection *Without Sanctuary: Lynching Photography in America* (Santa Fe, NM: Twin Palms, 2000) has brought the legacy of lynching back into the public consciousness. Allen's collection provided the impetus for the international conference on lynching, "Lynching and Racial Violence in America: Histories and Legacies," held at Emory University October 3–6, 2002. Johnson wrote her plays during the 1920s and 1930s when lynchings were occurring, predominantly in the South, and at a time when various antilynching bills were introduced in the United States Congress. Despite the efforts of organizations such as the NAACP, the federal government never enacted antilynching legislation, although several states did so. According to Fitzhugh Brundage, in 1953 the Tuskegee Institute announced that lynching "seems no longer to be a valid index" of race relations in the United States, but the language of the announcement itself speaks to the major role of lynching in enforcing racial boundaries up until the mid-twentieth century. See Brundage, *Lynching in the New South: Georgia and Virginia, 1880–1930* (Urbana: University of Illinois Press, 1993), 275. Lynching as a means of racial intimidation did not come to an end in the 1950s (as witness Emmett Till in 1955, Mack Charles Parker in 1959, Michael Donald in 1981, and James Byrd in 1998)

but by that time incidents like those portrayed in Johnson's plays had significantly declined, and black activist and civil-rights organizations turned their energies to other matters.

128. A possible mistake in assembling Johnson's Catalogue is that five plays numbered 7 through 11, and placed under the Category of Lynching Plays, are actually intended for inclusion under the category Plays of Average Negro Life. Judging from the summaries Johnson provided, none of the five plays deals with lynching. Instead, they offer more diverse and much lighter fare such as romance, interracial friendships, and postwar stories. *Miss Bliss* (see plot summary under Plays of Average Negro Life in the text), is a romance story of mistaken racial identity. *Heritage* encourages young people to value the inheritance of character over wealth. Obviously, these plays do not touch directly upon the subject of lynching, and summaries of the other three, *Midnight and Dawn*, *Camel Legs*, and *Money Wagon,* do not suggest any connection to the atrocity of lynching. Since the list of dramas under Plays of Average Negro Life ends at the bottom of a page with the summary of play number 6, I am suggesting that the list should continue with plays numbered 7 through 11, mistakenly listed under Lynching Plays. This decision is based on the fact that none of the five summaries refers to a lynching and none of the plays appears to be appropriate for the category. Furthermore, in correspondence dated as late as 1938, Johnson referred specifically to her "five lynching plays," and an earlier page from the Catalogue lists the five extant lynching plays alone on a single page. Since Johnson's Catalogue seems to have existed in several preliminary versions, it is highly possible that the mistake occurred in compiling the final version, and that instead of placing the synopses of plays numbered 7 through 11 after number 6 under Plays of Average Negro Life, Johnson, or someone else, mistakenly placed them after number 6 under Lynching Plays. Although previous scholarly studies have credited Johnson with writing as many as eleven lynching plays, she actually wrote five or, if the two different versions of *A Sunday Morning in the South* are counted separately (as Johnson lists them in her Catalogue), six lynching plays. I am suggesting these six plays are Johnson's complete body of work in the lynching-drama genre.

129. Hatch and Shine, *Black Theatre USA*, 232.

130. In *Lady Sings the Blues*, written with William Duffy, Holiday is quoted as saying the song *Strange Fruit* became her "personal protest" because of the way her father, Clarence Holiday, died. Apparently Clarence Holiday was stricken with pneumonia in Dallas, Texas, but he was refused care by one hospital after another because of jim crow laws. When a veterans' hospital finally accepted him, it was too late to save him. Holiday said of the song: "It reminds me of how Pop died. But I have to keep singing it, not only because people ask for it but because twenty years after Pop died the things that killed him are still happening in the South." Billie Holiday with William Duffy, *Lady Sings the Blues* (New York: Lancer , 1972), 68, 82–83.

131. Hull, *Color, Sex and Poetry*, 229 n. 19.

132. Harris, "Before the Strength, the Pain," 39, 41.

133. McHenry, *Forgotten Readers*, 276.

134. Claude McKay, "If We Must Die," in *The Portable Harlem Renaissance Reader*, ed. David Levering Lewis (New York: Penguin, 1994), 290.

135. Walter White to GDJ, 18 January 1937, box C-299, "Anti-Lynching Bill Play 1936–1938," NAACP Papers, Manuscript Reading Room, Library of Congress. All correspondence between Johnson and the NAACP is in this file.

136. Harry Elam Jr., "The Device of Race: An Introduction," in Elam and Krasner, *African American Performance*, 6.

137. As Brenda Murphy points out, portraying a serious social problem that was unresolved at the play's end was one of the hallmarks of "realism" as it was developed by early twentieth-century American dramatists. See Murphy, *American Realism and American Drama, 1880–1940* (New York: Cambridge University Press, 1987), xii.

138. Krasner, *Beautiful Pageant*, 150.

139. Walter White to GDJ, 18 January 1937, box C-299, Anti-Lynching Bill Play file, NAACP Papers.

140. Memorandum from Mr. Morrow to Miss Jackson, "Criticism of one-act play for radio skit," 25 January 1938, box C-299, Anti-Lynching Bill Play file, NAACP Papers.

141. See, for example, the Western Union telegram from the Writers League Against Lynching, 15 January 1935, box C-208, folder WLAG, NAACP Papers.

142. Copies of "Brotherhood Marching Song" (1945) are in the Glen Carrington Papers.

143. GDJ to Langston Hughes, 9 December 1955, and Hughes to GDJ, 15 December 1955, box 83, Langston Hughes Correspondence with Georgia Douglas Johnson, James Weldon Johnson Collection.

144. Floyd, *Black Music*, 6.

145. In her August 4, 1938, letter to Harold Jackman, Johnson describes her drama *Sue Bailey* as ". . . no moral to it . . . Simple entertainment. The sordid tale of a girl who lived the easy way . . . her conflicts . . . life's exactions and the final payment she made." Box 19, folder 20, Countee Cullen/Harold Jackman Memorial Collection.

146. McHenry, *Forgotten Readers*, 276.

147. Tate, *Selected Works*, lxvii.

148. See Marta Effinger, "Georgia Douglas Johnson," in *Dictionary of Literary Biography: Twentieth Century American Dramatists*. Both Effinger and Lambert presented papers on Johnson at the 2002 annual conference of the Black Theatre Network. Lambert's "Ar'n't I A Woman? Georgia Douglas Johnson's *Blue Blood*," explored Johnson's portrayal of the sexual exploitation of black women, while Effinger's "The (In)humanity of Place: An Examination of Georgia Douglas Johnson's Lynching Dramas" examined racism in America against the backdrop of Johnson's settings. Both papers were part of the panel "Georgia Douglas Johnson: Pioneer-

ing Poet and Playwright." Actress, director, and playwright Dorothy E. King portrayed Johnson, in conversation with the audience, discussing her work and literary salon. See "Georgia Douglas Johnson Panel: 'A First' Presented at the 2002 BTN Conference in San Francisco," *Black Theatre Network News* 13, no. 1 (Fall 2002): 3. For other feminist approaches to Johnson's plays see Megan Sullivan's "Folk Plays, Home Girls and Back Talk: Georgia Douglas Johnson and Women of the Harlem Renaissance" *CLA Journal* 38, no. 4 (June 1995): 404–19, and Judith Stephens's "Politics and Aesthetics, Race and Gender: Georgia Douglas Johnson's Lynching Dramas as Black Feminist Cultural Performance," *Text and Performance Quarterly* 20, no. 3 (July 2000): 251–67. For a discussion of Johnson's work within the context of cosmopolitanism, see C. C. O'Brien, "Cosmopolitanism in Georgia Douglas Johnson's Anti-Lynching Literature," *African American Review* 38, no. 4 (2004): 571–87. For a cogent analysis of plays by Grimke, Burill, Dunbar-Nelson, and Johnson as foundational scripts of antilynching drama see Koritha Mitchell, "A Different Kind of 'Strange Fruit': Lynching Drama, African Identity, and U.S. Culture" (Ph.D. dissertation, University of Maryland, 2005).

Johnson as a youth. Reprinted with permission of the Moorland-Spingarn Research Center of Howard University.

Johnson as a young woman. Reprinted with permission of the Moorland-Spingarn Research Center of Howard University.

Johnson with a frilly hat. Reprinted with permission of the Moorland-Spingarn Research Center of Howard University.

Johnson, young, with dark headband. Reprinted with permission of the Moorland-Spingarn Research Center of Howard University.

Johnson in mid-life. Reprinted with permission of the Moorland-Spingarn Research Center of Howard University.

Johnson with striped headband, 1949. Reprinted with permission of the Photographs and Prints Division, Schomburg Center for Research in Black Culture, The New York Public Library, Astor, Lenox and Tilden Foundations.

Johnson with Rufus Clement, president of Atlanta University, 1963, three years before her death. From the *Atlanta University Bulletin* (July 1963), p. 25. Reprinted by permission of the Atlanta University Center of the Robert W. Woodruff Library.

Georgia Douglas Johnson's home, "Half-Way House," 1461 S Street NW, Washington D.C., as it was undergoing renovation. Photo by Kathy Perkins; reprinted by her permission.

PART I

Primitive Life Plays

Blue Blood
(1926)

Characters:

MAY BUSH
MRS. BUSH
JOHN TEMPLE
MRS. TEMPLE
RANDOLPH STRONG
These characters are *Negroes*

Place:
Georgia

Time:
Shortly after Civil War

Scene
Large kitchen and dining room combined of frame cottage, showing one door leading into back yard. One other door (right side of room facing stage) leading into hall. One back window, neatly curtained. Steps on right side of room leading upstairs. (Enter Randolph Strong with large bunch of white roses and a package. He places the package, unnoticed, on the table—still holding the roses.)

RANDOLPH STRONG: How is my dear Mother Bush?

MRS. BUSH: Feeling like a sixteen-year-old! That's right, you come right on back here with me. *(notices roses)* Oh! What pretty roses! Snow white!

RANDOLPH STRONG: Like um? Thought you would . . . May likes this kind!

MRS. BUSH: She sho'ly do. Pore chile! She's turning her back on the best fellow in this town, when she turned you down. I knows a good man when I see one.

RANDOLPH STRONG: You are always kind to me, Mother Bush. I feel like the lost sheep tonight, the one hundredth one, out in the cold, separated by iron bars from the ninety and nine! Bah! What am I doing? The milk's spilt! *(arranges flowers)* Put these in here?

MRS. BUSH: Sure! My, but they look grand. There ain't many young doctors so handy-like!

RANDOLPH STRONG *(half to himself)*: The first time I saw her she wore a white rose in her hair . . .

MRS. BUSH: Jest listen! May's plum blind! Oh! If she'd a only listened to me, she'd be marrying you to-night, instead of that stuck up John Temple. I never did believe in two "lights" marrying, no how, it's onlucky. They're jest exactly the same color . . . hair . . . and eyes alike too. Now you . . . you is jest right for my May. "Dark should marry light." You'd be a perfect match.

RANDOLPH STRONG *(groans)*: Hold, hold for goodness sake! Why didn't you lend that little blind girl of yours your two good eyes?

MRS. BUSH: Humph! She wouldn't hear me. *(goes up to him, speaking confidentially)* 'Tween you and me, I shorely do wish she'd a said "yes" when you popped the question las' Christmas. I hates to see her tying up with this highfalutin' nothing. She'll re'lize some day that money ain't everything, and that a poor man's love is a whole sight better than a stiff-necked, good-looking dude.

RANDOLPH STRONG: It can't be helped now, Mother Bush. If she's happy, that's the main thing!

MRS. BUSH: But is she going to be happy . . . that's jest it!

RANDOLPH STRONG: Let us hope so! And yet, sometimes I think—do you know, Mother Bush *(lowering his voice)*: sometimes I think May cares for me.

MRS. BUSH *(confidently)*: Do you know, honey, somehow, sometimes I do too!

RANDOLPH STRONG *(excitedly)*: You do too!! Oh, if I could fully believe that—even now—at the last minute—*(snaps his finger)* Oh, what's the use? *(constrainedly)* Is everything ready?

MRS. BUSH: You bet! I'm all dressed under this apron. *(swings it back and discloses a brilliant and much decorated gown. Then with a start)* Lord save us! That Lyddie Smith ain't brought that my'nase dressing yet. Vowed she'd have it here by eight sharp, if she was alive. What time you got?

RANDOLPH STRONG *(looking at his watch)*: Eight thirty.

MRS. BUSH: Eight thirty? Good gracious!

RANDOLPH STRONG: I'll run over and get it for you.

MRS. BUSH: Oh yes, honey! Do hurry. Oh, what a son-in-law you would'a made!

RANDOLPH STRONG: Good joke . . . but I can laugh!

(He goes. Mrs. Bush busies herself with the table arrangements and finally notices a package that had been left by Strong; she opens it and discloses a beautiful vase and reads aloud the card attached)

MRS. BUSH *(reading)*: For May and her husband, with best wishes for your happiness, Randolph. *(she sets it aside without saying a word—only wiping her eyes—thinks a while; shakes her head; picks up the vase again and calls toward the stairway)* May! May! Run down here a minute. I've got something to show you. *(Mrs. Bush polishes the vase with her apron and holds her head to one side looking at it admiringly. Enter May in negligee. Mrs. Bush—with vase held behind her)* Not dressed yet? . . . Gracious! There . . . look . . . Randolph brought it!

MAY BUSH: Oh! . . . did he? *(reads card)* Randolph is a dear! *(fondles vase and looks sad)*

MRS. BUSH: He brought theses roses, too . . . said you liked this kind.

(May Bush takes roses and buries her face in them, then thoughtfully changes them into Randolph's vase; looks at it with head on side, then breaks off one rose, fondles it, places it in her hair)

MRS. BUSH: May—May—are you happy?

MAY BUSH: Why—why—*(dashing something like a tear from her eye)* of course I am.

MRS. BUSH: Maybe you is . . . May . . . but, somehow, I don't feel satisfied.

MAY BUSH *(kisses her mother)*: Oh, Ma, everything is all right! Just wait until you see me dressed. *(noise at door)* Oh, somebody's coming in here!

(May retreats partly up the stairway. Enter Mrs. Temple, talking. Voices and commotion heard as if coming from the front of the house, where heated argument is going on at front door, Mrs. Temple's muffled voice being heard. Hall kitchen door opens suddenly. Enter Mrs. Temple, excitedly)

MRS. TEMPLE: Heavens! They tried to keep me from coming out here! The very idea of her talking that way to me—the groom's own mother! Who is that little upstart that let me in at the front door? I told her I was coming right out here in the kitchen, for even though we have not called on each other in the past, moving around—as you know—in somewhat different social circles, and, of course, not being thrown very closely together, yet now, at this particular time, Mrs. Bush, since our two children are determined to marry, I feel that my place to-night is right back here with you! *(glancing upward, Mrs. Temple discovers May upon the stairway)* Why, May, are you not dressed yet! You'll have to do better than that when you are Mrs. John Temple!

MRS. BUSH: Don't worry 'bout May; she'll be ready. Where's John? Is he here?

MRS. TEMPLE: Sure—he brought me in his car, but the fellows captured him and said they were going to keep him out driving until the last minute. *(Again glancing upward toward May)* Better hurry, May; you mustn't keep John waiting.

MAY BUSH *(slowly walking upstairs)*: Oh, John will get used to waiting on me. *(exit May)*

MRS. TEMPLE *(to Mrs. Bush)*: What's this . . . chicken salad? Is it finished?

MRS. BUSH: No, it ain't. The my'nase ain't come yet. I sent Randolph for it. I jest got tired waiting on Lyddie Smith to fetch it.

MRS. TEMPLE: My gracious . . . give me the things and I'll make the dressing for you in a jiffy.

(Mrs. Temple removes her white gloves and gets ready for her new role in the kitchen. Without waiting for Mrs. Bush's consent, she rapidly walks over to wooden peg on wall, takes down extra gingham apron and removes her hat and lightweight coat, hanging both upon peg)

MRS. BUSH *(remonstratingly):* I'm 'fraid you'll git yo'self spoiled doing kitchen work. Sich folks as you'd better go 'long in the parlor.

MRS. TEMPLE: Oh, no indeed. This is my son's wedding and I'm here to do a mother's part. Besides—he is a Temple and everything must be right.

MRS. BUSH *(takes materials for making the mayonnaise from kitchen safe and reluctantly places them before Mrs. Temple):* You needn't worry 'bout this wedding bein' right. It's my daughter's wedding—and I'll see to that!

MRS. TEMPLE *(breaking and stirring eggs for the dressing):* You'll have to admit that the girls will envy May marrying my boy John.

MRS. BUSH *(stopping her work suddenly and with arms akimbo):* Envy May!!! Envy May!!! They'd better envy John!!! You don't know who May is; she's got blue blood in her veins.

MRS. TEMPLE *(laughing sarcastically):* You amuse me. I'll admit May's sweet and pretty, but she is no match for John.

MRS. BUSH *(irately):* She's not, eh? If I told you something about my May—who she is—you'd be struck dumb.

MRS. TEMPLE *(nervously stirring the mayonnaise, replies in a falsetto or raised tone, denoting sarcasm):* Remarkable . . . but I am curious!

MRS. BUSH *(proudly):* I bet you is—you'd fall flat if I told you who she is.

MRS. TEMPLE *(suspending the operation of the mayonnaise and curiously assuming a soft, confidential tone):* Pray, Mrs. Bush, tell me then. Who is May?

MRS. BUSH: Who is May? Huh! *(proudly tossing her head)* Who is May? *(lowering her voice, confidentially)* Why . . . do you know Cap'n Winfield McCallister, the biggest banker in this town, and who's got money 'vested in banks all over Georgia? That 'ristocrat uv 'ristocrats . . . that Peachtree Street blue blood—Cap'n McCallister—don't you know him?

MRS. TEMPLE *(starts at the mention of the name but recovers herself in a moment):* Y—e—s, I've heard of him.

MRS. BUSH *(like a shot out of a gun):* Well, I'd have you to know—he's May's daddy!

MRS. TEMPLE *(agitatedly):* W-h-y . . . I . . . I . . . I can't believe it!

MRS. BUSH *(flauntingly):* Believe it or not, it's the bounden truth so help me God! Ain't you never seen him strut? Well, look at May.

Walks jest like him—throws her head like him—an' she's got eyes, nose and mouth jest like him. She's his living image.

MRS. TEMPLE *(almost collapsing, speaking softly and excitedly):* You . . . you terrify me. Mrs. Bush . . . Captain McCallister can't be May's father!

MRS. BUSH: Can't be May's father! Well, I reckon I ought to know who May's father is! What do you know 'bout it anyhow? What do you know 'bout Cap'n McCallister?

MRS. TEMPLE: Do you mean to tell—

MRS. BUSH *(interrupting):* I mean jest whut I said. I'm telling you that my daughter—May Bush—has got the bluest blood in America in her veins. Jest put that in your pipe and smoke it! *(Mrs. Bush here proudly flaunts herself around the kitchen, talking half at Mrs. Temple and half to herself)* Huh! Talkin' 'bout May not bein' a match fur John. I should say they don't come no finer than May, anywhere.

MRS. TEMPLE *(again collecting herself and speaking in a soft, strained, pleading voice):* Mrs. Bush, Mrs. Bush, I have something to say to you and it must be said right now! Oh, where can I begin? Let me think—

MRS. BUSH: This ain't no time to think, I'm going to act! *(takes mayonnaise from Mrs. Temple's apathetic hands)* My chile's gotter get married and get married right. I . . .

MRS. TEMPLE *(breaking in):* Please, please, be still a minute for heaven's sake! You'll drive me mad!

MRS. BUSH: Drive you mad! The devil I will. *(abruptly runs and stands in a belligerent attitude in front of Mrs. Temple)* Say, look here, Miss High-and-Mighty, what's you up to? Git out of here, you ain't going to start no trouble here. *(tries to force Mrs. Temple toward the door)*

MRS. TEMPLE *(breaking down in tears and reaching for Mrs. Bush's hands):* Please, please, Mrs. Bush, you don't understand, and how can I tell you—what a day!

MRS. BUSH *(standing squarely in front of Mrs. Temple):* Look here, is you crazy? Or just a fool?

MRS. TEMPLE: Neither, Mrs. Bush, I'm just a broken-hearted mother and you must help me, help me, for May's sake, if not for mine!

MRS. BUSH: For May's sake! 'Splain yourself! This is a pretty come off. *(sarcastically)* For May's sake.

MRS. TEMPLE: It's a long story, but I'll tell you in a few words. Oh, oh, how I've tried to forget it!

MRS. BUSH: Forget what! Look here, what time is it? *(Mrs. Temple looks at her watch)*

MRS. TEMPLE: A quarter of nine.

MRS. BUSH *(excitedly)*: Lord, woman, we ain't got no time fur story telling. I've got to hustle!

MRS. TEMPLE *(hysterically)*: You must hear me, you must, you must!

MRS. BUSH: Well, of all things, what is the matter with you?

MRS. TEMPLE: Be quiet, just one minute, and let me tell you.

MRS. BUSH: You'd better hurry up.

MRS. TEMPLE: Once . . . I taught a country school in Georgia. I was engaged to Paul Temple . . . I was only nineteen. I had worked hard to make enough to pay for my wedding things . . . it was going to be in the early fall—our wedding. I put my money in the bank. One day, in that bank, I met a man. He helped me. And then I see he wanted his pay for it. He kept on—kept writing to me. He didn't sign his letters, though. I wouldn't answer. I tried to keep away. One night he came to the place where I boarded. The woman where I boarded—she helped him—he bribed her. He came into my room—

MRS. BUSH: The dirty devil!

MRS. TEMPLE *(continuing her story)*: I cried out. There wasn't any one there that cared enough to help me, and you know yourself, Mrs. Bush, what little chance there is for women like us in the South, to get justice or redress when these things happen!

MRS. BUSH: Sure, honey, I do know!

MRS. TEMPLE: Mother knew—there wasn't any use trying to punish him. She said I'd be the one . . . that would suffer.

MRS. BUSH: You done right . . . and whut your ma told you is the God's truth.

MRS. TEMPLE: I told Paul Temple—the one I was engaged to—the whole story, only I didn't tell him who. I knew he would have tried to kill him, and then they'd have killed him.

MRS. BUSH *(interrupting)*: That wuz good sense.

MRS. TEMPLE: He understood the whole thing—and married me. He knew why I wouldn't tell him the man's name—not even when—when that man's son was born to me.

MRS. BUSH: You don't mean John?

MRS. TEMPLE: Yes . . . John. And his father. . . .

MRS. BUSH: Oh no . . . no. . . .

MRS. TEMPLE: Yes. *(with a groan)* Winfield McCallister . . . is John's father, too.

MRS. BUSH *(clasping her hands excitedly)*: My God! My God! *(whimpering, between sobs)* Whut kin we do? Just think of my poor dear chile, May, upstairs there—all dressed up jest lak a bride—'spectin' to git married—and all them people from everywhere—in the parlor—waiting for the seymoaney! Oh, whut kin we tell her . . . whut kin we tell them?

MRS. TEMPLE *(Looking at watch. Gets up, walks up and down excitedly)*: Yes . . . we've got to think and act quickly! We can't tell the world why the children didn't marry . . . and cause a scandal. . . . I'd be ruined!

MRS. BUSH *(getting irate)*: So far as you is consarned . . . I ain't bothered, 'bout your being ruined. May'll be ruined if we don't tell. Why—folk's all be saying John jilted her, and you can bet your sweet life I won't stand fur that. No siree! I don't keer who is hurts . . . I'm not agoin' to see May suffer . . . not ef I kin help it!

MRS. TEMPLE *(bursting into tears)*: Oh! Oh! We must do something!

(enter Randolph Strong, breathlessly, with mayonnaise dressing from Lyddie Smith's—placing large glass jar of mayonnaise on kitchen table)

RANDOLPH STRONG: Good evening, Mrs. Temple. I'm a little late, Mrs. Bush, but here's what you sent me for. *(he notices Mrs. Temple in tears)* My, my, why, what's wrong?

MRS. BUSH: Randolph, my dear boy . . .

RANDOLPH STRONG: What's the matter? What's happened since I left you awhile ago?

MRS. BUSH *(slowly and feelingly)*: Sump'n . . . sump'n terrible!

RANDOLPH STRONG: Has anything happened to May?

MRS. BUSH: Not only to her—to all of us!

RANDOLPH STRONG: All! Heavens!

MRS. BUSH: Listen, Randolph, and help us, for God's sake! May and John can't get married!

RANDOLPH STRONG *(turning to Mrs. Temple)*: Can't get married! Why?

MRS. TEMPLE: It's a long story. I've told—I've explained everything to Mrs. Bush. She—she understands.

RANDOLPH STRONG: You can trust me. I'm like one of the family. You both know that I have always cared for May.

MRS. BUSH *(to Mrs. Temple)*: Kin I tell him? *(Mrs. Temple silently and tearfully nods her assent)* May mus' know it too—right away. Let's call her down. May! May! Oh, May! My dear chile come down here a minute—quick—right away! My poor chile . . . my poor chile!

MRS. TEMPLE: What a day! What a day!

MAY'S VOICE: Coming, Ma! *(enter May Bush, coming downstairs in her wedding gown)* Am I late? *(noting Randolph)* The roses are beautiful. See. *(points to one in her hair)*

MRS. BUSH: Randolph . . . Randolph remembered the kind you like, honey.

MAY BUSH *(to Randolph)*: Just like you!

RANDOLPH STRONG: How sweet of you to wear one!

MAY BUSH *(proudly walking across room toward Mrs. Bush)*: How do I look, Ma?

MRS. BUSH *(tenderly kissing her daughter several times)*: Beautiful, my darlin' *(adding softly)* poor chile!

MAY BUSH *(walking toward and kissing Mrs. Temple)*: How do you like me—my other mama?

MRS. TEMPLE: Charming—God protect you, my dear!

MAY BUSH *(noticing the sad expression on the faces of both mothers)*: My, you all look so sad; why so doleful? What is the matter with them, Randolph?

RANDOLPH STRONG: Why . . . I'm wounded, but smiling. The ladies . . .

MRS. BUSH *(impatiently interrupting)*: Oh, children, don't waste this precious time. We've called you together to tell you sump'n . . . (stuttering) we've got sump'n to tell you, and we got to tell you right now!

(Mrs. Bush draws May aside toward Mrs. Temple, hastily and cautiously locking kitchen hall door)

MRS. BUSH *(continuing)*: Listen, May. Come here, come here, Randolph, for I feel that both of you are my children. May, you got to be strong—for if ever you needed wits, now's the time to use 'em. May God forgive me—and Mrs. Temple there, both of us—I just got to tell you 'bout it quick—for all them folks are in the parlor and if we don't do something quick, right now, this whole town will be rippin' us to pieces—all of us, you and me—Mrs. Temple—and—and—the las' one of us! There ain't time to tell you the whole story—but—May—my poor chile—I know you kin trus' you own, dear ma that far?

MAY BUSH *(excitedly)*: Yes, Ma, yes, but what is it?

MRS. BUSH: May, you and John can't marry—you jest can't marry!!

MAY BUSH *(aghast)*: Can't marry! Can't marry!

MRS. BUSH: No, never!

MAY BUSH: But why—why!

MRS. BUSH: Your father, and John's father—is—is—

MAY BUSH: You don't mean . . .

MRS. TEMPLE: Yes, May. John's father is you father.

MAY BUSH *(wrings her hands)*: Oh, I'd rather die—I'd rather die than face this . . .

MRS. BUSH *(crooning)*: I know, honey . . . I know . . . God forgive me . . . God forgive that man. Oh, no . . . I don't want Him to forgive him.

MAY BUSH: O why, why did this have to happen to me—oh!! I wish I were dead!

RANDOLPH STRONG: May—don't say that. You mustn't say that.

MAY BUSH: I do. Oh, God—I've kept out of their clutches myself, but now it's through you, Ma, that they've got me anyway. Oh, what's the use . . .

RANDOLPH STRONG: May!

MAY BUSH: The whole world will be pointing at me . . .

MRS. BUSH: Ah, honey, honey, I'll be loving you . . .

MAY BUSH: I wish I could die right now.

RANDOLPH STRONG: Will you listen to me, now, May?

MAY BUSH: Those people in there—they'll be laughing . . .

(knocking is heard)

MRS. TEMPLE: It's John. We can't let him come in here now. He mustn't know . . .

MRS. BUSH: No. We can't let him know or he'll kill his own father . . .

MRS. TEMPLE: What are you going to do, May?

MRS. BUSH: Yes, May—what are you going to do?

RANDOLPH STRONG: We are going to run away and get married, aren't we, May? Say yes, May—say yes!

MAY BUSH: John . . . *(the knocking is heard again)*

MRS. BUSH: Keep it from him. It's the black women that have got to protect their men from the white men by not telling on 'em.

MRS. TEMPLE: God knows that's the truth.

RANDOLPH STRONG: May! Come with me now!

MAY BUSH: Randolph—do you want me?

RANDOLPH STRONG: I want you like I've always wanted you.

MAY BUSH *(shyly)*: But—I don't love you.

RANDOLPH STRONG: You think you don't . . .

MAY BUSH: Do you want me now?

RANDOLPH STRONG: I want you now.

MAY BUSH: Ma, oh, Ma!

MRS. BUSH *(in tears)*: Quick, darlin'—tell him.

MAY BUSH: My coat.

MRS. BUSH: I'll get your coat, honey.

MRS. TEMPLE: Here, May, take my coat!

MRS. BUSH: What we going to tell John—and all the people?

MAY BUSH: Tell 'em—Oh God, we can't tell 'em the—truth?

RANDOLPH STRONG: Mother Bush—just tell them the bride was stolen by Randolph Strong!

(Strong puts the coat around her and they go out the door, leaving the others staring at them)

(Curtain)

Plumes

A ONE-ACT PLAY

(1927)

Characters:

CHARITY BROWN, *The Mother*
EMMERLINE BROWN, *The Daughter*
TILDY, *The Friend*
DR. SCOTT, *Physician*

Time:

Present

Setting

The kitchen of a two-room cottage. A window overlooking the street. A door leading to street, one leading to the back yard, and one to the inner room. A stove, a table with shelf over it, a wash tub. A rocking chair, a cane bottom chair. Needle, thread, scissors, etc., on table.

Scene opens with Charity Brown heating a poultice over the stove. A groaning is heard from the inner room.

CHARITY: Yes, honey, mamma is fixing somethin' to do you good. Yes, my baby, jus' you wait—I'm a coming.

(Knock is heard at door. It is gently pushed open and Tildy comes in cautiously.)

TILDY *(whispering):*—How is she?

CHARITY: Poorly, poorly. Didn't rest last night none hardly. Move that dress and set in th' rocker. I been trying to snatch a minute to finish it but don't seem like I can. She won't have nothing to wear if she—she—

TILDY: I understands. How near done is it?

CHARITY: Ain't so much more to do.

TILDY *(takes up dress from chair, looks at it):*—I'll do some on it.

CHARITY: Thank you, sister Tildy. Whip that torshon on and turn down the hem in the skirt.

TILDY *(measuring dress against herself):* How deep?

CHARITY: Let me see now *(studies a minute with finger against lip)* I tell you—jus' baste it, cause, you see—she wears 'em short, but—it might be—*(stops)*

TILDY *(bowing her head comprehendingly):* Eughhu, I see exzackly. *(sighs)* You'd want it long—over her feet—then.

CHARITY: That's it, sister Tildy. *(listening)* She's some easy now. *(stirring poultice)* Jest can't get this poltis hot enough somehow this morning.

TILDY: Put some red pepper in it. Got any?

CHARITY: Yes. There ought to be some in one of them boxes on the shelf there. *(points)*

TILDY *(goes to shelf, looks about and gets the pepper):* Here, put a plenty of this in.

CHARITY *(groans are heard from the next room):* Good Lord, them pains got her again. She suffers so, when she's 'wake.

TILDY: Poor little thing. How old is she now, sister Charity?

CHARITY: Turning fourteen this coming July.

TILDY *(shaking her head dubiously):* I sho hope she'll be mended by then.

CHARITY: It don't look much like it but I trusts so—*(looking worried)* That doctor's mighty late this morning.

TILDY: I expects he'll be long in no time. Doctors is mighty onconcerned here lately.

CHARITY *(going toward inner room with poultice):* They surely is and I don't have too much confidence in none of 'em. (*You can hear her soothing sick girl.*)

TILDY (*listening*): Want me to help you put it on, sister Charity?

CHARITY (*from inner room*): No, I can fix it. (*coming back from sick room shaking her head rather dejectedly*)

TILDY: How's she restin' now?

CHARITY: Mighty feeble. Gone back to sleep. My poor little baby. (*bracing herself*) I'm going to put on some coffee now.

TILDY: I'm sho glad. I feel kinder low spirited.

CHARITY: It's me that's low sperited. The doctor said last time he was here he might have to operate—said she might have a chance then. But I tell you the truth, I've got no faith a-tall in 'em. They takes all your money for nothing.

TILDY: They sho do, and don't leave a thing for putting you away.

CHARITY: That's jest it. They takes every cent you got and then you dies jest the same. It ain't like they was sure.

TILDY: No, they ain't sure. That's it exzactly. But they takes your money jest the same, and leaves you flat.

CHARITY: I been thinking 'bout Zeke these last few days—how he was put away—

TILDY: I wouldn't worry 'bout him now; he's out of his troubles now.

CHARITY: I know . . . but it worries me when I think about how he was put away . . . that ugly pine coffin, jest one shabby old hack and nothing else to show—to show—we cared more than that about him.

TILDY: Shoo . . . hush, sister, don't you worry over him. He's happy now anyhow.

CHARITY: I can't help it . . . then little Bessie. We all jest scrouged in one hack and took her little coffin in our lap all the way to the graveyard. (*breaks out crying*)

TILDY: Do hush, sister Charity. You done the best you could. Poor folks have to make the best of it. The Lord understands.

CHARITY: Yes. I know . . . but I made up my mind when little Bessie went that the next one of us what died would have a sho nuff fun'ral, everything grand—with plumes! So I saved and saved and now—this doctor—

TILDY: All they think about is cuttin' and killing and taking your money. I got nothin' to put 'em doing.

CHARITY *(goes over to wash tub and rubs on clothes):* Me neither. Now here's these clothes got to get out. I needs every cent.

TILDY: How much that washing bring you?

CHARITY: Dollar and a half. It's worth a whole lot more. But what can you do?

TILDY: You can't do nothing—look, sister Charity, ain't that coffee boiling?

CHARITY *(wipes her hands on apron and goes to stove):* Yes, it's boiling good fashioned—come on, let's drink it.

TILDY: There ain't nothing I'd rather have than a good strong cup of coffee. *(Charity pours Tildy's cup)*

TILDY *(sweetening and stirring hers):* Pour you some. *(Charity pours her own cup)* I'd been dead too long if it hadn't been for my coffee.

CHARITY: I love it but it don't love me, gives me the shortness of breath.

TILDY *(finishing her cup, taking up sugar with spoon):* Don't hurt me. I could drink a barrel.

CHARITY *(drinking more slowly, reaching for coffee pot):* Here, drink another cup.

TILDY: I shore will. That cup done me a lot of good.

CHARITY *(looking into her empty cup thoughtfully):* I wish Dinah Morris would drop in now. I'd ask her what these grounds mean.

TILDY: I can read 'em a little myself.

CHARITY: You can? Well, for the Lord's sake look here and tell me what this cup says. *(Offers cup to Tildy. Tildy wards it off.)*

TILDY: You got to turn it round in your saucer three times first.

CHARITY: Yes, that's right, I forgot. *(turns cup round counting)* One, two, three. *(starts to pick it up)*

TILDY: Eughn nhu *(meaning no)* Let it set a minute. It might be watery. *(after a minute while she finishes her own cup)* Now let me see. *(takes cup and examines it very scrutinizingly)*

CHARITY: What you see?

TILDY *(hesitatingly):* I ain't seen a cup like this one for many a year. Not since—not since—

CHARITY: When?

TILDY: Not since jest before ma died. I looked in the cup then and saw things and . . . I stopped looking.

CHARITY: Tell me what you see, I want to know.

TILDY: I don't like to tell no bad news—

CHARITY: Go on. I can stan' any kind of news after all I been thru.

TILDY: Since you're bound to know I'll tell you. *(Charity draws nearer)* I sees a big gethering!

CHARITY: Gethering, you say?

TILDY: Yes, a big gethering—people all crowded together. Then I see 'em going one by one and two by two. Long lines stretching out and out and out!

CHARITY *(softly)*: What you think it is?

TILDY *(awed like)*: Looks like *(hesitates)* a possession.

CHARITY: You think it is?

TILDY: I know it is. *(Just then the toll of a church bell is heard and then the steady and slow tramp, tramp of horses' hoofs. Both women look at each other.)*

TILDY *(in a hushed voice)*: That must be Bell Gibson's funeral coming way from Mt. Zion. *(gets up and goes to window)* Yes, it sho' is.

CHARITY *(looking out of window also)*: Poor Bell suffered many a year; she's out of her pain now.

TILDY: Look, here comes the hearse by!

CHARITY: My Lord, ain't it grand. Look at them horses—look at their heads—plumes—how they shake 'em! Land O'mighty! Ain't it a fine sight?

TILDY: That must be Jeremiah in that first carriage, bending over like, he shorely is putting her away grand.

CHARITY: No mistake about it. That's Pickett's best funeral turnout he got.

TILDY: I bet it cost a lot.

CHARITY: Fifty dollars, so Matilda Jenkins told me. She had it for Bud. The plumes is what cost.

TILDY: Look at the hacks. *(counts)* I believe to my soul there's eight.

CHARITY: Got somebody in all of 'em, too—and flowers—she shore got a lot of 'em. *(Both women's eyes follow the tail end of the procession, horses' hoofs die away as they turn away from window. The two women look at each other significantly.)*

TILDY *(significantly):*—Well—*(They look at each other without speaking for a minute. Charity goes to the wash tub.)*—Want these cups washed up?

CHARITY: No, don't mind 'em. I rather you get that dress done. I got to get these clothes out.

TILDY *(picking up dress):* Shore, there ain't so much more to do on it now.

(Knock is heard on the door. Charity answers knock and admits Doctor.)

DR. SCOTT: Good morning—how's my patient today?

CHARITY: Not so good, doctor. When she ain't asleep she suffers so, but she sleeps mostly.

DR. SCOTT: Well, let's see—let's see. Just hand me a pan of warm water and I'll soon find out just what's what.

CHARITY: All right, doctor, I'll bring it to you right away. *(Bustles about fixing water.) (Looking toward dress Tildy is working on.)* Poor little Emmerline's been wanting a white dress trimmed with torshon a long time—now she's got it and it looks like—well—

TILDY: Don't take on so, sister Charity—The Lord giveth and the Lord taketh.

CHARITY: I know—but it's hard—hard—*(Goes to inner door with water. You can hear her talking with the doctor after a minute and the doctor expostulating with her—in a minute she appears at the door, being led from the room by the doctor.)*

DR. SCOTT: No, my dear Mrs. Brown. It will be much better for you to remain outside.

CHARITY: But, doctor—

DR. SCOTT: No. You stay outside and get your mind on something else. You can't possibly be of any service. Now be calm, will you?

CHARITY: I'll try, doctor.

TILDY: The doctor's right. You can't do no good in there.

CHARITY: I knows, but I thought I could hold the pan or somethin'. *(lowering her voice)* Says he got to see if her heart is all right or somethin'. I tell you—nowadays—

TILDY: I know.

CHARITY *(softly to Tildy):* Hope he won't come out here saying he got to operate. *(goes to wash tub)*

TILDY: I hope so, too. Wont' it cost a lot?

CHARITY: That's jest it. It would take all I got saved up.

TILDY: Of course if he's goin' to get her up—but I don't believe in 'em. I don't believe in 'em.

CHARITY: He didn't promise tho—even if he did, he said maybe it wouldn't do any good.

TILDY: I'd think a long time before I'd let him operate on my chile. Taking all your money, promising nothing and ten to one killing her to boot.

CHARITY: This is a hard world.

TILDY: Don't you trust him. Coffee grounds don't lie!

CHARITY: I don't trust him. I jest want to do what's right by her. I ought to put these clothes on the line while you're settin' in here, but I hate to go out doors while he's in there.

TILDY *(getting up)*: I'll hang 'em out. You stay here. Where your clothes pins at?

CHARITY: Hanging right there by the back door in the bag. They ought to dry before dark and then I can iron tonight.

TILDY *(picking up tub)*: They ought to blow dry in no time. *(goes toward back door)*

CHARITY: Then I can shore rub 'em over tonight. Say, sister Tildy—hist 'em up with that long saplin' prop leaning in the fence corner.

TILDY *(going out)*: All right.

CHARITY *(standing by table beating nervously on it with her fingers—listens—and then starts to bustling about the kitchen)*

(Enter doctor from inner room)

DR. SCOTT: Well, Mrs. Brown, I decided on the operation—

CHARITY: My Lord, doctor—don't say that!

DR. SCOTT: It's her only chance.

CHARITY: You mean she'll get well if you do?

DR. SCOTT: No, I can't say that. It's just a chance—a last chance. And I'll do just what I said, too, cut the price of the operation down to fifty dollars. I'm willing to do that for you.

CHARITY: Doctor, I was so in hopes you wouldn't operate—I—I—and you say you ain't a bit sure she'll get well—even then?

DR. SCOTT: No, I'm not sure. You'll have to take the chance. But I'm sure you want to do everything—

CHARITY: Sure, doctor, I do want to—do—everything I can do to—to—Doctor, look at this cup. *(picks up fortune cup and shows doctor)* My fortune's been told this very morning—look at these grounds—they—says—*(softly)*—it ain't no use, no use a-tall.

DR. SCOTT: Why, my good woman, don't you believe in such senseless things. That cup of grounds can't show you anything. Wash them out and forget it.

CHARITY:—I can't forget it, doctor—I feel like it ain't no use. I'd jest be spendin' the money that I needs—for nothing—nothing.

DR. SCOTT: But you won't, tho—You'll have a clear conscience. You'd know that you did everything you could.

CHARITY:—I know that, doctor. But there's things you don't know 'bout—there's other things I got to think about. If she goes . . . If she must go . . . I had plans . . . I had been getting ready . . . now . . . Oh, doctor, I jest can't see how I can have this operation—you say you can't promise—nothing?

DR. SCOTT: I didn't think you'd hesitate about it—I imagined your love for your child—

CHARITY *(breaking in)*: I do love my child. My God, I do love my child. You don't understand . . . but . . . can't I have a little time to think about it, doctor . . . it means so much—to her—and—me!

DR. SCOTT: I tell you. I'll go on over to the office and as soon as you make up your mind get one of the neighbors to run over there and tell me. I'll come right back. But don't waste any time now, every minute counts.

CHARITY: Thank you, doctor. Thank you. I'll shore send you word as soon as I can. I'm so upset and worried I'm half crazy.

DR. SCOTT: I know you are . . . but don't take too long to make up your mind . . . It ought to be done today. Remember—it may save her. *(doctor exits)*

(Charity goes to door of sick room, looks inside for a few minutes, then starts walking up and down the little kitchen first holding a hand up to her head and then wringing them. Enter Tildy from yard with tub under her arm)

TILDY: Well, they're all out, sister Charity—*(stops)* What's the matter?

CHARITY: The doctor wants to operate.

TILDY: *(softly)* Where he—gone?

CHARITY: Yes—he's gone, but he's coming back—if I send for him.

TILDY: You going to? *(puts down tub and picks up white dress and begins sewing)*

CHARITY: I don't know—I got to think.

TILDY: I can't see what's the use myself—he can't save her with no operation—coffee grounds don't lie.

CHARITY: It would take all the money I got for the operation and then—he can't save her—I know he can't—I feel it . . .

TILDY: It's in the air . . .

(Both women sit tense in the silence. Just then a strange strangling noise comes from the inner room.)

TILDY: What's that?

CHARITY *(running toward and into the inner room):*—Oh, my God! *(from inside)* Sister Tildy—come here—no,—some water, quick.

(Tildy with dress in hand starts toward inner room. Stops at door, sighs, and then goes hurriedly back for the water pitcher. Charity is heard moaning softly in the next room, then she appears at doorway. Leans against jamb of door.)

CHARITY: Rip the hem out, sister Tildy.

(Curtain)

PART II

Historical Plays

Frederick Douglass

A ONE-ACT PLAY

(1935)

Characters:

FRED DOUGLASS, *Young slave man*
ANN, *His sweetheart freewoman*
BUD, *Ann's brother*
JAKE, *An old slave*

Time:

Slavery days

Place:

Baltimore, Maryland

Scene

A kitchen in an humble two-room hut at the corner of a street in the poor section of the city near the railroad, the home of Ann and her brother Bud, both free. There is an open door leading to the front room and another door leading to the backyard and street. There is a small window with a calico curtain before it on the side-street side. Against the wall between the window and door is a table with a red checked cloth covering one-half of it. On the uncovered side are a water bucket and yellow bowl. Near the bucket is a gourd, and hanging on the wall are a towel and a small piece of broken looking glass. On a shelf nearby are a plate, knife, mugs, spoons, a can of molasses. Near the back door is a small iron cook stove; on it is a tea-kettle; and a half-knitted sock is seen over the edge of the sewing box.

Ann is seen stooping as she pushes a pan of ginger bread into the oven to bake. She straightens up, goes to the table and with a finger wipes around the bowl and tastes ginger-cake batter.

ANN: Eugh-Good. *(She goes to window and looks up and down the street expectantly. She then goes to the bit of looking glass, stands before it and primps her hair. A knock sounds at the door of the front room. She gives her hair another pull or two, calling out as she does so.)* All right! *(She hurries through the open door to the front door and voices are heard in the next room. She immediately returns to the kitchen with* DOUGLASS *in pursuit. He tries to kiss her but she eludes him. He puts some papers he brought in with him on the tablecloth.)*

No kissin' tell we're married. I promised Ma.

FRED: I can wait—you're worth it. Won't be long now. Look a-here! *(he takes a handful of silver from his trouser pocket and shows it to Ann)*

ANN: Whooee—how much?

FRED: Seventeen dollars and fifty cents—most enough for me to steal away to freedom an' marry with up North. *(chuckling to himself)* Honey, do you know something funny happened tonight? When I gave Marse Tom his ten dollars I worked an' made fur him this week, he was tickled to death an' said "Here, Fred, take this here quarter an' buy yourself somethin'." He ain't got no idea how much extra money I picks up during the week. You see I'm a-workin' for freedom an' you.

ANN *(shyly)*: Oh, Fred! I hopes he don't fin' out 'bout it 'fore we gits away.

FRED: I'm scareful. I hides my money an' just brought it along tonight to show you how I'm a-doin'.

ANN: How many mo' Saddays 'fore you goin' to have enouf fur us to go on?

FRED: Mebbe four more, an' then, little honey, *(he snaps his finger exultantly)* I'm a-goin' to that free country, learn all I can an' then I'm a-goin' to help the rest of my poor down-trodden people to get out from under this yoke.

ANN: You sho look grand when you talk like that. *(hesitatingly)* You won't want me then, speck.

FRED *(putting his arms about her fondly)*: Oh my little honey, I'm goin' to love you all my life. We goin' to work together, you an' me, in that great big free country up North.

ANN: Free country! *(she stands with hands clasped as though she saw a vision, then, as if dropping back to earth, continues)* But look, I got somethin' good fur you. *(advancing toward the stove)* Guess whut?

FRED *(advancing a step or two behind her)*: Not gingy bread, now?

ANN *(opening stove door with her apron)*: Course 'tis—you done smelled it.

FRED *(peeping in stove from behind her and making a noise of whiffing spicy flavor)*: My, that spice sholy smells good—like, like singin' in the meetin' house! I want you to make a gingy bread for us when we get married, honey.

ANN: I'm a gonner mek one with white icing fur that.

FRED *(pensively)*: Here I am talkin' 'bout marryin' an' cake an' such like an' me just a poor slave! *(sighs deeply and then goes over to table and starts putting down sums for the lessons)*

ANN *(going over to him consolingly)*: Tain't fur long, Fred, you boun' to be free—I feels it—you got them big free ways.

FRED *(caressingly)*: Honey, you jes' like a rock in a weary land . . . weary land *(drops his head into hands and repeats softly)* weary land! *(A train whistle blows and the sound of a train passing is heard. Both listen.)*

ANN *(moving toward the window)*: The South boun'! Come look at the lights from the train winders.

FRED *(following her to window, shaking his head)*: She's headed the wrong way—South!

ANN *(thoughtfully)*: Yes, she sho is. *(goes over to stove to look at ginger bread and turn it around)*

FRED *(facing room observantly)*: Ann, this here little bit of kitchen of yours is the nearest I ever been to heaven since I been born. *(going over to table where papers are, starts putting down sums again)*

ANN *(reprovingly)*: You forgittin' your own Ma's cook kitchen, ain't you? *(quickly)* I mean the white folkses' kitchen what owned her?

FRED *(sadly)*: I never saw it—I never saw my own Ma but one time in my whole life.

ANN: Jes' one time; Good Lawd!

FRED: 'Twas when I was around six years old. I remember wakin' up long about midnight . . . I never will forget it. She was huggin' and kissin' me an' her tears was fallin' all down in my face like rain. She said "My poor baby . . . my poor baby . . . I'm your ma, honey," an' she went on callin' me sweet names an' cryin'; then all sudden like, she almost throwed me down on the palatte an' darted out through the door like mad!

ANN: I wonder why she done that?

FRED: I found out from Aunt Dinah that my Ma had to walk forty miles goin' an' comin' that night just to see me. She had to be back to her new master's plantation before sun-up . . . I never seen her since.

ANN: Lawd! Lawd! *(going up to him and patting him on the shoulder)* Don't you fret. We going' to fin' her one uv these days an' till you do, I'm a gointer make it all up to you—I'll be yore wife an' ma all rolled into one.

FRED *(thoughtfully)*: You look like she did that night—your eyes—but come on an' get some lessons now; we won't wait for Bud. His boat in yet?

ANN *(moving over toward the stove)*: Yes, it's in. I heard her blow at the dock before you come in. *(taking ginger bread from oven and putting it on top of the stove)* You cummon an' eat a piece uv cake an' mebbe by then Bud'll be here. *(cuts a piece and hands it to him, leaving cake on back of stove)*

FRED *(going over to stove near her)*: Sure! But what you reckin' is keeping Bud so late; he knows Sadday night is lesson night. *(takes cake and tastes it)* Good!

ANN *(beaming appreciatively)*: He must er stopped down there in some uv them saloons an' got a drink er two. He sho worries me most to death. I promised Ma 'fore she died that I would keep him straight, but Lawd!

FRED: When I get away from here up North I'll take charge of Bud for he'll hafter live with you an' me, you know!

ANN: Oh, Fred, you so good, teachin' me an' Bud to read an' figger an' ev'rything. Whus more, Bud likes you an' you know he don't like nobody much—he jes' loved Ma and that's all!

FRED: Bud loves you, Ann.

ANN: Oh jes' since Ma's been dead he kinder hankers after me, but he ain't loved nobody relly but Ma. I do everythin' for him now. Let me finish this sock while we's waitin' for him. *(she picks up a sock)*

FRED: But I want you to do some sums now. *(pulls her on over to the table)* You got to learn a lot cause you got to help me when we get away, honey.

ANN: Let me finish this sock while we's waitin' an' you go on an' tell me how 'twas you got all that book learnin'. Slaves roun' here can't read nothin', even down to free ones don't know nothin'. Look at me an' Bud!

FRED *(still holding pencil and absently tapping the paper on the table):* Well, you see I used to play with young Marse Tom. We both was around eight an' old Miss would read to us an' teach us, but old Marse got mad when he found out about it an' stopped her.

ANN: He did! *(she stops knitting a minute in her excitement)*

FRED: Yes. But that didn't stop me; I'd got a start an' I kept right on—picked up scraps of printin' from the streets an' wet gutters, dried 'em, hid 'em an' kept a-learnin'.

ANN: But sho'ly you couldn't read an' learn all by yourself!

FRED: I didn't. When I got hold of hard words I couldn't spell, I'd say to some one of the white boys when I'd meet one on the street—"Say, I bet you can't read this here word," an' I'd show it to him. He would always spell it out jest to show off. I played lots of tricks like that to get more learnin'.

ANN: But want you skered they'd ketch you an' beat you?

FRED: They caught me an' nearly killed me many a time. They took all my papers away, but pshaw! I whirled right around an' found some more an' learned harder than I ever had. Something inside of me just drove me to it!

ANN: I b'leve you. You ain't like nobody round here. You so—so wonderful like. I'll sho be glad when you git to git away, free!

FRED: It won't be long now till . . . *(a cautious knock is heard at the back door of the kitchen)*

ANN: Who at that back door, you reckin? I ain't spectin' nobody but Bud. *(she goes over to the door and calls)* Who dere?

VOICE: It's me, Jake, open de door.

ANN *(to Fred):* It's Jake.

JAKE *(comes in panting as if he'd been running):* Look here, Fred, I heered somethin' tonight you ought to know.

FRED *(excitedly):* What, Jake?

JAKE: Marse Tom's brother, Marse George, come in on dat las' boat an' he swore at Marse Tom an' said he was a gonner take you back wid him in de morning down on de Eastern Shore agin. Sed he was gonner put you back in de field an' break ye damn sperrit!

FRED: But he give me to Marse Tom.

JAKE: He screeched at Marse Tom, "Youser spilin' him, youser spilin' him lettin' him work out fer wages—Fore long you won't have him, he'll run away."

FRED: He's damn right! *(then agitatedly)* But what can I do? *(slaps his hand to his forehead)* In the mornin' . . . In the mornin' . . . I got to do something before mornin'.

JAKE: You sho is.

ANN: Whut kin you do?

FRED: I don't know, I don't know but I got to get away . . . got to!

JAKE: You mout hide in de woods tell you could git away, mebbe!

FRED: Yes, but there ain't no safe places to hide in roundabouts!

ANN *(excitedly)*: You got money to ride the train, ain't you?

FRED *(thoughtfully)*: That's so! *(then shakes his head despondently)* But I can't ride the train without a pass.

JAKE: Dat's so. Now where could you git one?

ANN *(with sudden animation)*: Bud's got one!

FRED *(brightly)*: That's so! *(then rather colorlessly)* But he wouldn't let me take it away.

ANN: For me he would.

JAKE: But where is Bud? You got to git it now—tonight!

ANN: He'll be lon' soon. His boat's done docked long time ago. *(then with sinking spirits)* I hopes he's sober.

FRED: We can't reason with him if he's drunk, but we got to somehow!

ANN: Yes, we got to.

FRED *(excitedly striking his forehead with his hand)*: I just thought of something. I got to have a sailor's suit.

JAKE: Whut fer?

FRED: They tell me that you get by easy when you're a sailor, the white folks don't bother them a-tall. I got to have a suit! *(to Jake)* Jake, you take this dollar an' go down by the docks an' rent me one quick. Somebody'll let you have one for a few days. I'll send it back to Ann here with the pass, if I get it. *(hands Jake the money and pushes him toward the door)*

JAKE: I'll do my bes'. You'se lak a son to me, boy!

FRED *(emotionally)*: Thankee, thankee, Jake. Hurry!

JAKE *(poking his head back in at the back door)*: You'll better lay low cause Marse might be lookin' down here fur you. All de niggers knows you come down here on Sadday night!

(door closes)

FRED: He's right, Ann, we'd better fix that window an' move that light.

ANN *(nervously)*: All right, Fred. *(they quickly close the curtains and take the lamp from the table and set it in a corner on the floor)*

FRED: That's better.

ANN *(anxiously)*: Bud's mighty late! Lawd! I hope he's sober.

(goes to stove and pokes at the fire)

FRED *(nervously walking up and down)*: If he is an' we can't get it, I'll have to take to the woods I reckon! *(A noise is heard at the door as if some one fumbling with the latch. Both start.)*

ANN *(excitedly rushing toward the door)*: That's him now!

(Bud stumbles in)

FRED: Hello, Bud! Too late for your lessons tonight.

BUD *(thickly)*: Eughn nhu. *(meaning no)* Sor-i-e, Fred. *(falls heavily into a chair)*

FRED: It's all right.

ANN *(going over to stove and cutting a piece of ginger bread)*: Eat a piece of gingy bread, Bud, it's hot yet. *(comes over to him with a piece)*

BUD *(drawlingly)*: I ain't hungry. *(slouches down lower in chair)* I wanna sleep.

ANN *(hands cake to Fred, looks at him significantly and pats Bud on shoulder coaxingly)*: Oh, Bud, I want you to do somethin' fur me. *(he doesn't answer)* Hear me, lissen, I wants you to lemme have yore pass fur a little while. Lemme see it. Where is it, Bud?

BUD *(fretfully)*: G'on. *(shakes her off)* Lemme lone! *(Ann looks helplessly at Fred. Fred shakes his head despondently)*

FRED: I reckon I'll have to take to the woods. *(looks resigned)*

ANN *(droopingly)*: Ef he wan't drunk he'd be all right. *(then brightening up sudden as if struck with an idea)* I know . . . I know . . . I'll make some tea!

FRED *(repeats rather absently)*: Tea?

ANN *(to Fred in a stage whisper):* It sobers him! See ef the kittle's boilin'. *(Fred goes to stove, looks in kettle. Ann goes to table, gets tea and puts some leaves in small saucepan, goes to stove with it.)*

FRED *(motioning toward kettle):* It's hot.

ANN *(putting saucepan on stove):* Pour on some. *(she stirs it)* Git a mug.

(Fred goes to table and gets mug) (While they are fixing tea a noise is heard at back door. Jake enters cautiously with bundle under left arm.)

JAKE *(with bated breath):* I got 'em. Got de p . . .

FRED: Sh' . . . *(stopping him, points to Bud slouched on chair, and in lower voice)* He won't.

JAKE *(understandingly):* Oh! *(gives Fred bundle)*

FRED: Thanks, Jake. *(Fred takes bundle listlessly and drops it on the cot carelessly)*

JAKE *(following Fred to cot):* What you gonner do?

FRED: Ann's givin' him tea to sober him an' then . . . maybe . . . *(Jake goes into a deep study)*

ANN *(coaxingly holding mug for Bud):* Drink this tea, Bud, it's strong an' hot. *(holds it close to his nose)* Don't it smell good?

BUD *(smelling):* Gimme! *(drinks and brightens at once)*

JAKE *(excitedly to Fred):* Yaw'll wait, I kin git it, watch me! *(goes over close to Bud)* Got any leaves in dat mug, Bud? *(Fred beckons to Ann and explains to her in pantomime what Jake is trying to do).*

BUD *(looking inside):* Yeah!

JAKE: Wamme to talk wid de sperrits in yore leaves?

BUD *(with interest):* Y-e-a-h! Reckin you could talk wid Ma?

JAKE *(taking mug):* Lemme see! *(looks in mug as if seeing something, then softly and confidentially to Bud)* Yes, Bud, yore Ma's sperrit is here. She got a message fur you. You ready?

BUD *(hitching his chair close to Jake, eagerly):* Yeah, go on. *(Fred and Ann hover around on qui vive while Jake proceeds)*

JAKE *(as if listening to some one speaking from the mug):* I's a-lissenin'. *(as if repeating message)* Tell Bud I can't res' in my grave tell he quits that drinkin'. I'm miser'ble here twix heben an' earth. Tell him I heered his sister ax fur his pass tonight an' it hurt my soul when he didn't give it. Tell him to han' it to her quick an' then run down to the sycamoo tree at the corner of de fence in de back yard, an' fall down on his knees an' pray. My sperrit is on de way ther now to bless him whilst he prays. Tell him to do all I said now this very minute. *(Jake shakes himself as if throwing off a trance and then looks at Bud who seems dazed)* You heered yore Ma, Bud? *(Bud starts up as if to go to the door)*

ANN: Ma said . . .

BUD *(hurriedly reaching down into his boot top for pass, hands it to Ann who has followed him)*: Heah! *(he rushes out of doors) (As Bud reaches for pass and hands it to Ann, Fred snatches the bundle of clothes from the cot, leaving the cap there in his haste. He rushes to inner room. Jake picks up cap, brushes it off on his trousers, follows Fred.)*

ANN *(holding pass in hands exultantly)*: Thank God fur this! Jake done it. *(she hurries over to stove and gets a piece of the ginger bread and wraps it up in a piece of cloth for Fred's lunch)*

JAKE *(emerging from other room helping Fred into his coat)*: Yeah, but ef yu goin' to ketch de North Boun', you gotter fly.

FRED *(putting his money into his sailor pants pocket)*: It won't take me a minit to cut across to the junction; she ain't blowed yet.

JAKE: No, but it's time fur her. *(urging Fred toward the door)*

ANN *(handing him the pass and the cake)*: Here 'tis. *(slips cake into his pocket)* Eat that when you is hongry. *(Pushes him toward door. As Fred lingers she urges him on.)* Don't stop to say good bye. Hurry!

(train is heard blowing at a distance)

JAKE *(at door holding it slightly ajar)*: Fur God's sake, cummon, man, you ain't got a minute to lose.

FRED *(with one arm around Ann at door)*: Bye, Ann. I'll send for you, honey.

ANN *(pushing Fred out door, agitatedly)*: Bye, Fred. Hurry! Hurry! *(Ann turns quickly and goes to window, pushes back curtain and looks out. She listens. The rumble of the train can be heard as it nears the junction. All is still a few minutes and then the sound of the train bell is heard to ring and the gradually accelerating sound of a train gaining momentum is heard. There is a long whistle. Ann seems satisfied.)* Thank God! *(She falls down beside the cot as if in prayer as the curtain falls.)*

(End)

William and Ellen Craft

A ONE-ACT PLAY

(1935)

Characters:

WILLIAM CRAFT, *Brown Slave*
ELLEN CRAFT, *Octaroon slave*
AUNT MANDY, *Old slave*
SAM, *Young slave*

Time:

Slavery Time, Late April

Place:

On the Upper Mississippi

Scene

A log cabin with a window open toward the west. A door to the right of the window. A fireplace at right with sweet potatoes baking in the ashes. At center a table. At left a sheet drawn across the room to screen the bed. A box of light-wood knots beside the fireplace. Two chairs (cane bottom) near the table. By the side of one chair is a tin box with thread, scissors, and a cloth in it. On the back of one chair an old black coat with a needle in it, which is being darned. Near the window a bench on which are a bucket of water and a gourd. Ellen is discovered looking out of the window at the setting sun. There is a red glow. She seems to be in deep thought and worry. Picks up articles of clothing and ties them in a bundle. Hearing a knock at the door she throws the bundle behind the curtain and taking the coat begins darning.

ELLEN: Who dere?
MANDY (*entering*): It's me. Mandy. Want you spectin' me?
ELLEN: Course—but I's so nervous an' figety.

MANDY: An' skeered too, I be boun'. You better be, cause . . .

ELLEN *(breaking in):* 'Cause what?

MANDY: 'Cause I got bad news for you.

ELLEN: Bad news? What you mean, bad news?

MANDY: Chile, ole Missus done foun' out 'bout the undergroun' railroad an' now can't none ov you git away. Dey watchin' you alls hidin' places like hawks. *(Ellen drops her sewing and puts her hands to her face moaning)*

MANDY *(picks up sewing and starts to darn):* I'll finish dis coat for you, chile. I reckon you lowed William was goin' to wear it tonight, didn't you?

ELLEN *(brokenly):* Eugh-hu. But, Aunt Mandy, do they know 'bout our last secret hidin' place in the woods where Cap'n Smith meets the slaves an' takes um to the boat?

MANDY: Yes, honey, dey knows all 'bout ev'ything. You sho can't go now 'cause de'll ketch you.

ELLEN: But, I got to go! I got to!

MANDY *(exasperated):* No you ain't, you can't. How ken you?

ELLEN: I don't know, I don't know. But sho'ly dere must be some way ayuther.

MANDY *(soothingly):* Po' chile! I know it's hard, but you got to ben' to do rod. You got to stan' it. *(looks at potatoes on hearth)* Don't no trouble las' all de time. Evething passes soon or late. Come on, less us eat one of these taters—I'll peel you one.

ELLEN *(shaking her head):* You go on an' eat. I'd choke. Dem traders will be here at sun up an' you knows they means to take me down the ribber!

MANDY *(peeling and eating potato):* I'll finish dis coat for you. Now chile be sensible—life's moughty sweet if it is bitter!

ELLEN *(agitatedly):* Oh, you don't know, you don't know what dey mean to make out of me do you?

MANDY *(soothingly):* Yes I knows . . . yo' pretty white face is yo' curse. Youse just the spittin' image of your daddy, ole Marse Charles.

ELLEN: I hate him! Hate him!

MANDY: Don't say dat. Don't say dat. He was good to you while he was alivin'. Now ole Miss is takin' out her spite out on you sendin' you down de ribber.

ELLEN: I hate her fur it. I'd ruther stay here an' work like a dog in de field than go down de ribber.

MANDY: No honey, your hands too white fur field work. Dey makes ladies outen sech as you.

ELLEN *(sarcastically)*: Lady! Eugh!

MANDY: If you was black an' ugly you would sho' get along lots better. Dem white debils!

ELLEN *(goes up to Mandy supplicatingly)*: Don't you see I just got to get away tonight?

MANDY *(shaking her head)*: Poor chile, youse just most plum crazy wid skeer but we's all in the han's of de good Lord. *(As she speaks a sound is heard at the door. William enters hurriedly. Ellen flies to him and flings herself into his arms crying.)*

ELLEN: Oh, William, Aunt Mandy says you can't go tonight.

WILLIAM *(excitedly)*: Whut you mean?

MANDY: De white folks done found all about de underground.

WILLIAM: Who tole em?

MANDY: Dey caught Jack and Sophie las night an' whupped em till dey tole all 'bout de secret plans an' meetin' places. Liza's boy Bill overheered em frum de kitchen door whiles dey was talkin' in de dinin' room. Dey said they want goin' to be no more gol darn niggers runnin' away soon, said dey'd shoot any nigger full o buck shot that sot foot nigh dat ribber bottom.

WILLIAM *(Putting his hand up to his face thoughtfully, then sinks weakly into a chair and puts both hands up to his face. Ellen drags over to the fireplace and cries hopelessly. There is a tense stillness in the cabin for some minutes, then William jumps to his feet his snapping finger.)*: I got it! I know whut I'll do!

ELLEN *(rushing over to him eagerly)*: Whut, William, whut?

WILLIAM *(walking up and down excitedly)*: If I kin get the things I needs we kin do it. I bet my life on it.

MANDY: What tomfoolery you goin' to start, William? I done tole you de white folks is spicious an' all de pateroles is out tonight. You can't git away!

WILLIAM: You don't understand Aunt Mandy. I got to git Ellen away from here tonight or I'll die tryin'.

ELLEN: You right William. I'd rather be dead than stay here till mornin', an' . . .

WILLIAM *(still nervously moving about)*: If I kin git some things I need we kin steal cross de corn fields an' ketch the north bound when she stops at de flag station. I done it many of times wit young Marse Charles when we used to go up to Philadelphia. *(stops dead still)* But I got to git a suit of Master's clothes.

MANDY: Lord sakes. Whut you mindin' to do wid em?

WILLIAM *(speaks excitedly)*: You see if I could git a suit of Master's clothes I could dress Ellen up like a white man an' I could go long an' be her slave. Jus like I done wid young Marse Charles.

MANDY: You crazy boy!

ELLEN: Oh, William, how could we do that?

WILLIAM: You see when I used to go off to school wit young Master I looked after everything for him. That's why he learned me to read an' write an' figger. I knows how to do travelin'. I kin do it—I must do it, but I got to get de clothes.

ELLEN: But where?

WILLIAM: I kin steal em from de big house. I knows where all ole Marse clothes is hung up. I kin sneak in there . . .

ELLEN *(breaking in)*: Oh William they might ketch you!

MANDY: Dat's mighty dangerus.

WILLIAM: Can't help it. Ellen can't stay here till mornin'. No matter whut happens I wunt let her!

ELLEN *(moaning)*: Oh Lord, whut's goin' to become a me?

WILLIAM *(rising)*: Stay wid her Aunt Mandy; I'm a goin' to git a suit ov clothes from somewhere.

MANDY: I thinks youse plum crazy William runnin' way like white folks, you an' Ellen—if dey ketches you—um-m-mh!

WILLIAM *(moving toward the door)*: Don't you all worry. I kin do it! I'm bleeged to do it. Young Marse used to say my head was too good for a nigger an' now I'm going to try it out.

ELLEN *(moving toward door with William solicitously)*: Be careful, William.

MANDY *(standing up hesitatingly, as if trying to make up her mind about something)*: Wait, William, I lows you done gone plum crazy an' loss your mind doin' this here thing. But since you gwine go anyhow, I'll help you! I got a suit!

WILLIAM *(turning back toward Mandy excitedly)*: A suit! You is?

MANDY: Yes, I is.

WILLIAM: Oh Aunt Mandy, where ya got it?

MANDY: In my lof'. You see ole Miss din't wunt nothin' lef round here to put her in de mind of dat terrible time when young Masser died. She told me to burn up all his close 'cause you know he had dat ketchin' sickness.

WILLIAM: It sho is lucky fur us! You didn't burn nothin' 'tall?

MANDY: Nothin' 'tall. After I done washed an' laid out young Marse Charles I took every stitch uv his close an burned sulfer thru em in my hut . . .

WILLIAM *(interrupting, lowering his voice earnestly)*: You ain't got his tall hat, is you?

MANDY: I sho is! Eben down to his walkin' stick.

WILLIAM: What a God send! Will—will you let Ellen wear em?

MANDY: Sho she kin, since you two goin' to play fool I kin do dis much to hep.

WILLIAM *(pulling Aunt Mandy up from chair)*: Hurry Aunt Mandy! Go an' get em, an' we kin ketch dat north bound at dat crossin' in no time.

ELLEN *(moving over to William)*: I'm skeered, William, I'm sho skeered.

WILLIAM: Shucks, buck up! You don't want to be here in de mornin', do you, when de slave traders come?

ELLEN: Oh, no, William, no. I'll go—I'll go.

WILLIAM *(urging Aunt Mandy toward the door)*: Do hurry, Aunt Mandy!

MANDY *(going toward the door)*: I'll be right back. Thase all right in my lof'.

WILLIAM: Put em in a quilt an' if anybody sees you tell em you comin' to do some quiltin' wid Ellen.

MANDY *(going out of the door)*: Don't you worry—I'm er ole fox, I knows.

ELLEN *(going up to William trembling)*: You sho you kin git us through, William?

WILLIAM: Sho honey; ain't I been on the train time an' time agin wid young Marse, an' can't I read and write?

ELLEN: But how kin I be like a young Marse? I'm all a shakin' now.

WILLIAM *(soothing her):* All you got to do is to walk. You don't have to talk, don't have to do a thing but just walk along bigity like a white man. See here. *(shows her how to walk)* Try it.

ELLEN *(tries to walk like him):* Dis way?

WILLIAM: You doin' fine! You see now you is supposed to be sick, you got a toothache, you goin' to a doctor in Philadelphia, you is nearly deaf, an' yo' nigger slave is takin' you—understand? Oh-o-o.

ELLEN: What's wrong?

WILLIAM: Nothin' 'tall. Gimme yo' shears. I got to cut yo' hair. You see you is a man now.

ELLEN *(despairingly):* Oh my hair! *(she gets the scissors from the sewing basket, and brings them to him)*

WILLIAM *(placing chair near table where the candle is lighted):* Set here. *(he goes to shutter, makes sure it is tight, walks back to Ellen, who has let down her long hair):* I hates to cut yo' pretty hair, but . . .

ELLEN *(resignedly):* Anything is better than goin' down de ribber.

WILLIAM *(takes a lock of hair to cut it when there is a sound of voices and footsteps outside of the door):* Specks you better git behind the curtain, somebody might drop in.

ELLEN: Yes. *(rising)* That tale-tellin' Sam's got a way of dropping in here right free lak.

WILLIAM: That would be terrible! He'd be sho to git suspicious.

ELLEN *(halting as she raises the curtain):* If he do drap in whut we goin' to say? How we goin' to git him out?

WILLIAM: Oh, I'll say you sick—got a headache or something other, an' gone to bed. I'll git a few horseradish leaves out of the garden an' lay one or two on de table to make it look natul like.

ELLEN *(entering into the spirit):* Yes, an' I'll put de coffee pot on some coal an' you kin say you makin' me some coffee to he'p me.

WILLIAM: You sho learn fass. You'se reel smart. I knows you'se goin' to make this trip perfect.

ELLEN *(beaming, moves toward the table as William moves toward the door):* Hurry William!

WILLIAM *(going out of door):* Awright, honey, put on the coffee.

ELLEN *(Takes some water from the bucket with the gourd, puts it in the coffee pot, puts some coffee in it, sets it on some coals at the fireplace.*

Goes to the window, cracks it open a little, looks anxiously down the road and sighs. After a moment there is a soft scraping at the door, then Mandy comes in with a big bundle tied up in a quilt.): Oh you got em!

MANDY *(placing bundle on floor)*: Sho, where's William?

ELLEN: He's in de garden gittin' some horseradish so's if anybody draps in we can play lak I'm sick behind the curtain here.

MANDY: Dat's right! I'll put dese things behind the curtain too. You can't never tell—dere's many a slip.

WILLIAM *(Coming in with leaves. Puts them on table; saying breathless to Mandy)*: Got em?

MANDY *(points)*: Sho, I put em behind the curtain.

WILLIAM: Smart.

MANDY: Dat coffee smells good!

ELLEN: You drink some Aunt Mandy while William's cuttin' off my hair over here behin' de curtain. We got to be careful now. *(Ellen goes behind curtain)*

MANDY: You'se right! I clean forgot 'bout yo' hair. William sho got a good head on him.

WILLIAM: If anybody happens to drop in please git rid o' 'em, Aunt Mandy. Tell 'em Ellen's sick, got a headache and I'm doctorin' it wid horseradish. *(takes scissors and follows Ellen behind screen)*

MANDY: Just leave it to me, I knows whut to do. *(pouring some coffee in a mug, tastes it)* Um-m-m, sho is good. Bof o' you better swallow a mug befo you starts tonight—it'll buck you up.

WILLIAM *(from behind curtain)*: You right, we sho will. Leave it where it'll keep hot.

ELLEN *(from behind curtain)*: Did you git some molasses for your coffee, Aunt Mandy?

MANDY: Yes, chile, I done sweetened it.

WILLIAM *(poking his head out from behind the curtain)*: You sho done fine Aunt Mandy! Dese things sho fit! I'll hep Ellen git into de britches an' she kin do de ress.

MANDY: Dey ought to fit for she's just de size of her haf brother, Marse Charles.

ELLEN *(from behind the curtain)*: Don't talk about dat Aunt Mandy!

WILLIAM *(coming out and pouring himself a mug of coffee)*: Well, dat's done.

MANDY: You got nuff money to git to Philadelphia?

WILLIAM *(snapping his finger)*: Goodness! I jest recollect I got my money buried under a tomato bush in de garden. I'm goin' to dig it up. *(drinks down his coffee)*

MANDY: It's high time!

WILLIAM *(goes to window, cracks shutter a little, peers into the darkness, then closes it)*: We ain't got much more time to lose. Hurry Ellen!

ELLEN *(from behind curtain)*: I's mos' ready.

MANDY: It sho would be too bad if you'd miss dat train.

WILLIAM: We got to start in half hour.

MANDY: I hope nothin' hinders you.

WILLIAM: Nothin' is goin' to.

ELLEN *(steps out from behind curtain dressed in a man's suit, tall silk hat, and a muffler, shrinkingly)*: Oh, I feels terrible!

MANDY *(admiringly)*: You looks just like Marse Charles. I would o' said you was him if I hadn't a laid him out myself.

WILLIAM *(standing up and looking her over critically, wrapping the scarf up around her face)*: Like dis. *(he then takes a large handkerchief from the pocket of the suit and pins it to her coat and puts one arm in it explaining)* You see you can't write so I make out you got rheumatism; now you won't have to sign for nothin'.

MANDY *(admiringly)*: You sho is smart, William.

ELLEN *(breathlessly)*: Do you think we will make it, Aunt Mandy?

MANDY: I sho hopes so. *(sighs)*

WILLIAM *(to Ellen)*: Now take a mug of coffee, while I go out and dig up dat money out of de garden. *(as he goes out of door, says)* Practice walkin' like a white man while I'm gone.

ELLEN: Awright, William. *(nervously)* You hurry. *(drinks coffee and walks up and down cabin, as William had shown her)*

MANDY *(solicitously)*: Got everything in your valise?

ELLEN: I think it is.

MANDY: Let me see. *(Gets valise from behind curtain, looks in it. Says um-m, then goes to cupboard.)* I'll put a piece of dis here bread an' some herring in it cause I hern tell you can't tell nothin' tall bout dem trains. *(fixes bread and herring and puts it in valise while Ellen is stalking up and down the cabin practicing) (listening)* Ain't dat some-body at de door?

ELLEN: 'Taint William. Who dat?

MANDY *(to Ellen):* You git behind de curtain. *(then sets valise behind curtain quickly) (louder)* Who dere?

VOICE *(outside):* It's me, Sam!

MANDY *(to Ellen, softly):* We better let him in.

ELLEN *(softly to Mandy):* Yes, but do get rid of him quick.

MANDY *(opening the door):* What you doin' running up an' down the road worrin' sick people fur tonight?

SAM *(coming in and looking around):* Who sick?

MANDY: Ellen. She got a terrible headache an' gone to bed.

SAM: Wher' William?

MANDY: Out in de garden.

SAM: Pretty time o night gardenin'.

WILLIAM *(entering rather upset and overhearing Sam's last remark):* I'm a trying out a new secret on my tomatoes this year. Everytime I gits a piece o' iron I buries it under em. Makes em blood red an' big as your fist.

SAM: I never hearn o' that. I'm going to watch yourn from now on.

WILLIAM *(to Mandy):* How's Ellen feeling?

MANDY: I think she's 'bout to drap off to sleep.

WILLIAM: May be we had better change the poltis on her head. *(takes up another horseradish leaf and bruises it)*

MANDY *(softly):* You gimme I'll put it on er, then we better put out the light an' let er go to sleep.

SAM *(riled):* You all putin me out?

WILLIAM: No, we ain't, but Ellen a got to get up before day in de mornin' to do some work fur ole Miss an' she got to git some sleep tonight.

SAM *(slyly):* I been hern an' tell the traders was comin' tomorrow an' there was some talk about ole Miss a sendin' Ellen down the ribber.

MANDY: Don't you pay no 'tention to dem low lak niggers talkin'. 'Taint no such thing. Ole Miss aint thunking about sending Ellen no wheres.

SAM *(rising slowly)*: Well, tain't none o' my business, no how. *(slyly)* Kin I have a drink o' water for I goes?

WILLIAM: Sho, take a gourd full. *(William moves toward the gourd but Sam wheels suddenly and ducks toward the curtain, peeping behind it. Ellen screams, then stifles it.)*

WILLIAM: You mangy dog! *(angrily)* What do you mean by doin' dat?

SAM *(sneeringly)*: So you is goin' to try to get away, is ya? *(moves toward the door)* Goin' to tell ole Miss goodbye?

WILLIAM *(excitedly)*: What you goin' to do?

SAM *(snarlingly)*: What you reckon, Mr. edicated nigger?

WILLIAM *(rushes to him and catches him about the throat)*: So you is goin' to tell! Spyin' on us! I sho ya!

MANDY *(jumping up overturning her chair in excitement)*: What you goin' to do, William?

WILLIAM: I'm a goin' to shut his mouth. Give me a piece er rag, Mandy.

MANDY *(hunts around the cabin, finds a piece of cloth in the sewing basket and brings it to William) (looking at Sam)*: Dirty pup!

WILLIAM *(stuffs cloth into Sam's mouth, while he presses him down into a chair with his knees) (to Mandy)*: Now get me Ellen's clothes line over there in the corner.

MANDY *(running to corner getting clothes line, bringing it to William excitedly)*: Lord, Jesus, hep us!

WILLIAM *(tying rope around Sam's arms with a loop knot) (to Mandy)*: Peep out first, then open de door. *(takes Sam and drags him out of the door as Ellen comes trembling from behind the curtain)*

ELLEN *(crying)*: What will we do now, Aunt Mandy?

MANDY *(shaking her head despondingly)*: Things look mighty bad, honey, I dunno.

(For a few minutes there is a strained silence in the cabin while the two women strain their ears listening for sounds outside. Ellen nervously moves about the room, picking up things and putting them down. Aunt Mandy picks up William's coat she has darned, shakes it.)

MANDY *(head on one side listening outside)*: Wonder what William is a doin' to Sam?

ELLEN *(tearfully)*: I dunno. I don't wunt to know.

MANDY: He brung it on his self.

WILLIAM *(entering disheveled and brushing his hands on his trousers, speaking hoarsely)*: Come on, Ellen, trains don't wait.

ELLEN: Oh, William! What ya done done?

MANDY *(holding William's coat for him to put on, as William slips off his sweater) (to Ellen)*: Don' worry about dat now, too late!

WILLIAM: I'm sorry, Aunt Mandy, but I had to do what I done to kiver you cause he saw you here. *(just then a train whistle blew, all listen and move excitedly)* Come on, Ellen, we jes kin make it by takin' the short cut, walk in fron' o' me an' don't say nothin' tall to nobody. I'll do de talkin'. Keep you arm in de sling. *(breathlessly)* Goodbye, Aunt Mandy, goodbye.

MANDY: You ain't gone yet.

(Ellen, whimpering, as she hesitates at door)

MANDY *(to Ellen)*: Buck up, chile, white men don't cry!

WILLIAM *(to Mandy)*: I hope no harm don' come to you for this night's work, Aunt Mandy.

MANDY *(appreciatingly)*: Huh! After I done suckled all ole Miss children, gone chile, I kin take ker myself.

WILLIAM: Well, goodbye, Aunt Mandy. *(kisses her) (to Ellen)* You go first, Ellen. I'll walk behind you in de light but I'll walk wid you in de dark. Hurry!

(Ellen throws arms around Mandy, kisses her, then dashes out)

MANDY: God bless you, William.

(Mandy closes door, goes to shutter, cracks it a little, and peers out. It is quiet for a few minutes. A train whistle is heard in the distance. Mandy drops down on her knees on the floor, while the candle sputters and goes out.)

(Curtain)

PART III

Plays and Stories of Average Negro Life

Paupaulekejo

A THREE-ACT PLAY

(c. 1926)

Georgia Douglas Johnson (writing as John Tremaine)

Characters:

PAUPAULEKEJO, *(half caste) Son of Zoagoa*
ZOAGOA, *Chief of the tribe of Tshaka*
CLAIRE, *Daughter of missionary*
DUGLEY MCKENZIE, *Missionary*
EDWARD LONSDALE, *Cynic, trader*
SAHDJI, *Dancer*
MISCELLANEOUS, *Warriors, Witch Doctor, Wives*

ACT I

Scene 1

Scene opens in a jungle clearing in interior of Africa. In the left center, a fire around which are warriors squatting, the women in the rear standing. In the right center to right of fire, a little back stage, three tom-toms, a rattler, reed-blower.

Curtain rises on Sahdji dancing to jungle music. This dance is significant to Paupaulekejo. Sahdji throws her beads at Paupaulekejo's feet.

Curtain falls on this scene, slowly.

Interior of a trader's store, printed cloths of cotton and cheap silk, gaudy jewelry, glass beads. Open packing case showing cheap toys, tobacco and cheap candies in glass jars, crates of soda crackers, demi-johns of cheap liquor, sawdust floors, kerosene lamps, cheap print pictures on walls. Door to back right center, window to left of door with cheap print muslin curtain, couple of folding chairs. Scene opens with Lonsdale talking to missionary.

CYNIC: So this is the great day your daughter will be here. You'll be happy, eh?

MISSIONARY: Yes. Haven't seen her for five years. I suppose she'll be a big girl now.

CYNIC: How old is she?

MISSIONARY: Let me see. She—Oh, there she is now. *(rushes out of doorway)*

(Offstage, you can see him pass by the window running. Sounds from without, dropping of ropes, snorts, grunts, then from without is heard girl's voice.)

(from without) "Father, Father!"

(The missionary's voice is heard) My darling! *(They pass the window, arms about each other, she impeding his steps)*

(enter Missionary and Claire)

MISSIONARY: How was the trip on—

CLAIRE *(breaking in):* Oh wonderful, wonderful!

MISSIONARY: How did you leave Aunt Roberta?

CLAIRE: Distressed to death! Said the natives would kill us both!

MISSIONARY: Bah! This is my little girl, Claire McKenzie—the apple of my eye.

CYNIC: Little girl—ho! She's a great dame. Glad to see you. Good for the eyes. Hope you'll like these parts.

CLAIRE: Oh, I'll like it! Seems very interesting already.

MISSIONARY *(patting daughter on back lovingly):* Wait, dear, I'll speak to my men outside, then we'll go over to my hut. *(goes outside)*

CLAIRE: The natives have such splendid physiques.

MISSIONARY: Yeh, the blacks have big healthy bodies. They're so bloody lazy they ought to have.

CLAIRE: They seem very kind—pleasant.

CYNIC: Wait 'til you see 'em drunk; they're awful then.

CLAIRE: You'd never believe it to see them now.

CYNIC: By and by—

CLAIRE *(cutting him off)*: You have lots of British goods here. So far from England. What's this? *(picks up fetish)*

CYNIC: Some black tomfoolery! That's the sort of thing they bring in here and trade for rum.

CLAIRE *(noticing book with pictures in it, then laughing)*: Do you sell these to the natives too?

CYNIC: Oh no, there's only one of 'em here with brains enough even to look at the pictures *(afterthought)* and he's half white.

CLAIRE: Oh, I think I must have seen him—a big, handsome specimen of manhood. He was leading a troop of blacks. He was marching like a king! I wondered who he was. He wasn't—well—black like the rest!

CYNIC: Paupaulekejo!

CLAIRE: Whom did you say?

CYNIC: Paupaulekejo. He thinks he's the king around here; a sort of despot.

CLAIRE: Tell me about him.

CYNIC: Well, his father's black; his mother came out from England, at least, they say so.

CLAIRE: How singular!

CYNIC: Not strange. He was a handsome black and she—well she came out without a man.

CLAIRE: This is going to prove interesting.

CYNIC: Oh yes—*(interrupted by missionary's return)*

MISSIONARY *(entering speaking)*: Well, everything is ready, darling. Let's go.

CLAIRE *(turning to Cynic)*: It has been very pleasant to have known you and—and I'd like to know more about—

CYNIC: Oh, you'll learn.

(Curtain)

ACT I

Scene 2

Missionary's hut. Rude sitting room. A wooden center table with books. A rudely constructed bookshelf with rows of books. A door leading to a small room that Claire occupies. A door leading into another room back. Front door leading to the porch and window to the left of door. A settee near book-cases.

Claire and missionary discovered in sitting room having tea as curtain rises.

MISSIONARY: Well, darling, what do you think of my bringing black souls to Christ?

DAUGHTER: I think you've been a perfect St. Xavier, considering all the difficulties you encounter here.

MISSIONARY: I don't think I have been so great as all that, but at least I have been successful in planting the Spirit of the Master here among many other gods. The natives seem to take to Christianity well enough, but they don't seem to think that they are under obligation to give up their false gods.

DAUGHTER *(thinking, somewhat):* I—I—from what I've seen of them, I think they make good Christians, provided they could be persuaded to adopt a more civilized dress.

MISSIONARY: That also is one of the serious drawbacks. They seem to think that the body is something to be proud of and shown at all times.

DAUGHTER: I do think they have splendid bodies, but the flesh is not everything.

MISSIONARY: That's just it! The flesh is not everything and they must learn to overcome the desires of the flesh if they would be good Christians.

DAUGHTER: I think I shall be able to offer some suggestions, whereby, you will be able to make further progress, provided, of course, they are acceptable and practicable to you.

MISSIONARY *(somewhat beaming):* I am glad to hear you say that, since for so long I have labored here without the help or suggestion of anyone genuinely interested in the work.

DAUGHTER: First, I would suggest that we get in touch with the most influential leaders, whoever they are.

MISSIONARY: I have met and talked with most of the leaders, but—

DAUGHTER: Are they sympathetic?

MISSIONARY: Yes, at least as far as I can see.

DAUGHTER: How about inviting the most influential one to a sort of conference here?

MISSIONARY: That's a good idea. We might send for Paupaulekejo. He's the most influential native. King in fact.

DAUGHTER: Oh yes. He is the one that—that reads the picture books.

MISSIONARY: Yes—if only we can influence him—but I've tried. God knows I have, but—

DAUGHTER: Now father, nothing beats a trial but a failure and I do want to help.

MISSIONARY: I'll do it. I'll send for him. *(calling)* Sahdji!

SAHDJI: Yes, Teacher. [The script originally called for African word for "Master" which was crossed out by hand, and replaced with the word "Teacher"]

MISSIONARY: Sahdji, I wish you to go to Paupaulekejo. Tell him—ask him to come here, please.

SAHDJI: He no come. Me go for he though. *(exits)*

MISSIONARY *(rising):* It is always best to humor the natives, to *ask* for Paupaulekejo. *(laughs slightly)*

DAUGHTER *(also rising):* Now father, you go and take a smoke. I'll finish clearing off the tea dishes. *(gently pushes him to the door)*

MISSIONARY: Yes, daughter. I will take a walk through the garden, but I will be back before Paupaulekejo arrives or Sahdji returns with his no.

DAUGHTER: I think he will come. Now out with you. *(shoos Missionary on)*

MISSIONARY: It won't be the first time he has sent a refusal! *(exits wagging his head)*

DAUGHTER *(Daughter makes busy over the dishes, humming the Kashmir song. Every now and then she speaks to herself.):* If no other way works, a picture Bible might. That's it, a picture Bible. *(stoops before a bookcase in corner away from door, humming Kashmir song)*

(A native enters, stands with folded arms, and speaks)

PAUPAULEKEJO: I am Paupaulekejo. *(She stands abruptly; the books in her lap fall. Sees Paupaulekejo.)*

(Curtain)

ACT II

Scene I

Three months have elapsed between Act I and Act II. Living room. Sahdji is dusting around. Offstage in distance can be heard a male voice singing love song, bizarre. Sahdji listens, dusts dilatorily. Paupaulekejo enters.

SAHDJI: Paupaulekejo!

PAUPAULEKEJO: Where is your mistress?

SAHDJI: She here.

PAUPAULEKEJO: Tell her I am here.

SAHDJI: She come—bymby.

PAUPAULEKEJO: Sahdji, I am here!

(Sahdji leaves room. Paupaulekejo looks around furtively, then tips over to bookcase, gets Bible, and tips out. Returns in a few moments and is curiously looking at prints on the wall when Claire enters.)

CLAIRE: Well, I see you are on time.

PAUPAULEKEJO: What this? *(pointing to picture on wall)*

CLAIRE: That is the Pantheon.

PAUPAULEKEJO: What that?

CLAIRE: Oh, a building that—but never mind, we will get to our lesson first. *(goes to bookcase, searches)* Where is that Bible? *(Calls)* Sahdji.

SAHDJI *(entering)*: Yes, tasmamy?

CLAIRE: Where did you put the Bible?

SAHDJI: Me put him there. *(goes to case)*

CLAIRE: But it's not there.

SAHDJI: Me put him there.

CLAIRE: Oh pshaw! Help me find it, Sahdji. *(they look)*

PAUPAULEKEJO: You tell me. All the same.

CLAIRE: Where is it? It was right here this morning.

PAUPAULEKEJO: You find him bimeby. You tell me.

CLAIRE *(absently)*: You will find it *soon*, Paupaulekejo.

PAUPAULEKEJO: Yes, you find him soon.

CLAIRE: Where on earth can it be? Sahdji, ask father! Or ask him to lend me another. *(Sahdji leaves)* Now, where did we leave off before? *(turns to Paupaulekejo)*

PAUPAULEKEJO: You say your God is love?

CLAIRE: Yes, and what did you learn?

PAUPAULEKEJO: To love everybody.

CLAIRE: Every *one.*

PAUPAULEKEJO: Sahdji?

CLAIRE: Yes.

PAUPAULEKEJO: Slaves?

CLAIRE: Yes.

PAUPAULEKEJO: That white man give me rum?

CLAIRE: Yes, Paupaulekejo, everyone. That is God's message.

PAUPAULEKEJO: Love you?

CLAIRE *(embarrassed):* Yes, of course. Now what?

PAUPAULEKEJO: Love much?

CLAIRE *(blushing):* Yes, you must love everyone—everyone!

PAUPAULEKEJO: I no like to love everyone!

CLAIRE: But you must! That's what I have been—

PAUPAULEKEJO: I love you!

CLAIRE: That is right, but—

PAUPAULEKEJO: I no love Sahdji!

CLAIRE: Oh Paupaulekejo, but you must.

PAUPAULEKEJO: You love Sahdji?

CLAIRE: Of course.

PAUPAULEKEJO: Me?

CLAIRE: Yes, every—

PAUPAULEKEJO: Love long time?

CLAIRE: Always, everyone.

PAUPAULEKEJO: I no want you love everyone.

CLAIRE: Paupaulekejo, stop it. I want to teach you.

PAUPAULEKEJO: I know how to love.

CLAIRE: Then do it, love everyone!

PAUPAULEKEJO: Can I call your name?

CLAIRE: *May I,* Paupaulekejo.

PAUPAULEKEJO: Claire—you here—night time—tom-tom go boom, boom, boom!

CLAIRE: Yes, but—

PAUPAULEKEJO: An' air in grass blowing by young bucks, sound sweet—like song?

CLAIRE: Yes, Paupaulekejo, but that is not the lesson.

PAUPAULEKEJO: Yes him is. That my men, tom-tom love for you, for me.

CLAIRE: All right now.

PAUPAULEKEJO: And I sing for wind to bring to you love song like this. *(sings, Claire listens) Him go Goaro njubomotbo sale.* I sing him for you.

CLAIRE: But you mustn't, Paupaulekejo. It's wrong.

PAUPAULEKEJO: What wrong? I love you?

CLAIRE *(faintly):* Yes.

PAUPAULEKEJO: But you say, your God say love; I love you more everybody.

CLAIRE: But you mustn't, Paupaulekejo, not like that.

PAUPAULEKEJO: I only know one love. I love you that one.

CLAIRE: Please.

PAUPAULEKEJO: Love you that one all time. Claire, Claire, make sound like love song in grass; Claire sound like love song on wind. Paupaulekejo sound like love song on tom-tom. Love song on wind, you Claire, love song on tom-tom, me. Go all time together. Paupaulekejo and Claire.

CLAIRE: Please, Paupaulekejo, it isn't right.

PAUPAULEKEJO: You no love me?

CLAIRE: Yes, but—

PAUPAULEKEJO: You put your lip on my lip.

CLAIRE *(frantically):* No!

PAUPAULEKEJO: Then Paupaulekejo no think your God.

CLAIRE: But a kiss doesn't mean love. Judas kissed Christ.

PAUPAULEKEJO: You love me then?

CLAIRE: In my country, a white woman must not love a—a—black man.

PAUPAULEKEJO: In your country no think your God?

CLAIRE: Oh, God yes! But—Oh, I can't explain.

PAUPAULEKEJO: You no love me?—Your God no love me?

CLAIRE: I do love you—I do—Oh, God, what have I said?

PAUPAULEKEJO: I do love you—Claire—*(kisses her warmly)*

CLAIRE: Stop—Father might—*(pushes him away)*

PAUPAULEKEJO: Paupaulekejo love you, love your God—love Sahdji—love everybody—everyone—*(father enters)* Me know—my mother—she white—my father, him black—she think your God—you no think Him.

CLAIRE: But I do—I—

PAUPAULEKEJO: Then you love me?

CLAIRE: I—I can't say.

PAUPAULEKEJO: Him mean yes.

CLAIRE: Paupaulekejo:

PAUPAULEKEJO: You love me? Put you lip on my lip.

CLAIRE: If Father should hear you.

PAUPAULEKEJO: Him tell me your God—him think Him.

CLAIRE: I know, but—

PAUPAULEKEJO: Claire love me?

CLAIRE: It cannot be—not here or anywhere on God's green earth.

PAUPAULEKEJO: Why—why?

CLAIRE: Because—Oh, Paupaulekejo—

MISSIONARY *(enters, looks vexed):* Better stop the lesson for the night, Claire! Let Paupaulekejo go!

CLAIRE: Why father! *(turning to Paupaulekejo)* We'll take this up next Friday Paupaulekejo.

(Missionary walks up and down agitatedly. Paupaulekejo gathers his books and paper, looks perplexed, salutes and leaves hastily. Sahdji is seen darting out of the door in the wake of Paupaulekejo. Missionary is glowering as curtain descends.)

ACT III

*Scene 3 same as scene 2, one day later.**

CLAIRE *(whispering to Sahdji):* Sahdji, run and find Paupaulekejo. Tell him to come right away. *(Sahdji, with peculiar expression, hurries out. Claire, getting things together in a grip perturbedly, stands in doorway. Enter Paupaulekejo quietly and Sahdji enters behind him.)*

CLAIRE: Run without, Sahdji! *(Sahdji leaves reluctantly)*

PAUPAULEKEJO: You send for Paupaulekejo?

CLAIRE: Yes, I had to see you to—er—say good-bye.

PAUPAULEKEJO: Good-bye—what you mean?

CLAIRE: I'm going away. I take the next ship. It leaves shortly. I've enjoyed teaching you.

*Johnson's numbering of scenes appears incorrect here since Act III has only one scene. Perhaps she meant the setting for Act III is the same as Act II, one day later; or perhaps text is missing.

PAUPAULEKEJO: You what? You go leave Paupaulekejo? You say good-bye all time—never see Paupaulekejo again, no?

CLAIRE: Yes, Paupaulekejo. Father says I must go. He is angry with me. I must go.

PAUPAULEKEJO: Why you want to leave Paupaulekejo?

CLAIRE: I don't want to, but I must.

PAUPAULEKEJO: No, you stay.

CLAIRE: My father forbids and I—I—Oh you can't understand!

PAUPAULEKEJO: I do. You love me and I love you. What more?

CLAIRE: Everything. We are different. I can't live as you live. We're different, different!

PAUPAULEKEJO: You don't want to go. Stay. Paupaulekejo marry you. Me buy you everything—big house, pretty dress—me get him.

CLAIRE: No, I cannot live your life. It's terrible.

PAUPAULEKEJO: What wrong!

CLAIRE: I'm bewitched! Bewitched!

PAUPAULEKEJO: No. No you not. You love. You happy with me, yes.

CLAIRE: Yes, happy! Too happy! But you must go. Father will be returning. He said he would kill you.

PAUPAULEKEJO: Kill me? I ready. My braves outside; they wait; I know and ready, trick with trick.

CLAIRE: But you mustn't shed blood!

PAUPAULEKEJO: Ha! Shed blood! I make the rivers red with blood for you. For you, Paupaulekejo drown the world in blood!

CLAIRE: Hush! You must leave now! I'm sorry we met.

PAUPAULEKEJO: Sorry? You sorry?

CLAIRE: I mean since we must—must part.

PAUPAULEKEJO: Part? Must? Claire, once more your lip on my lip once last time, then Paupaulekejo go. Come!

CLAIRE: Last time. Good-bye. *(they embrace)*

PAUPAULEKEJO: We go same God. Your God, my God. We same there; we love there. Your heart, Claire, my heart. We go together!

(Swiftly he plunges knife into Claire's heart and then into his own. They fall on couch.)

(Sound of returning voices. Sahdji enters hastily, rushes across room, looks around quickly, dashes to couch and throws her hands up in horror. Screams

and moans, pulls Paupaulekejo away from Claire and falls with her arms about him. Missionary and Cynic enter and then both stop in horror. Missionary slowly advances and kneels at the side of his dead daughter.)

(Curtain)

Starting Point

A ONE-ACT PLAY IN THREE SCENES

(1938)

Characters:
FATHER, *Henry Robinson*
SON, *Tom Robinson*
MOTHER, *Martha Robinson*
GIRL, *Belle*

Place:
Charleston, South Carolina

Props:
Kitchen table—stove—cabinet—five chairs—dishes—food for meal

SCENE 1

Martha discovered laying table for dinner—takes a letter from apron pocket and with a pleased expression places it under her husband's plate.

ROBINSON *(enters stage right, walks over to his wife and kisses her lightly on the cheek):* Hello Martha—how you feeling?

MARTHA: Oh—a little tired Henry, but I've had good news today.

ROBINSON: Good news, what kind of good news?

MARTHA: It'll wait—eat your supper first—I know you're tired and hungry after being on your feet all day long at the beck and call of Tom, Dick and Harry.

ROBINSON: You're mighty right—my feet seem like they don't belong to me a'tall they're that tired—let me get my slippers—*(goes off stage left)*

(Martha puts food on table)

(Robinson reenters—sits down at head of table and asks blessing—they begin to eat—)

MARTHA: How's things at the bank today?

ROBINSON: Well, there's been a whole lot of howdy do down there today over Jim Boyd's son Toby—you know, from in Cat fish row [Catfish Row]—seem like he's been writing numbers for the white folks round the bank, and them federal investigators caught him red-handed.

MARTHA: You don't say—poor Jim—I know he's all broke up—he set such store on that boy of his—Suppose there's anything we can do to help 'em out?

ROBINSON: I don't know, I'll ask him tomorrow. We got a lot to be thankful for, our son's doing so fine up there in the doctor's school in Washington.

MARTHA: It sure is—it won't be long now before he gets his doctor's license—Euhm hum—*(she smiles)*

ROBINSON: I can see him now, going about from house to house.

MARTHA: Doctoring sick folks now! My but I'll be proud!

ROBINSON: Proud's no name for it. Thank God he's got a fine profession and won't have to set at no white man's door fetching and carrying all his life like me.

MARTHA: Yes, and he'll make a lot of money and help you like you helped him.

ROBINSON: Sure he'll want to, fine boy—but I don't need him to help me—I can get along alright—I just want him to be a man and stand up on his own two feet, that's all—be a real man!

MARTHA *(gets up, lifts up Henry's plate and discloses letter underneath)*: Here's your surprise Henry, read it! *(proudly)*

(Robinson takes letter and looks at it quizzingly)

MARTHA: Read it out loud.

ROBINSON *(reading)*: Dear mother and dad: I'm coming home for a day or two. Will be there almost as soon as this letter. Have a surprise for you. Your loving son, Tom.

I wonder what's bringing him home.

MARTHA: I wonder what the surprise is.

ROBINSON: School's not through yet.

MARTHA: Maybe he's got his license already—maybe that's the surprise.

ROBINSON *(scratching his head)*: I don't believe that's it—it's something else.

MARTHA: Go long Henry, you know—Tom's a smart boy—why couldn't they give it to him already.

ROBINSON: Maybe they might, but seems like to me that's too good to be true. *(They hear a voice from outside calling, "Dad, Mother, Dad." The two look at each other startled.)*

MARTHA *(excitedly)*: Oh my lands, Henry—here we've been talking ourselves to death and here's the child already. Go see.

(Henry goes out stage right. Martha bustles about kitchen snatching off her apron. Noise of greeting in yard comes faintly into kitchen. Martha listens perplexedly, then draws back upon noticing the dazed expression on her husband's face—as he enters.)

(Robinson walks toward Martha and puts his arm tenderly around her shoulder as Tom and Belle follow upon his heels.)

TOM: Mother! *(dashes over and kisses her)*

MARTHA: My little boy—my son—my! *(Then notices the girl just behind Tom's shoulder. She stops short again as Tom leaves her, approaches the girl and leads her back to his mother.)*

TOM: My surprise, Mother, your new daughter Belle—!

MARTHA *(Staggers—swallows—as though to collect herself. Then putting out her arms slowly embraces the girl.) (then faintly)*: Belle—welcome. My, but I'm glad to see you. I'm so surprised—I don't know what to say,—I, I, thought maybe you—

TOM: Don't worry little mother—*(fondles her)* I'm o.k.

MARTHA: But, ——Well, supposing you go upstairs children a little while—you must be dead beat out, riding on the train all that way.

TOM: Oh, we're not tired mother. How about a little snack. *(goes over to the stove and peers in the pots)* What you got to eat?

MARTHA: You go long Tom and take Belle to wash up, she's dusty I know. I'll fix you all something and call you in no time.

BELLE: Don't bother about me—I'm not hungry and you oughtn't put your mother out either, Tom, after all the hot dogs you ate on the train.

TOM *(takes the hint from Belle)*: Come to think of it, I'm not hungry—a bit. It's just the smell of ma's good cooking and bein' home, I guess, that's what I was hungering after. My stomach and my heart is both full—Now I got you too.

TOM: Come on up Belle and wash up.

(As Tom and Belle exit—the father looks in blank amazement toward the door they passed through, turns his gaze from the door to Martha—then wearily drags himself to the table and falls down limply into a chair—his head falling on his outstretched arms. Martha walks over quietly to him, leans over him tenderly and pats him on the shoulders.)

(End of Scene 1)

SCENE 2

Time:

An hour later

Same scene

Table is cleared. Father and Mother are seated at the table. Father playing a game of solitaire and Mother darning a pair of socks—looking up furtively now and then at her husband who holds one card looking at it as if he has forgotten where to put it.

TOM: *(hurries in from stage left, coat off, collar open)* Gee, it's great to be home. Same old place—same old kitchen.

MARTHA *(smiling)*: It's good to see you too, son.

TOM: It's sure sweet of you to take Belle right in, but I knew you would.

ROBINSON *(grunts)*: Eughn.

MARTHA: Well son—your happiness is our happiness. Tho, we did think maybe you'd get your license. We thought that was the surprise you had for us.

TOM: Well, you see Mother—*(Belle's voice is heard in a popular blues song off stage. All three lift their heads with varying expressions. Father and Mother taken aback look askance at each other because of the type of song and rowdy music.) (proudly)* That girl's a wow! She sure can sing. Knocked 'em cold in Washington! *(continues with broken speech)* Well, as I was saying. It's like this. They're as tricky as they can be at these schools—always trying to put stumbling blocks in your path and making you go through a lot of red tape. I won't finish this year at all.

(Belle has caught the last few words of his sentence as she hesitates for a minute in the doorway stage left.)

TOM: You see *(haltingly as he looks at Belle)* I won't get my medical degree until next year.

BELLE: What kind of cock and bull story is that you're pulling on your folks, Tom?

(Father and Mother look from Belle to Tom wonderingly)

ROBINSON: What does she mean, Tom?

BELLE: I mean *(Tom looks at her imploringly)* Tom's not in school.

MARTHA *(aghast):* Not in school!

BELLE: No, he's not in school.

ROBINSON *(looking from Belle to Tom):* What do you mean, not in school?

BELLE: Come on, Tom, make a clean breast of it. Tell them the truth.

TOM *(sheepishly):* Well—No. Father, I had to have some money, I couldn't ask you or ma for any more—so—well, I had to get busy.

ROBINSON: Busy, busy doing what?

TOM *(hesitatingly):* Well—

BELLE: For God's sake, be honest. Tell 'em. They've got a right to know. *(pauses, she waits for Tom to speak)* He's in the number racket.

ROBINSON: My God!

MARTHA *(whispers):* My son!

TOM: Well, I had to do something.

MARTHA: You should have told us. We would have helped you.

ROBINSON: What a mess—what a mess. *(knock heard at door)*

*(*TOM *goes to front door through entrance stage right)*

MARTHA *(absently):* I wonder who's that knocking so sharp this time of night.

ROBINSON *(mechanically):* I don't know.

(Tom reenters with a telegram in his hand)

MARTHA: A telegram! Who's it for?

TOM *(who's torn it open with a quick jerk and is now reading it with a worried expression)*

BELLE: What is it Tom?

ROBINSON: Yes, what is it?

TOM *(flicking the telegram with one hand then quickly jabbing it into his pocket):* Oh, it's nothing. Just a little line from a friend in Washington.

BELLE: Quit stalling, Tom—come clean—you've got bad news—spill it.

ROBINSON: Yes, what is it? I demand to know.

MARTHA: Now, Henry, don't be harsh with the boy. What is it son?

BELLE *(going up to him):* Here, give it to me Tom. If you won't say what's in it, I'll find out for myself.

TOM *(reluctantly drags telegram from his pocket and reads):* "Your—place raided. Town's hot. Don't come back."

(looks of consternation pass between Mother and Father)

BELLE *(stands knitting her brow—arms a-kimbo):* Well, that's that. What's the next move?

TOM: Oh, it'll blow over—we've been in jams before—we can go back undercover when this has all quieted down.

BELLE: Oh, no we don't either. I told you before if this happened again, either go straight now or never. *(looks at parents)* I'm sorry, I know it's tough on you but we've got to face it. Looks like he'll have to stay here.

TOM *(heatedly):* Now wait a minute Belle. I've been man enough to make my own decisions up to now. You shut your mouth. I'll decide what I'm going to do and I'm not going to stay in this dead hole—there's other fields for a smart fellow like me. I can go to New York, Chicago, Pittsburgh—

BELLE *(shouting):* Oh no you won't. Over my dead body. You've been cock of the roost too long now. You've got to take low. *(pleadingly)* Please Tom, you know it's the toughest game in the world, you can't beat it.

TOM: I'm beating it—nobody's going to tell me what to do.

ROBINSON: Oh yes they are—you listen to me boy—you've had your way long enough. You've fooled your mother and me up till now. But, my God, I'm going to have my say and you're going to do as I say if I have to thrash you to bring you to your senses.

TOM: Who in the hell do you think you are? You're only my father, you're not God.

(Father rushes at Tom and slaps him)

MARTHA: Henry!—Tom! *(faints)*

(Curtain)

SCENE 3

Time:

Early next morning

Scene opens with Belle and Tom entering kitchen

BELLE *(continuing argument that evidently has been going on all night)*: I don't understand how you can't see it, Tom. It's plain as the nose on your face. You can't go back. You've got to start anew and from scratch.

TOM: Scratch! Why I got enough now to buy up everybody in this little burg!

BELLE: Got! What you got? A car—a few dollars and a few suits of clothes—that's what you've got, and that don't amount to a hill of beans!

TOM: That's what you say . . . but I got mother wit and that's worth a million dollars!

BELLE: Humph—that's what all hustlers think, and where do they wind up? Behind bars! The easy way is the hardest way and after all's said and done, it don't pan out the way you want it to. You've already found that out Tom. So don't be a sucker. After all, what kind of sport are you? You always prided yourself on the fact that everyone said you were one of the squarest shooters in the game. Well, what about it—here you have two of the finest folks in the world. How about giving them a break? What about what you owe them? You've taken everything and given them nothing . . . They bet on you and you failed them. Don't you see, Tom, you've got to square yourself.

TOM: Square myself, for what? I didn't ask to be born.

BELLE: So you are a heel. You've only been a big bluff—a whole lot of wind. I drew the booby prize for a husband. *(She walks away from him, walks over to the stove, lights a cigarette. Father comes in with Mother leaning weakly on his arm. He seats her at the table)*

MARTHA: Good morning son . . . good morning Belle.

ROBINSON: Morning Belle.

MARTHA: Did you sleep well children . . . seems like to me you were up pretty late.

BELLE: I hope we didn't keep you awake. I've got some breakfast ready for you.

MARTHA: Thank you child . . . I just want a cup of strong coffee . . .

(Belle and Martha are watching the two men furtively. Robinson exits stage right and comes right back in carrying the morning paper. Tom is fidgeting about the kitchen nervously.)

BELLE *(to Robinson who is glancing through the paper timidly)*: Father, your breakfast is on the table.

(A tense silence is felt in the room. Martha sips her coffee in the electric atmosphere)

ROBINSON: Thank you, Belle.

TOM: I'm . . . I'm sorry about last night Dad.

ROBINSON: That's all right son—we all make mistakes, but it's never too late to start over again. Now I been thinking, and your Ma and me figured that since I'm old and about played out, you could step in and take my place. I feel almost certain my boss would be willing.

TOM: You mean?

ROBINSON: Yes, son.

(Tom looks at Belle who stands with clasped hands . . . looks at Tom imploringly and nods her head approvingly)

ROBINSON *(rises, gets hat, walks a step or two, turns to Tom)*: Ready now?

TOM *(stands irresolutely looking at the three of them as if for direction, then with a sudden turn, exits left)*: Just a minute Dad.

(Robinson walks over and kisses Martha who is quietly weeping then walks to Belle and tenderly kisses her. As he walks toward the door, Belle moves toward Martha and stands behind her protectingly.)

TOM *(off stage left):* I'm coming Dad.

(Curtain)

PART IV

Lynching Plays

A Sunday Morning in the South

A ONE-ACT PLAY IN TWO SCENES

(c. 1925)

White Church Version

Characters:

SUE JONES, *The grandmother, around 60*
TOM GRIGGS, *Her grandson, aged 19*
BOSSIE GRIGGS, *Her grandson, aged 7*
LIZA TWIGGS, *A friend, around 60*
A WHITE GIRL
FIRST OFFICER
SECOND OFFICER
ROBERT MANNING, *Judge*
USHER
TWO WHITE MEN

Place:
A town in the South

Time:
1924

SCENE 1

Sue Jones' kitchen

Kitchen in Sue Jones' two-room house. There is a window in the left wall, a door at back, and a door leading to front room; a stove against back wall, and a table near it: four chairs, an old time kitchen safe, a wooden water bucket with shiny brass bales on a shelf near the door, with a dipper hanging beside it.

As curtain rises, Sue Jones is seen putting the breakfast on the kitchen table. She wears a blue bandanna handkerchief on her gray hair, a big brown gingham apron tied around her waist, and big black old lady comfort shoes. She moves back and forth from the stove to the table as fast as her rheumatic legs will allow her.

SUE *(lifting her voice):* Tom, Tom, you and Bossie come on out here and eat your breakfast. Harry up cause I got hot rolls.

TOM *(from next room):* All right Gramma, we're coming.

SUE: You better. *(She opens the stove door and looks at the rolls, then starts humming an old fashioned camp meeting tune)* "Oh poor sinner Eughumn—Now is the time—oh poor sinner Eughumn—What you gointer do when the lamp burns down?" *(As she finishes the song, Tom and Bossie hurry into the kitchen, get their chairs and put them to the table. There is one there already for Sue.)*

SUE *(taking rolls out of stove and bringing the pan over to the table):* It's as hard to git you all out here to eat on Sunday morning as it is to pull hen teeth.

TOM: Gramma, I tell you the truth, my back feels all unjointed like. I ain't never gointer try to lift no more boxes, big and heavy like as them was yesterday all by myself.

SUE: I hader oughter rubbed it last night with some of my snake-oil liniment before you went to bed. But you was fast asleep before I was done washing up the supper dishes.

TOM: Yessum, I sholy did. I must a got to sleep long before eight o'clock and didn't I sleep—boy I was tired!

BOSSIE *(eating rolls):* Eughm, those rolls is sure good, Gramma; I could eat the whole pan myself.

SUE: Eat and keep your mouth shut. When you git big and work hard and make money like your brother, you kin eat two pans full; wheat flour is high and we got to 'lowance ourselfs.

BOSSIE *(looking doleful):* I ain't never gointer work hard like Tom and break my back. I'm gointer learn to be a preacher and—

SUE *(catching sight of someone passing the window and approaching the door):* Look, there comes Liza Twiggs. I bet she smelled these rolls and coffee way over to her house. *(a knock is heard at the back door)* Let her in Bossie!

(Bossie jumps up from the table and goes to the door, opens it, and lets the visitor in)

LIZA *(sniffling)*: Mawning yawll. I'm on my way to service but I thought I'd drop in a minute. Coffee smells good.

SUE: 'Tis good too. Come and swaller a cup with one of these good hot rolls.

LIZA: Don't mind if I do. *(draws a chair and is helped to coffee and rolls as Bossie looks on disapprovingly)*

SUE: Well, whut you know good?

LIZA: Good? I don't know nothing good, but I did hear as how they's got the police all out going up and down hunting another poor Nigger man who they says 'tacked a white 'oman right about here at the corner of Broad and 1st Street last night. If they git him, they'll lynch him sho—

SUE: Yes, they make short of work of 'em. And do you know Liza, I don't believe half of 'em is tellin' the truth. They holler out "rape" at the drappin' of a hat. Half these tales is lies, jest lies.

LIZA: Why I knows it fer a fact that they lynched a man in Texas last year and found out most a mont afterwards that a white man done it—he blacked his face and put it on the poor Nigger.

SUE: Pity we can't let the whole world know 'bout sich. I heared a lot of unbelievable things in my time that's been laid at the black man's door.

LIZA: Me too. I sho wish I could read and write and talk proper. I'd make folks set up.

TOM: You know. I gointer get a good schooling some day so as I can help my folks get away from this terrible thing. I wonder sometimes what would I do if it happened to me—

SUE: It couldn't happen to you, Sonnie; everybody knows you wouldn't harm a flea.

LIZA: No, sir, it ain't your kind theyse after. Its them poor onnerry devels that does enough devilment to git things pinned on 'em—thems the kind they picks on.

TOM: I tell you whut. I—*(There is a quick rap at the back door and it is pushed open and at the same time an Officer enters. The four at the table look up in consternation.)*

FIRST OFFICER: Tom Griggs live here?

SUE *(starting up excitedly, stammering)*: Yes sir—

FIRST OFFICER *(to Tom)*: You Tom Griggs?

TOM: Yes sir.

FIRST OFFICER: Where were you last night at ten o'clock?

SUE: Right here. He was right here, why whut you want to know fer?

FIRST OFFICER *(to Sue)*: You keep quiet. *(to Tom)* Say you, answer up. Can't you talk? Where were you last night at ten o'clock?

TOM: Gramma told you. I was here, right here at home.

FIRST OFFICER: Who else knows you were here?

SUE: Say Mr. Officer, whut you trying to do? My grandson was here at ten o'clock, in bed. 'Fore God he was. I saw him and his little brother there saw him, didn't you Bossie?

BOSSIE *(frightened whisper)*: Yes mam.

FIRST OFFICER *(to Bossie)*: Shut up. Your word's nothing, now yours either. You'd lie for him. *(Looking at Sue. He makes a sign to Officer Number Two, then looks at a paper he is holding in his hand, and reads it slowly.)* Age about 20, five feet five or six, light brown. *(he looks at Tom as he reads each item)* Eughum, fits like a glove.

(Sue, Liza and Tom look from one to another in amazement and growing terror. Officer Number Two supports a white girl by the arm at the back door where she peeps in furtively.)

FIRST OFFICER *(to girl)*: Do you recognize him?

WHITE GIRL *(hesitatingly)*: He looks something like him.

SECOND OFFICER: Look good. He fits the description we got perfect. He's the only Nigger 'round here it could have been. Fits your description to a tee. Same size, color, and had to pass down by the corner of Broad and 1st Street to come here from his work. Niggers down the street told us you did. *(he urges the girl)* You say he looks like him?

WHITE GIRL *(still hesitatingly)*: Y—e—s! *(she finally finishes, then covering her face with her hands, turns and is led away)*

(First Officer taking a step toward Tom and slipping handcuffs quickly on his wrists before he is aware of what he is doing.)

SUE *(Screams and rushes up to the First Officer. Liza stands cowering behind her as Bossie looks from one to the other sniffling and crying as he wipes his nose from time to time with his fist.):* Whut you doing? Whut you doing? You can't 'rest my granson—You can't 'rest him!

FIRST OFFICER *(to Sue):* Stand back, old woman. I'm just going to take him along to the sheriff to question him some more.

SUE: But you can't do that! You can't! He don't know nothing about that girl. He want there—you can't take him!

TOM *(utterly bewildered):* Gramma, don't take on so. I'll go along with him to the Sheriff. I'll 'splain to him as how I couldn't of did it—I was here—sleep all the time. I never saw that white lady before in my life.

SUE: 'Course you ain't—*(to First Officer)* Mr. Officer, she ain't seen him befo'—All Niggers looks alike to her—that white girl ain't never laid eyes on my grandson befo'.

FIRST OFFICER *(to Sue as he pulls Tom along):* You just keep quiet Grannie. If your grandson's innocent, he'll be all right. *(to Tom)* And the quieter you come on along, the better it will be for you.

TOM *(looking back at his grandma with terror in his eyes):* I'll be all right Gramma, don't cry. *(keeps talking as he is pulled out of the door)* I'll be right back soon as—

LIZA *(standing with her hands clasped together, her head bowed over and swaying emotionally from side to side):* Sweet Jesus, do come down and hep us this mornin'. *(she turns her ear as if listening to some sound outside, gives one look at Sue who has fallen down into a chair moaning and groaning with her face on her hands on the table, while Bossie crouches whimpering at her feet, and then hurries out through the back behind the First Officer and Tom.)*

BOSSIE *(between sobs):* Whut they going to do with my brother, Grannie? What they going to do?

SUE *(brokenly):* God knows, honey. God only knows. Oh Jesus! Oh Jesus! Hep my poor little motherless chile.

LIZA *(rushing in at the back door, speaks breathlessly):* Sue, Sue, there's a passle uv white mens out there a followin' Tom and that police, I heered 'em say—"She done 'dentified him, cummon, we ain't a going to let no coat [court] house cheat us—let's git him" and they started out arguing wid the police whut had him.

SUE *(jumped to her feet when Liza began her tale and is now frantically gyrating from side to side):* My God—My God—*(she pants hoarsely as she looks despairingly at Liza)* Whut you reckin'—Whut kin I do? *(she repeats shrilly)* Whut kin I do? *(Bossie has jumped up and stands crying afresh and clinging to his grandmother's apron)*

LIZA: Ef I was you, I'd go and git some good white man to hep him right away—befo' it's too late.

SUE *(looking at Liza helplessly):* You don't think—

LIZA: Ef you'd a seed 'em—

SUE: Jesus hep me—lemme see—*(thinks)* Lemme see! *(looks up quick)* I know—Jedge Mannin!

LIZA: But kin you fin him—on Sunday?

SUE *(going toward the door as fast as she can):* Yes, I'll fin him—I'll fin' him! Ef he's on the topside of the yearth, I'll fin' him!

BOSSIE *(following her as she goes out, cries):* Gramma! Gramma! Take me wid you—Take me wid you! *(he runs out of the door behind his Grandmother and Liza stands with one hand up to her face)*

(End of First Scene)

SCENE 2

Outside of small church. An usher can be seen standing near the door as Sue comes up panting with Bossie running along behind her. The choir can be heard singing. She goes up the church steps to the door and speaks to the usher. The sound of the organ and voices float out.

"Jesus Savior, pilot me, over life's tempestuous sea—
Unknown waves before me roll, hiding rock
And treacherous shoal
Chart and compass come from Thee
Jesus Savior, pilot me."

(The music drowns out Sue's lowered voice as she talks to the Usher)

SUE: I got to see Judge Manning.

USHER: But you can't. He's in church.

SUE *(wildly gesturing):* I knows he is, but its life and death—I got to see him!

USHER *(trying to wave her away):* But—

SUE *(more wildly):* Tell him its Sue Jones—Tell him to step to the do' jes a minute—I got to see him now, this minute!

USHER *(still waving her away):* But I—

SUE *(trying to push past him):* Ef you won't tell him, I'll go in myself—I got to see him!

USHER *(With a gesture of resignation, disappears inside church. She wrings her hand and rocks from foot to foot. The singing continues.):*

"When at last I near the goal
And the fearsome breakers roll . . .

(Judge Manning appears at the church door looking vexed. Sue urges him by gestures to come away from the doorway. He moves away and halts a little further down in front of the church as the singing ceases and the preacher's voice is faintly heard lifted in prayer.)

SUE: Jedge Manning, 'skuse me please from coming here, but you got to hep me, got to. I ain't got nobody else to turn to—you got to be quick. They done took my grandson Tom and I hears they gonner take him from the police and—and God knows whut'll happen—Do fur God's sake, go take charge of him and save him. He ain't done no harm—'fore God he ain't!

JUDGE MANNING *(trying to calm Sue):* I expect you're all roused up over nothing—you go home and I'll see what I can do right after services.

SUE *(hysterical):* No! No! No! Jedge—that mout be too late—come now, right away—

JUDGE MANNING: But it's Sunday morning. Nobody's going to do anything to your grandson today.

SUE *(pleadingly):* But Jedge, you don't know these bad white folks lak I do—You'se good—they'd do anything, anything Jedge, Please sur cummon!

JUDGE MANNING: I think you are being foolish to worry so, but—*(he decides)* I'll get my hat and go. Wait here!

SUE: Oh, Jedge, you don't need no hat anyone pritty head. Oh, why can't you see—why can't you—

(The Judge smiles slightly at the old woman's flattery as he turns and walks rapidly back up to the steps into the church. She stands stooped and bowed

with the resignation of despair as she waits for his return. The Judge has been inside the church but a minute or so when Two White Men come slowly talking rather loudly)

FIRST WHITE MAN: Well we strung him up all right. But when he kept hollering, "Granny, Granny", it kinder made me sick in the belly.

(Sue follows them with her eye as they disappear from sight, then clutches at her heart and reels to the ground as the music comes from the church):

Going home, going home, yes I'm going home *(the melody from Dvorak's World Symphony)*

(The Judge comes from the church steps, hat in hand, and halts stunned by the tableau of the old woman dead on the ground with the little boy kneeling, crying beside her. The music continues to come from the church softly as the curtain slowly falls.)

(Finis)

Johnson's handwritten arrangement of "O Poor Sinner," written to accompany *A Sunday Morning in the South* (white church version). Source: Papers of the Federal Theatre Project, Music Division, Library of Congress.

Johnson's handwritten arrangement of "Going Home" from "New World" Symphony (Symphony No. 9) by composer Antonin Dvorák (1841–1904), written to accompany *Sunday Morning in the South* (white church version). Source: Papers of the Federal Theatre Project, Music Division, Library of Congress.

A Sunday Morning in the South

A ONE-ACT PLAY IN ONE SCENE

(c. 1925)

Black Church Version

Characters:

SUE JONES, *the grandmother, around seventy*
TOM GRIGGS, *her grandson, aged nineteen*
BOSSIE GRIGGS, *her grandson, aged seven*
LIZA TWIGGS, *a friend, around sixty*
MATILDA BROWN, *a friend, around fifty*
A WHITE GIRL
FIRST OFFICER
SECOND OFFICER

Place:

A town in the South.

Time:

1924

Scene

(Kitchen in Sue Jones' two-room house. A window on left, a door leading to back yard and another leading to front room. A stove against the back wall, a table near it, four chairs, an old-time safe with dishes and two bottles—one clear and one dark—a wooden water bucket with shiny brass bales, and a tin dipper hanging near it on a nail.)

As the curtain rises Sue Jones is seen putting the breakfast on the kitchen table. She wears a red bandanna handkerchief on her grey head, a big blue gingham apron tied around her waist and big wide old lady comfort shoes.

She uses a stick as she has a sore leg, and moves about with a stoop and a limp as she goes back and forth from the stove to the table.)

SUE *(calling):* Tom, Tom, you and Bossie better come on out here and git your breakfast before it gits cold; I got good hot rolls this mornin!

TOM *(from next room):* All right Grannie, we're coming.

SUE: You better ef you know whut's good for you. *(opens stove door, looks at rolls, then begins humming and singing)*

Eugh . . . eu . . . eugh . . .
Jes look at the morning star
Eugh. . . . eu . . . eugh . . .
We'll all git home bye and bye . . .

(As she finishes the song Tom and Bossie come hurrying into the kitchen placing their chairs at the table; there is one already at the table for Sue. Sue takes rolls out of stove with her apron and brings them to the table) It's as hard to git yawll out of the bed on Sunday morning as it is to pull hen's teeth.

TOM *(eating. The church bell next door is heard ringing):* Eugh—there's the church bell. I sho meant to git out to meeting this morning but my back still hurts me. Remember I told you last night how I sprained it lifting them heavy boxes for Mr. John?

SUE *(giving Bossie a roll and a piece of sausage):* You hadn't oughter done it; you 'oughter ast him to let somebody hep you—you aint no hoss!

TOM: I reckin I oughter had but I didn't know how heavy they was till I started and then he was gone.

SUE: You oughter had some of my snake oil linament on it last night, that's whut!

TOM: I wish I hader but I was so dead tired I got outer my clothes and went straight to bed. I muster been sleep by nine er clock I reckin.

SUE: Nine er clock! You is crazy! T'want no moren eight when I called you to go to the store and git me a yeast cake fur my light rolls and you was sleeping like a log of wood; I had to send Bossie fur it.

BOSSIE: Yes, and you snored so loud I thought you would a choked. *(holding out his plate and licking his lips with his tongue)* Grannie kin I have some more?

SUE: Whut? Where is all thot I jest give you?

BOSSIE *(rubbing his stomach with his other hand and smiling broadly):* It's gone down the red lane struttin'.

SUE: Well this is all you gointer git this mornin. *(helping him to more rolls and sausage)* When you git big and work like Tom you kin stuff all you wants to.

BOSSIE: I aint never gointer break my back like Tom working hard—I'm a gointer be a—a preacher that's whut and . . .

SUE *(catching sight of someone passing the window as she approached the back door):* I b'leve that's Liza Twiggs must be on her way to church and smelled these light rolls and coffee. *(a knock is heard at the back door)* Let her in, Bossie!

(Bossie jumps up from the table, hurries to the door and opens it)

LIZA *(enters sniffling):* Mawning yawll.

SUE: Morning Liza—on your way to church?

LIZA: Yes, the first bell just rung and I thought I'd drop in a minute. *(whiffs again)* Coffee sho smells good!

SUE: Tastes better'n it smells—Pull up a cheer and swaller a cupful with one of these light rolls.

LIZA *(drawing up a chair):* Don't keer if I do. *(She is helped to coffee and rolls while Bossie looks at her disapprovingly. To Sue)* How is your leg gitting on?

SUE. Well as I kin expect. I won't never walk on it good no mo. It eats and eats. Sho is lucky I'm right here next door to church. *(to Tom)* Open that winder, Tom, so I kin hear the singing. *(Tom opens window. To Liza)* Folks don't like to set next to me in church no mo. Tinks its ketching—a cancer or somethin'. *(then brightly)* Whut you know good?

(From the church next door is heard the hymn, drifting through the window:)

"Amazing grace how sweet the sound / That saves a wretch like me . . ." (long meter)

LIZA *(listening):* They done started . . . "Amazing grace." *(music continues as a background for their talk. Still eating)*

"I once was lost but now I'm found
Was blind but now I see.

Amazing grace, how sweet the truth
In a believer's ear,
It heals his sorrows, heals his wounds,
And drives away each tear."

LIZA *(still eating)*: That music sho is sweet but I got to finish eatin' first, then I'll go . . .

SUE: I ast you whut you know good.

LIZA: Well, I don't know nothin tall good, but I did hear as how the police is all over now trying to run down some po Nigger they say that's 'tacked a white woman last night right up here near the Pine Street market. They says as how the white folks is shonuff mad too, and if they ketch him they gointer make short work of him.

SUE *(still drinking coffee)*: Eugh, eugh, eugh, you don't say. I don't hold wid no rascality and I b'leves in meting out punishment to the guilty but they fust ought to fine out who done it tho and then let the law hanel 'em. That's what I says.

LIZA: Me too, I thinks the law oughter hanel 'em too, but you know a sight of times they gits the wrong man and goes and strings him up and don't fin out who done it till it's too late!

SUE: That's so. And sometimes the white uns been knowed to blackin they faces and make you b'leve some po Nigger done it.

TOM: They lynch you bout anything too, not jest women. They say Zeb Brooks was strung up because he and his boss had er argiment.

LIZA: Sho did. I says the law's the law and it ought er be er ark uv safty to pertect the weak and not some little old flimsy shack that a puff of wind can blow down.

TOM: I been thinking a whole lot about these things and I mean to go to night school and git a little book learning so as I can do something to help—help change the laws . . . make em strong . . . I sometimes get right upset and wonder whut would I do if they ever tried to put something on me . . .

LIZA: Pshaw. Everybody knows you . . . nobody would bother you . . .

SUE: No sonnie, you won't never hafter worry bout sich like that but you kin hep to save them po devels that they do git after.

(Singing comes from the church next door.)

Shine on me, shine on me,
Let the light from the lighthouse shine on me,
Shine on me, shine on me,
Let the light from the lighthouse shine on me.
(common meter)

TOM: It takes a sight of learning to understand the law and I'm gointer . . .

(a quick rap is heard at the door and it is almost immediately pushed open and an Officer enters as the four at the table look up at him in open-mouthed amazement)

FIRST OFFICER: Tom Griggs live here?

SUE *(starting up excitedly)*: Yes sir. *(stammering)*

FIRST OFFICER *(looking at Tom)*: You Tom Griggs?

TOM *(Puzzled)*: Yes sir.

FIRST OFFICER *(roughly)*: Where were you last night at ten o'clock?

SUE *(answering quickly for Tom)*: Right here sir, he was right here at home. Whut you want to know fer?

FIRST OFFICER *(to Sue)*: You keep quiet, old woman. *(to Tom)* Say, you answer up. Can't You talk? Where were you last night at ten o'clock?

TOM *(uneasily)*: Gramma told you. I was right here at home—in bed at eight o'clock.

FIRST OFFICER. That sounds fishy to me—in bed at eight o'clock! And who else knows you were here?

SUE: Say Mr. Officer, whut you tryin' to do to my granson. Shore as God Almighty is up in them heabens he was right here in bed. I seed him and his little brother Bossie there saw him, didn't you Bossie?

BOSSIE *(in a frightened whisper)*: Yessum, I seed him and I heered him!

FIRST OFFICER *(to Bossie)*: Shut up—Your word's nothing. *(looking at Sue)* Nor yours either. Both of you'd lie for him. *(steps to back door and makes a sign to someone outside, then comes back into the room taking a piece of paper from his vest pocket and reads slowly, looking at Tom critically as he checks each item)* Age around twenty, five feet five or six, brown skin . . . *(he folds up the paper and puts it back into his vest)* Yep! Fits like a glove. *(Sue, Liza and Tom look from one to the other with growing amazement and terror as Second Officer pushes open the door and stands there supporting a young White Girl on his arm.)*

SECOND OFFICER *(to Girl):* Is this the man?

WHITE GIRL *(hesitatingly):* I—I'm not sure . . . but . . . but he looks something like him . . . *(holding back)*

FIRST OFFICER *(encouragingly):* Take a good look, Miss. He fits our description perfect. Color, size, age, everything. Pine Street Market ain't no where from here, and he surely did pass that way last night. He was there all right, all right! We got it figgered all out. *(to Girl, who looks down at her feet)* You say he looks like him?

WHITE GIRL *(looking at him again quickly):* Y-e-s. *(slowly and undecidedly)* I think so. I . . . I . . . *(then she covers her face with her arm and turns quickly and moves away from the door, supported by Second Officer. First officer takes a step toward Tom and slips handcuffs on him before any one is aware what is happening.)*

SUE *(holding on to her chair and shaking her cane at the officer, while Bossie comes up close to her and snivels in her apron):* Whut you doing? Whut you doing? You can't 'rest my granson—he ain't done nothing—you can't 'rest him!

FIRST OFFICER: Be quiet, old woman. I'm just going to take him along to the sheriff to question him and if he's telling the truth he'll be right back home here in no time.

SUE: But you can't 'rest him; he don't know no mo bout that po little white chile than I do—You can't take him!

TOM *(utterly bewildered):* Gramma, don't take on so. I'll go long with him to the sheriff. I'll splain to him how I couldn't a done it when I was here sleep all the time—I never laid eyes on that white lady before in all my life.

SUE *(to Tom):* Course you ain't. *(to officer)* Mr. Officer, that white chile ain't never seed my granson before—all Niggers looks alike to her; she so upset she don't know whut she's saying.

FIRST OFFICER *(to Sue as he pulls Tom along):* You just keep cool Grannie, he'll be right back—if he's innocent. *(to Tom)* And the quieter you comes along the better it will be for you.

TOM *(looking back at his grandma from the doorway with terror in his eyes):* I'll be right back granny—don't cry—don't cry—Jest as soon as I see—*(the officer pulls him out of the doorway)*

LIZA *(standing with her hands clasped together, her head bowed and swaying from side to side with emotion. She prays):* Sweet Jesus, do come down and hep us this mornin. You knows our hearts and you knows this po boy ain't done nothing wrong. You said you would hep the fatherless and the motherless; do Jesus bring this po orphan back to his ole cripple grannie safe and sound, do Jesus!

BOSSIE *(crying and pulling at his grandma's apron):* Grannie, grannie, whut they gointer do to my brother? Whut they gointer do to him?

SUE *(brokenly):* The good Jesus only knows, but I'm a talking to the Lord now asting Him to—*(A rap is heard at the door; it is almost immediately pushed open and Matilda Brown enters hurriedly and excitedly.)*

MATILDA *(breathlessly):* Miss Liza, as I was coming long I seed Tom wid the police and there was some white mens wid guns a-trying to take him away from the police—said he'd done been dentified and they want gointer be cheated outen they Nigger this time. I, I flew on down here to tell you, you better do somethin'.

SUE *(shaking nervously from side to side as she leans on her cane for support):* Oh my God, whut kin I do?

LIZA *(alertly):* You got to git word to some of your good white folks, that's whut and git 'em to save him.

SUE: Yes . . . That's whut . . . Lemme see . . . *(She stands tense thinking a moment.)* I got it . . . Miss Vilet . . . I got to git to Miss Vilet . . . I nused her when she was a baby and she'll do it . . . Her pa's the Jedge.

LIZA: That's right! I'll go. You can't go quick.

MATILDA: No. Lemme go; I kin move in a hurry, lemme go!

SUE: All right Tildy. Tell Miss Vilet her ole nuse Sue is callin on her and don't fail me; tell her they done took Tom and he is perfect innercent, and they gointer take him away from the police, and ax her to ax her pa the Jedge to go git Tom and save him fur God's sake. Now hurry, Tildy, fly!

BOSSIE *(to Sue):* Lemme go long; I knows how to git there quick cutting through the ole field.

LIZA: Yes, they knows Bossie and he kin hep tell.

SUE: Yes Bossie, gone, yawll hurry, hurry! *(Matilda and Bossie hurry out of the back door and Sue sinks down into a chair exhausted while Liza comes over to her and pats her on the back.)*

LIZA: Now, now ev'rything's gointer be all right . . . Miss Vilet 'll fix it . . . she ain't gointer let her ole mammy call on her for nothing . . . she'll make her pa save him.

SUE: Yes, she's a good chile. . . . I knows she'll save him.

(Sue moves her lips in prayer. From the church next door comes the sound of singing; the two women listen to the words with emotion)

Alas, and did my savior bleed
And did my sovereign die
Would he devote his sacred head
For such a worm as I.
Must Jesus bear the cross alone
And all the world go free,
No, there's a cross for every one
And there's a cross for me.
(long meter)

(Sue rocks back and forth in chair, head buried in her apron. Liza walks up and down the floor, throws her hands up imploringly now and then)

LIZA: Oh Lord, hep us to bear our cross! Hep us!

SUE *(drooping):* Liza I'm feeling sorter fainty lack; git me my bottle of camphor out of the safe yonder.

LIZA *(going to safe):* Yes chile, I'll git it. You done gone through a whole lot this mornin, God knows. *(takes up a bottle and holds it up for Sue to see)* This it?

SUE *(shaking her head):* Eugh eugh, that's my sweet oil. It's the yuther one in the black bottle . . . see it?

LIZA *(taking out bottle and smelling it):* Yes here it is. Strong too. It'll do you good. I has them sinkin spells too sometimes *(comes over to Sue with stopper out of bottle and holds it to her nose)* There, draw a deep bref of it; feel better?

SUE: I'll feel better toreckly. My old heart is gittin weak.

LIZA: Set back comfortable in your cheer and listen to the singin; they all sho talkin to the Lord fur you in that church this mornin. Listen! *(The church is singing):*

I must tell Jesus, I cannot bear my burdens alone
In my distress he surely will help me
I cannot bear my burdens alone.
I must tell Jesus, I cannot bear my burdens alone
Jesus my Lord he surely will help me
Jesus will help me, Jesus alone
(common meter sung as background to talking)

LIZA: That's all, that's all we kin do jes tell Jesus! Jesus! Jesus please bow down your ear! *(walks up and down mumbling a soft prayer as the singing continues mournfully)*

SUE: I reckin Tildy's bout on her way back now. I knows Miss Vilet done got her pa by now, don't you reckin, Liza.

LIZA *(sympathetically):* Course; I spects Tom'll be coming back too any minit now. Everybody knows he ain't done no harm.

SUE *(listening to running feet at the door and sitting up straight in chair):* Who dat coming? *(Matilda pushes open the door and comes in all excited and panting while Bossie follows her crying)* Whut's the matter? Didn't you find Miss Vilet?

MATILDA *(reluctantly):* It want no use.

SUE: No use?

LIZA: Whut you mean?

MATILDA: I mean—I mean—

LIZA: For God's sake Tildy, whut's happened?

MATILDA: They—they done lynched him.

SUE *(screams):* Jesus! *(gasps and falls limp in her chair. Singing from church begins. Bossie runs to her, crying afresh. Liza puts the camphor bottle to her nose again as Matilda feels her heart; they work over her a few minutes, shake their heads and with drooping shoulders, wring their hands. While this action takes place the words of this song pour forth from church)*

Lord have mercy.
Lord have mercy,
Lord have mercy over me.
(long meter—sung first time with words and repeated in a low hum as curtain slowly falls)

(Curtain)

Johnson's handwritten arrangement of "Eugh-eu-eugh" written to accompany *A Sunday Morning in the South* (black church version). Source: Papers of the Federal Theatre Project, Music Division, Library of Congress.

Johnson's handwritten arrangement of John Newton's hymn "Amazing Grace How Sweet the Sound" (1779), written to accompany *A Sunday Morning in the South* (black church version). Source: Papers of the Federal Theatre Project, Music Division, Library of Congress.

Johnson's handwritten arrangement of Isaac Watt's hymn "Alas and Did My Savior Bleed" (1707), written to accompany *A Sunday Morning in the South* (black church version). Source: Papers of the Federal Theatre Project, Music Division, Library of Congress.

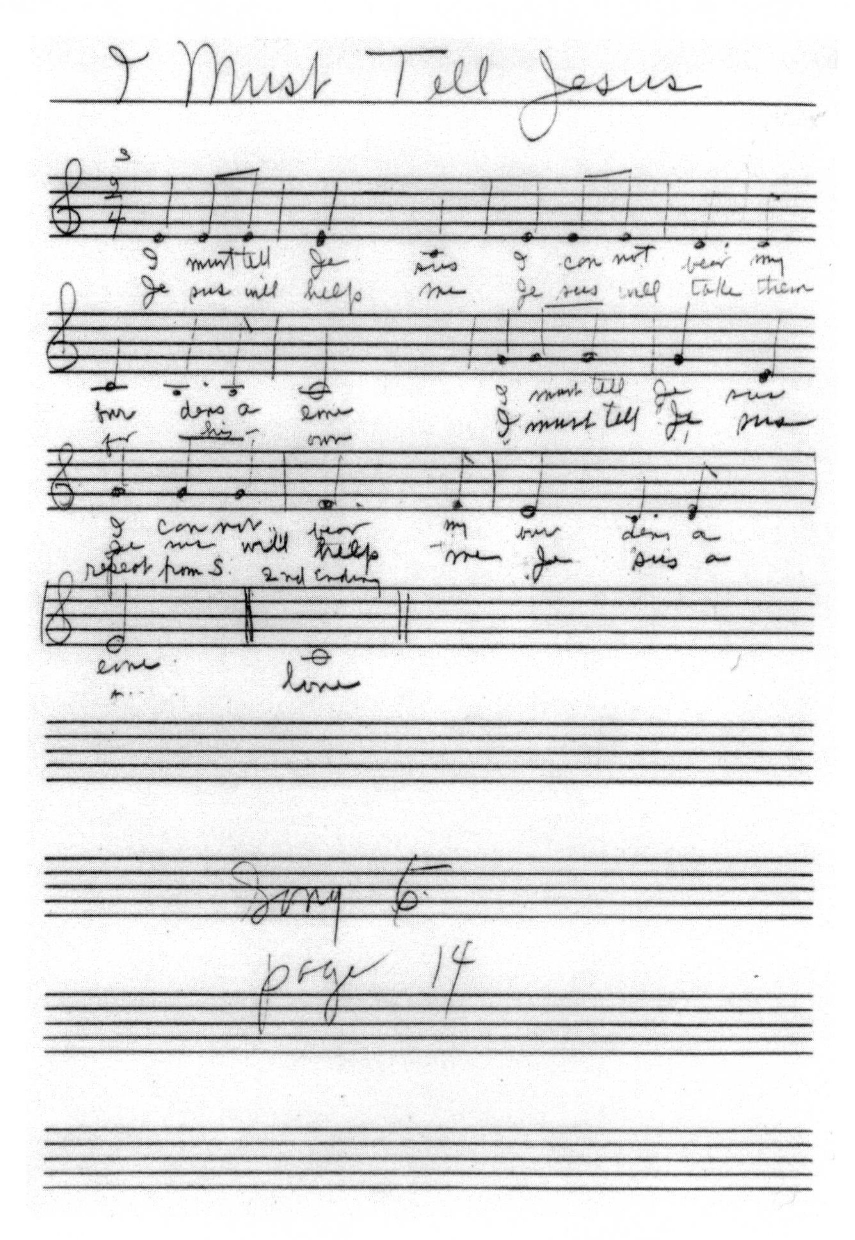

Johnson's hand written arrangement of Elisha A. Hoffman's hymn "I Must Tell Jesus" (1893), written to accompany *A Sunday Morning in the South* (black church version). Source: Papers of the Federal Theatre Project, Music Division, Library of Congress.

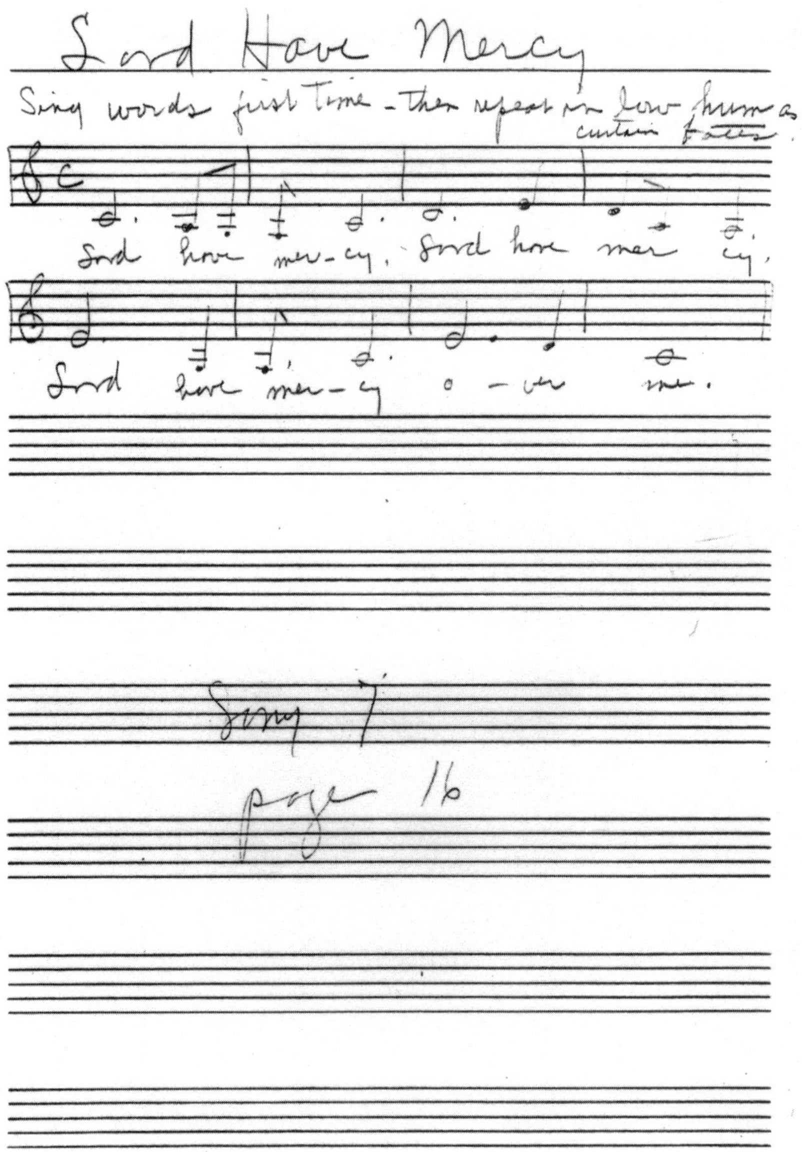

Lord Have Mercy

Sing words first time - then repeat in low hum as curtain falls.

Lord have mer-cy, Lord have mer cy.

Lord have mer-cy o - on me.

Song 7

page 16

Johnson's handwritten arrangement of "Lord Have Mercy," written to accompany *A Sunday Morning in the South* (black church version). Source: Papers of the Federal Theatre Project, Music Division, Library of Congress.

Safe

A PLAY ON LYNCHING

(c. 1929)

Characters:

LIZA PETTIGREW, *The Wife*
JOHN PETTIGREW, *The Husband*
MANDY GRIMES, *Liza's Mother*
DR. JENKINS, *Physician*
HANNAH WIGGINS, *Neighbor*

Place:

Southern Town

Time:

1893

Scene

Front room of Pettigrew home

Front room of a three-room cottage. Back door leading to kitchen. Door on left leading to Liza's room. A front door and a cot along the wall. A table and oil lamp, three chairs, baby garments, a basket of socks, newspapers, etc.

Scene Opens: Liza is discovered sewing on some small white garments. John is reading the evening paper by an oil lamp on the table.

LIZA *(lifting her voice)*: Ma, come on outer that kitchen—jest stack up them supper dishes and come on and set down and rest—you hear?

MANDY *(from kitchen)*: All right, Liza, I'm coming out in a minute now.

LIZA *(to John)*: Ma's been on her feet all day long. She don't know how to rest herself.

JOHN *(absently)*: Eughhu. She sho don't. *(continues reading)*

LIZA *(calling again):* Come on, Ma.

MANDY *(appearing in the kitchen doorway):* I hate to leave them dishes all dirty overnight, but if I must, I must. *(She looks about the room for something to do.)* I reckon I will jist mend John's socks while I'm setting here. *(She brings a basket with socks, needle and thread in it over near the table light with a chair.)*

LIZA: No, Ma, you lay down on your cot and stretch out a while and rest—first thing you know I'll be down and then you got to be up and around waiting on me—so rest now while you kin.

MANDY *(obediently putting up the sewing basket):* All right, honey. I'll stretch out a minute or so if you wants me to. *(She goes over to her cot against the wall and falls down heavily with a sigh upon it.)* My, this feels good to my old bones.

LIZA: Of course, it do—you're plum wore out; you done a sight of washing today.

MANDY *(yawning):* Yes, I been going pretty steady today. What you making on now?

LIZA: Just hemming some little flannel belly bands. *(She holds up one for her mother to see.)* I got all the night gowns ready now. My time's pretty nigh near.

MANDY: Yes, it's jest about time—nine months I count it.

[indecipherable line]

JOHN *(lowering the paper):* Well, well, well. I see they done caught Sam Hosea and put him in jail.

MANDY: When they ketch him?

JOHN: Paper says this morning. I reckon his ma is plum crazy if she's heered they got him.

LIZA: I knows her. She's a little skinny brown-skinned woman. Belong to our church. She use to bring Sam along pretty regular all the time. He was a nice motherly sort of boy, not mor'n seventeen I'd say. Lemme see. 'Twant no woman mixed up in it, was it?

JOHN: No, seems like he and his boss had some sort of dispute about wages—the boss slapped him and Sam up and hit him back they says.

MANDY: Eugh eugh—that's mighty unhealthy sounding business for this part of the country. Hittin' a white man, he better hadder made tracks far away from here I'm er thinking.

(Just then there's a soft knock at the door.)

JOHN: I wonder who that is.

LIZA: Go see!

(John goes to the door. Hannah Wiggins enters.)

JOHN: Howdy, Miss Wiggins, come in and take a cheer.

HANNAH *(still standing and excited like):* Howdy! I jist thought I'd drop over here, being as Liza was so near her time and, and—

MANDY *(Sitting up on the cot):* Go on Hannah—what's the matter, You look all flusterated—what's up?

LIZA: Set down, Miss Hannah, there's a cheer.

HANNAH *(sitting down on the edge of the chair uneasily):* I, I come over here to see how Liza was—most special—then I wanted to see if yaw'll knowed about the trouble—

MANDY: Liza's fine. But what trouble is you're talking 'bout? We ain't heered nothing 'tall—

JOHN: I saw in the papers they done caught Sam Hosea—we all thought he'd got out of town—I jest read bout it.

HANNAH: Yes, but that ain't all. *(shakes her head.)*

LIZA: What else is it? Tell us!

HANNAH *(looks around the room, again floundering):* You see I heered they done formed a mob downtown and it mout be there'll be hell to pay tonight!

JOHN *(excitedly):* Who told you that?

HANNAH: Jim Brown told me bout it. He dropped in our house jest now and said as how things didn't look good at all downtown—So I thought I better run over and tell yaw'll.

JOHN: Ain't they gointer call out the soldiers, did he say?

HANNAH: No, he jest said the crowds was gathering and it didn't look good in town.

LIZA *(in awed tones):* You don't reckon they'll take Sam out of the jail, do you, John?

JOHN: I don't know. *(He gets up and goes to the door.)* I think I'll step down the streets and see what they knows down by Briggze's store.

MANDY (to JOHN): You think you oughter go out?

LIZA: Be keerful and don't stay long.

JOHN: I'll be right back. Don't yaw'll worry. *(goes out.)*

LIZA: I been settin here thinking bout that poor boy Sam—him working hard to take kere of his widder mother, doing the best he kin, trying to be a man and stan up for hissef, and what do he git—a slap in the face.

HANNAH: Chile, that ain't nothing—if he gits off with a slap—These white folks is mad—mad—he done hit a white man back—

MANDY: They ain't gointer stan' for it—I done seen it happen before.

LIZA: What's little Nigger boys born for anyhow? I sho hopes mine will be a girl.—I don't want no boy baby to be hounded down and kicked round—No, I don't want to ever have no boy chile!

MANDY: Hush, honey—that's a sin—God sends what he wants us to have—we can't pick and choose.

HANNAH: No, we sho can't. We got to swaller the bitter with the sweet.

(just then a shot is heard.)

MANDY *(Jumping up):* What's that?

HANNAH: Sho sounded like a shot to me. I b'lieve them white folks is up to something this night.

LIZA: Listen—ain't that noise coming this a way?

HANNAH: It sho sounds like it. *(Goes over to the door, cracks it, peeps out and listens)* They's coming—a big crowd headed this way.

MANDY: *(excitedly):* We better put out the light and pull that curtain way down.

HANNAH: Yes, that's right, you can't tell what them devils might git it in they heads to do.

(There is an increasing sound.)

LIZA *(in awed tones):* They wouldn't come in here? Would they?

MANDY *(consolingly):* No, they wouldn't, but then we better keep it dark.

(Another shot rings out. The women jump and look at each other in fear.)

LIZA *(plaintively):* I wonder where John is—

MANDY: He oughter been back here before now. *(She goes to the window and peeps cautiously out from behind shade. Hannah follows and then Liza.)*

HANNAH: You stay back, Liza. You oughtenter see sich things—not in your delicate state.

LIZA: But what they doing? Where they goin to?

MANDY: Yes—go back, Liza, and set down—let us watch.

(a confusion of many footsteps, tramping horses as the roar becomes louder)

LIZA *(beginning to walk up and down the room restlessly):* Ma, Ma, do you think they got him—do you think they'll hang him—

MANDY *(patting Liza on the shoulder):* I don't know. You try and keep quiet. You hadn't ought to hear all this screeching hell—God help you! *(goes back to window)*

HANNAH: She sho oughten—It's a sin and a shame! Coming right by here, too—

(Then a voice rises above the din outside—"Don't hang me, don't hang me! I don't want to die! Mother! Mother!")

LIZA *(Jumping up):* That's him—That's Sam—They got him. *(She runs to the door and looks out. Hannah and Mandy follow her quickly and drag her back, shutting the door quickly.)*

MANDY: They'll shoot you—You can't do that—they're mad—mad!

LIZA *(crumpling up on the chair shivering, her teeth chattering):* Oh, my God, did you hear that poor boy crying for his mother—He's jest a boy—jest a boy—jest a little boy!

(The roar outside continues.)

HANNAH *(to Mandy):* This is mighty bad for her, mighty bad—

MANDY *(looking at Liza critically):* Yes, it sho is. *(She thinks a minute.)* I hates to ast you, but John ain't got back and we ought to git a doctor—Could you steal out the back and git him?

HANNAH: Yes, I'll go—I kin steal down the back ways.

MANDY: Better hurry, Hannah. I don't like the looks of her.

(Hannah goes out through back.)

LIZA *(continues to shiver and shake):* Oh, where is John—Where is John?—What you reckon has happened? Oh, that poor boy—poor little Nigger boy!

MANDY: Try not to worry so, honey. We's in the Lord's hands. *(shaking her head)* My poor, poor chile. I'll heat a kettle of water, then I'm gointer fix your bed so as you kin lay down when you feel like it.

(Hoarse laughter is heard outside as the noise grows less and less. Mandy goes into small bedroom adjoining kitchen for a moment, then comes back, looks at Liza, shakes her head. Then Liza gets up and begins walking up and down the floor all doubled over as if in pain. She goes to the window occasionally and looks out from behind the shade. The noise of countless passing feet are heard and an occasional curse or laugh. She trembles slightly every time she looks and begins pacing up and down again.)

MANDY *(coming over from the bedroom):* Come on and lay down now, Chile—the doctor'll be here to reckly. I'll git all your little things together for you. *(Goes over and begins to gather up the little white garments Liza had been sewing on.)*

LIZA *(stands stooped over in the opening of her bedroom door):* Did you hear him cry for his mother? Did you?

MANDY: Yes, Honey chile, I heard him—but you musn't think about that now—. Fergit it, remember your own little baby—you got him to think about—You got to born him safe!

LIZA *(looks at Mandy wild-eyed):* What you say?

MANDY: Born him safe! Born him safe! That's what you got to do.

LIZA *(turning her head from side to side as she stands half stooped in the doorway. She repeats.):* Born him safe!—safe—*(She hysterically disappears into the next room.)*

MANDY *(sighs and continues picking up the little garments, smoothing them out nervously. Just then the door opens and John enters.):* Oh, where you been, John? Why didn't you come back before now?

JOHN: I tried to but I got headed off—they come right by here too—It was terrible—terrible—where's she?

MANDY: In the room. I done sent fur the doctor; he'll be here any minute.

JOHN *(nervously going toward Liza's bedroom):* I'll go in and see her. Poor little Liza.

(enters room)

MANDY *(goes to the window and peers out and listens as scattering footsteps sound outside on the sidewalk. Then she busies herself about the room, turns down her bed, lights the lamp and turns it down low. Just then there is a knock at the kitchen door. Calling):* John! John! *(John comes to the door.)* See if that ain't Hannah at the back door with the doctor.

JOHN *(hurrying):* All right. *(He goes through the kitchen and returns with Dr. Jenkins.)*

MANDY: I'm sho glad you come, Doctor; she's right in there, please hurry.

DR. JENKINS *(to Mandy):* Get me some hot water.

MANDY: I got it ready for you. John, git the kettle! *(John goes in kitchen.)* She's terrible upset, Doctor, terrible.—

DR. JENKINS: I know—Hannah told me all about it; she stopped at her house a minute or two, but said tell you she'd be here to help.

(John returning with kettle): Here 'tis.

MANDY: Set it in the room.

(The doctor goes into the room with his bag and John comes out.)

MANDY: How is she?

JOHN: Mighty upset.

MANDY: She ain't never seen no lynching[,] not before, and it was terrible—her being so nigh her time too.

JOHN: Do you think she'll git through all right?

MANDY: I pray God she do. But she's sho shook to pieces.

JOHN: I oughter been here myself, but I didn't know I was gointer be cut off—

MANDY: Course you didn't. We's all in the hands of the Lawd.

JOHN *(drops his hands helplessly on his knees):* What a terrible night—

MANDY: I wish Hannah would come on back. I'm that nervish.

JOHN: She was right brave to go for the doctor.

MANDY: Want she.

(Just then a baby's cry is heard from the next room and both of them jump up and look toward the closed door. They take a step forward and wait.)

JOHN: You reckon she's all right?

MANDY: I hope so, but—

JOHN: But what?

MANDY: I don't know zactly; I never did see her look like she looked to-night.

JOHN *(groaning):* I wish the Lord this night was over.

MANDY: God knows I do too—my poor, poor chile.

(They wait for what [seems] like an eternity listening to the muffled sounds in the next room. Then the doctor appears at the door, closing it behind him. His face looks distressed.)

MANDY *(Nervously):* How is she? Can I go in?

JOHN *(agitatedly):* How is she, Doc?

DR. JENKINS *(holding up one hand):* Wait a minute, calm yourselves. I've got something to tell you, and I don't hardly know how—

MANDY *(bursting into tears):* She ain't dead, is she? Doc, my Chile ain't dead?

JOHN *(biting his lips):* Tell us, Doc, tell us! What is it?

DR. JENKINS: She's all right and the baby was born all right—big and fine—you heard him cry?—

JOHN: Yes—

MANDY: Yes, we heard—

DR. JENKINS: And she asked me right away, "Is it a girl?"

JOHN, MANDY *(stretching their necks out further to listen):* Yes, yes, Doc! Go on!

DR. JENKINS: And I said, "No child, it's a fine boy," and then I turned my back a minute to wash my hands in the basin. When I looked around again she had her hands about the baby's throat choking it. I tried to stop her, but its little tongue was already hanging from its mouth—It was dead! Then she began, she kept muttering over and over again: "Now he's safe—safe from the lynchers! Safe!"

(John falls down on a chair sobbing, his face in his hands, as Mandy, stooped with misery, drags her feet heavily toward the closed door. She opens it softly and goes in. The doctor stands, a picture of helplessness as he looks at them in their grief.)

(The Curtain Falls)

Blue-Eyed Black Boy
(c. 1930)

Characters:
PAULINE WATERS, *The Mother*
REBECCA WATERS, *Daughter*
DR. THOMAS GREY, *Fiancé of Rebecca*
HESTER GRANT, *Pauline's Best Friend*

Scene
A kitchen in Mrs. Waters's cottage. A stove with food keeping warm and an iron heating, ironing board in the corner, a table with a lighted oil lamp and two chairs. Door, slightly ajar, leads to the front room and window opening on to a side street.

Scene Opens: Pauline is discovered seated in a large rocker with her left foot bandaged and resting on a low stool.

PAULINE *(calling to the other room):* Rebecca, come on. Your iron is hot now, I know.

REBECCA *(answers from the front room):* I'm coming now, Ma—*(She enters holding a lacy garment in her hands.)* I had to tack these bows on. How you like it now?

PAULINE *(scanning the long night dress set off with little pink bows that Rebecca is holding up for her inspection):* Eugh-hu, it shure is pretty. I don't believe anybody ever had as fine a wedding gown in this whole town.

REBECCA: Humph! *(She shrugs her shoulders proudly as she tests the iron to see if it is hot and then takes it over to the board and begins to press the gown.)* That's to be expected, ain't it? Everybody in the Baptist Church looks up to us, don't they?

PAULINE: Sure they do. I ain't carried myself straight all these years for nothing. Your father was sure one proud man—he put us on a pinnacle!

REBECCA: Well, I sure have tried to walk straight all my life.

PAULINE: Yes, and I'm shore proud—Now here you is getting ready to marry a young doctor—My my! *(then she suddenly says)* Ouch! I wish he would come on over here to change the dressing on my foot—Hope I ain't going to have lock jaw.

REBECCA: You won't. Tom knows his business. *(She tosses her head proudly. She looks over to the stove and goes on.)* Wish Jack would come on home and eat his supper so's I could clean up the dishes.

PAULINE: What time is it?

REBECCA *(goes to the middle door and peeps in the next room):* The clock in position to exactly five minutes after seven. He oughter been here a whole hour ago.

PAULINE: I wonder what's keeping him?

REBECCA: Well, there's one thing sure and certain: he's not running after girls.

PAULINE: No—he shore don't—just give him a book and he's happy—says he's going to quit running that crane—and learn engineering soons you get married. He's been mighty tied down since your father died—taking care of us.

REBECCA: Everybody says he's the smartest and the finest-looking black boy in the whole town.

PAULINE: Yes, he is good looking even if he is mine—some of 'em lay it to his eyes—

(She looks far off thoughtfully.)

REBECCA: Yes, they do set him off—It's funny that he's the only one in our family's got blue eyes though. Pa's was black, and yours and mine are black too—It certainly is strange; wish I'd had 'em.

PAULINE: Oh, you be satisfied—you're pretty enough, Sister, Hush. There's the doctor's buggy stopping now—go let him in—*(Rebecca goes to the door while Pauline bends over, grunting and touching her foot. Dr. Grey enters, bag in hand, with Rebecca.)*

DR. GREY: Well, how's my patient feeling—better, I know.

PAULINE: Now don't you be kidding me, Doctor—my foot's been paining me terrible—I'm scared to death I'm going to have the lock jaw. For God's sake done let me—.

(Rebecca places chair for him near her mother.)

DR. GREY *(unwinds the bandages, looks at foot and opens his bag):* Fine, it's doing fine—you'll have to keep off it for a week more, and then you'll be all right.

PAULINE: Can't walk on it for a week?

DR. GREY: Not unless you want to die of blood poisoning—lock jaw, I mean! *(He touches the foot with iodine and puts on new bandage.)* That was an old, rusty nail you stuck in your foot—a pretty close call—*(He looks lovingly at Rebecca.)*

PAULINE: Well, I'm tickled to have such a good doctor for my new son.

DR. GREY: You bet. *(then thoughtfully)* I saw some mighty rough looking hoodlums gathering on the streets as I came in—looks like there might be some trouble somewhere.

REBECCA: Oh, they're always having a squabble on these streets. You get used to 'em—and you will too after a while—

PAULINE: Yes, there's always something stirring everyday—I just go on and on and don't pay 'em no mind myself.

DR. GREY *(patting the foot tenderly):* Now that's all right. You keep off of it—hear me. Or I won't vouch for the outcome.

PAULINE: It's so sore—I can't stand up even if I was a kind to—[*(A knock is heard.)*] See who's at the back door, Rebecca—peeps first.

REBECCA *(goes to the door and cracks it):* Who there?

HESTER: Me, me, it's Hester—Hester Grant. Lemme in. *(Rebecca opens the door and Hester comes panting in. She looks around as if hating to speak before the others then blurts out.)* Pauline, it's Jack—your son Jack has been 'rested—'rested and put in jail.

PAULINE: 'Rested?

REBECCA: Good Lord.

DR. GREY: What for? *(moving about restlessly)*

HESTER: They say he done brushed against a white woman on the street. They had er argument and she hollered out he's attacking her—a crew of white men come up and started beating on him and the policeman, when he was coming home from work, dragged him to the jailhouse.

PAULINE: My God, my God—It ain't so—he ain't brushed up against no lady, my boy ain't. He's, he's a gentleman, that's what he is.—

HESTER *(She moves about restlessly. She has something else to say):* And, and Pauline—that ain't the worst—that ain't the worst—they, they say there's gointer to be a lynching tonight. They gointer break open the jail and string him up! *(She finishes desperately.)*

PAULINE: String him up—My son—they can't do that—not to my son—not him!

DR. GREY *(excitedly):* I'll drive over and see the Judge—he'll do something to stop it.

HESTER *(sarcastically):* Him—not him—he's a lyncher his own self—Don't put no trust in him—Ain't he done let 'em lynch six niggers in the last year jes' gone—him! *(She scoffs again.)*

REBECCA *(wringing her hands):* We got to do something. *(goes up to Dr. Grey)* Do you know anybody else—anybody at all, who could save him—

PAULINE: Wait, wait—I know what I'll do—I don't care what it costs—*(to Rebecca)* Fly in yonder—*(points to the next room)* and get me that little tin box out of the left hand side of the tray in my trunk—hurry—fly—*(Rebecca hurries out while Dr. Grey and Hester look on in bewilderment.)* Lynch my son—my son—*(She yells to Rebecca in the next room.)* Got it—You got it?

REBECCA *(from next room):* Yes, Ma, I got it—*(She hurries in with a small tin box in her hand and hands it to her mother.)*

PAULINE *(Feverishly tossing out the odd bits of jewelry in the box, finally coming up with a small ring—She turns to Dr. Grey):* Here, Tom, take this. Run, jump on your horse and buggy and fly over to Governor Tinkham's house and don't you let nobody, nobody—stop you. Just give him this ring and say, "Pauline sent this. She says they goin to lynch her son born twenty-one years ago." Mind you, say twenty-one years ago—Then say—listen close—"Look in his eyes and you'll save him."

DR. GREY *(listens in amazement but grasps the small ring in his hand and hastens toward the door saying):* Don't worry. I'll put it in his hands and tell him what you said—just as quick as my horse can make it. *(When he leaves the room, Rebecca and Hester look at Pauline* with open-mouthed astonishment.)

HESTER *(starting as if from a dream):* Well, well, well, I don't git what you mean, but I reckon you knows what you is doing. *(She and Rebecca watch Dr. Grey from the front window as he drives away.)*

PAULINE: I shorely do!

REBECCA *(comes over and throws her arms around her mother's neck):* Mother, what does it all mean? Can you really save him?

PAULINE *(confidently):* Wait and see—I'll tell you more about it after a while. Don't ask me now.

HESTER *(going over to the window):* I hope he'll git over to the Governor's in time. *(looking out)* Emp! There goes a bunch of men with guns now and here comes another all slouched over and pushing on the same way.

REBECCA *(joining her at the window, with bated breath):* And look, look! Here come wagons full. *(The rumble of wagon wheels is heard.)* See 'em, Hester, all piled in with their guns, too—

(Pauline's lips move in prayer; her head is turned deliberately away from the window. She sighs deeply now and then.)

HESTER: Do Lord! Do Lord! Help us this night.

REBECCA *(with trembling voice):* Hussies. Look at them men on horses! *(Horses' hooves are heard in the street outside. Rebecca cries lightly.)*

HESTER: Jesus, Jesus! Please come down and help us this night—

REBECCA *(running over to her mother and flinging her arms about her neck):* Oh, mother, mother! What will we do? Do you hear 'em? Do you hear all them men on horses and wagons going up to the jail? Poor brother—poor boy.

PAULINE: Trust in God, daughter—I've got faith in Him, faith in—in the Governor—He won't fail. *(She continues to move her lips in prayer.)*

(Rebecca rushes back to the window as new sounds of wagon wheels are heard.)

HESTER: *(at window):* Still coming!

REBECCA: Why don't Tom come back? Why don't he hurry?

HESTER: Hush, chile! He ain't had time yet.

PAULINE *(breaks out in an audible prayer)*: Lord Jesus, I know I've sinned against your holy law, but you did forgive me and let me hold up my head again. Help me again, dear Jesus—help me to save my innocent child—him who never done no wrong—Save him, Lord—Let his father—*(She stops and looks around at the two women, then cautiously speaks.)* You understand all I mean, sweet Jesus—come down and rise with this wild mob tonight—pour your love into their wicked hearts—Lord, Lord, hear my prayer.

HESTER *(at window)*: Do Lord—hear.

PAULINE *(restlessly looking toward the others)*: Any sight of Tom yet—

REBECCA: No, Ma—I don't see him nowhere yet.

HESTER: Give him time—

PAULINE: Time! Time! It'll be too late reckly—too late—*(She sobs, her head lifted, listening.)* What that?

HESTER *(peers out and listens)*: What?

PAULINE: The sound of many feet I hear.

REBECCA *(looks out interestingly)*: I see 'em—I see 'em—wait wait—Ma! Ma! *(hysterically)* It's the state troops—the Guards—it's the Guard, Ma—they's coming—Look, Miss Hester!

HESTER: They sure is, Jesus—sure as I'm born—them military—they's come—come to save him.

REBECCA: And yonder's Tom at the gate—he's coming.

DR. GREY *(rushing in as the others look at him in amazement)*: He's saved, Miss Waters, saved. Did the Governor send the troops?

Curtain

*And Yet They Paused**

A ONE-ACT PLAY IN FOUR SCENES

(1938)

Characters:

REVEREND TIMOTHY JACKSON
DEACON BROWN
FIRST SISTER
JOE DANIELS, *Victim*
BOY
HENRY WILLIAMS, *Delegate*
ELDER, *Jasper Greene*
REPORTER
GUARD
TELEGRAPH BOY
SENATOR
ENSEMBLE—CHURCH GROUP—SENATE GROUP

SCENE I

Time:
Early afternoon

Place:
Mississippi

Setting:
Interior of small, unpretentious church. Pulpit stage left, Bible open on altar. Three windows stage up. Double door stage right. Benches lined to within

* In her "Catalogue" Johnson lists the title as "And Still They Paused."

six feet of pulpit. Oil chandelier hanging from center of church. Deacon's chair left stage front.

Scene opens with Reverend Jackson and Deacon Brown busying themselves about the preliminaries of the meeting.

Note: Scenes 2 and 4 can be arranged in one minute by simply dropping a curtain or sheet down in front of church scene which will make the long Hall scene for Congress with door at one end and open hall corridor from other end.

REVEREND JACKSON *(looking at his watch):* 'Most time for the meeting to start by my watch. Folks ought to be here by now—Eh Deacon?

DEACON BROWN: Oh you know how 'tis with our folks, they're always late.

REVEREND JACKSON: But this ain't no time for foolin' around.

DEACON BROWN: Ain't it de truth—Rev?

REVEREND JACKSON: I'm sure glad we sent us a delegate on up to Washington to hear them Senators pass that bill.

DEACON BROWN: And we couldn't of picked out no better young feller than Henry Williams. He's got plenty of schoolin'. He'll get the news.

REVEREND JACKSON: Yes, Praise the Lawd! And it's none too soon. We sure need it.

(Sisters and Brothers start to come in. Business of greeting between them. Reverend Jackson goes to pulpit, clears his throat.)

REVEREND JACKSON: Let's begin this meeting singing that rousing song "Walls of Jericho." Sing it like you mean it. Because we sure are trying to pull down that wall of hatred that's got us all shut away from our rights.

(Chorus of Amen, Amen. Congregation sings Jericho. *Few more brothers and sisters straggle in, as they seat themselves, a sister stands.)*

SISTER 1: Reverend Jackson, I think it's my duty to report what I just heard. Something that just happened downtown. Since we're here praying for the bill that's gonna stop all this lynchin'.

REVEREND JACKSON: Speak on Sister.

SISTER 1: You know that young Joe Daniels that they beat and drove out of town for bootlegging?

(VOICE: *Yes, sister, we knows him.*)

SISTER 2: He oughta knowed they don't 'low no colored folks do no bootleggin' down here. That's white folks' business.

(VOICE IN MEETING FROM CORNER: *Dat's so Sister.*)

SISTER 1: Well, it 'pears like de white store keeper on the hill was killed last night and dey took up Joe Daniels on suspect.

REVEREND JACKSON: You don't say.

BROTHER 1: He sure ought'n come back. He might'a knowned these white folks would pin sumpn' on him.

SISTER 2: Yes, and the white folks already started to collect 'round the corners now. Putting their heads together and actin' 'spicious. I thought you ought know.

BROTHER 2: *(another late comer)* Yes Reverend Jackson, that's so and what's more, they're gone to round up the store keeper's kin-folks. Looks mighty bad!

(low murmurs among the members)

(Reverend Jackson lifts his arms to quiet the members)

REVEREND JACKSON: Brothers and Sisters, let us be calm. Don't you know these white folks won't make no move to stir up trouble while Congress is sittin' right now, trying to put a stop to this very thing! What we's got to do is to pray that these men see the light and have strength to do their duty and pass this just law that will lead us out "of our Egyptland." Let us pray.

(with bowed heads, the members begin to softly hum "Go Down Moses" throughout the Reverend's prayer)

REVEREND JACKSON: Oh Lawd, you know our hearts, you know our hopes—you know our down-sitting and our uprising. Like stumbling pilgrims trying to make our way through these dark shadows on and up to the precious light of day. You know Lawd, how long we've been in these low vales of sorrow. Dear Father, let the glory of your infinite love shine into the hearts of the men that make the laws and guide them to lift the heavy yoke that bows their brothers to the dust!

(Curtain)

SCENE 2

Time:
Mid-afternoon

Setting:
Outside the door of Congress. White guard stands beside double door stage left. Behind the closed doors, the murmurs of voices are occasionally heard. A curtain rises, three colored men walk on stage and approach guard at door.

GUARD: You can't go in, the gallery is packed.
WILLIAMS: We can listen here, can't we?
GUARD: Sure, that's all right—it's not permitted, but I guess you can this time. You can't block the door though. Two of you better stand to one side.
REPORTER: Maybe I can hear it best and tell you two.

(Other two nod in agreement and wave him to go ahead. The two men stand a move away from the door and reporter stands with ear at door listening. After a short pause during which loud noises of discussions are heard)

REPORTER *(to other two)*: They're arguing about the Fourteenth Amendment.

(then after another pause)

REPORTER: Now they're callin' the roll. *(pause)* Now they're saying they ain't got a quorum.
WILLIAMS: But you know they have. They've been here day after day and keep on saying they ain't got a quorum. You know they're playing for time.
ELDER: Of course, stallin'—

(continued uproar from behind doors)

WILLIAMS: What are they doing now?

REPORTER: Just the same handful of crackers holding out so's the bill can't be passed. They know what side their bread is buttered on. They want to come back to Congress—they know what they're doing!

WILLIAMS: It's enough to make a man's blood boil—having to stand here helpless while other men fight your battles.

ELDER: No truer words were ever spoken. I know I get so tired of waiting outside of doors, always outside waiting, but waiting is our part to do now—We mustn't forget the good men who long ago fought our battles behind closed doors too—Lincoln and Brown and a host of others fought, bled and died for this very hour, so have patience my son.

WILLIAMS: But I'm tired, tired of just waiting.

REPORTER *(Gestures to the two)*: They're trying something else—

(general uproar attending dismissal of meeting)

REPORTER *(continuing)*: They're breaking up now—calling a recess—they're going to have a night session.

ELDER *(shoulders sagging listlessly)*: Well we better snatch a cup of coffee too, over to the Union Station and then hurry back.

REPORTER: You two go. I better hang around and see what news I can pick up. It's a sin and a shame.

WILLIAMS *(bitterly)*: They don't want to finish. They want to keep us on the cross! I just can't see how men with any spark of human feeling, regardless of racial differences, can dilly-dally, while the very life-blood of a people hangs in the balance.

(walks dejectedly off stage)

(Curtain)

[In a slightly different version of the play, Williams' speech is as follows:

WILLIAMS: Playing around—stalling—trying to keep us on the cross. I can't see where their sense of justice is but I'm game. I'll stick to my guns and will fight this thing out if it takes eternity!]

(Curtain)

SCENE 3

Setting:

Same as Scene 1

Time:

Dusk

REVEREND JACKSON: Better light the lamp Deacon—it's getting dark and we are going to stay right here like "Wrestling Jacob" until the good word comes from Washington City that this Lynching Bill is passed—

(shouts of "Amen," "Praise the Lawd," etc. from the members)

(Deacon rises and lights the oil chandelier hanging in the center of church)

DEACON: Yes, Reverend—it sho is getting dark fast, clouding up like rain too.

REVEREND JACKSON: It surely is, but let us keep in good spirits and don't get weary—*(starts singing as he walks up and down the platform waving his arms)*

(Deacon sings and members join in)

Sisters don't get weary
Sisters don't get weary
Sisters don't get weary
For the work is 'most done

Brothers don't get weary
Brothers don't get weary
Brothers don't get weary
For the work is 'most done

(The last line of the song is interrupted by the sudden entrance of a young boy who pauses breathlessly inside of doorway and pants.)

BOY: They got Joe Daniels! *(He rushes to pulpit gesticulating as a few members rise to their feet in panic)* They put him on a school bus and they coming this way. Crowds of 'em is coming along with it. They're goin' to lynch him!

(a sister's voice heard hysterically "Jesus God!")

(Reverend stands with face uplifted and lips moving in silent prayer as boy dashes to nearest window and gasps)

BOY: They're coming! I see the torches 'round the bend.

(Member's voice shouts "Put out the lights!" In the meanwhile, a few members have moved over and huddled about the windows and peering surreptitiously out. A deathly silence pervades the church. Through the stillness a faint sound of the approaching mob is heard which gradually grows louder and louder until it seems abreast of the church when it becomes a roar. From outside, loud and angry voices piercing the hush of the church. "Kill him! Kill the Nigger," "the black so and so" among epithets and then, "I didn't do it, I ain't guilty! God knows I ain't guilty!" They go on past. The noise becomes less distinct as the mob ascends the hill a short distance beyond the church. Subdued murmurs in church as they listen.)

BOY: Look they's on top of Lynchin' Hill now!
SISTER: They's draggin' him! They must be chaining him to that old pine tree!

(members grunt sympathetically)

BROTHER: They're tearin' his clothes off of him! They're kicking him! They're beating him!

(voices of members—"Merciful Lawd—Poor boy!")

SISTER: What's the flame they got in their hands? Ain't no torch!
BOY *(frantically explodes)*: My GOD! It's a blow torch!

(An agonizing scream from outside. The members in church answer with a moan. A second scream, louder than the first is heard. Members begin to rock and moan.)

BOY: They're blowin' holes in him.

(Voice of member "Oh Lawd, how long?" A sudden red glow of fire illuminates the windows. Another wild scream from outside. Hilarious rejoicing of mob on hill outside, pierces the night.)

OLD BROTHER: They's through. They's burnin' him up. They's sot fire to him.

(A low chant of sorrow broken by occasional sound of feminine weeping. A clap of thunder is heard. Woman's voice plaintively heard "Lawd, take him in your arms!" A second clap of thunder, the sound of quick and sudden rain. Woman's voice from near window, "It rains!" Reverend Jackson, who has been standing in the same spot throughout the lynching episode, speaks.)

REVEREND JACKSON: The angels weep. *(pause)* *(He begins to pray)* Oh Merciful Lawd, forgive me if I sin in thy sight, but Father, I humbly pray that you sear the heart and conscience of these white people as they have seared the flesh of our brother and help us all to walk humbly and justly before Thee.

(Curtain)

SCENE 4

Setting:

Same as Scene 2

Time:

Night (stage lighted from above)

Senate has resumed session. Reporter again at door listening—Elder and Williams to one side as before.

WILLIAMS *(To Elder)*: Think they're going to pass it tonight?

ELDER: God knows we can just hope and pray.

(sounds of uproar and a gavel rapping is heard from inside of doors)

REPORTER *(turning to the two waiting men)*: They're at it again—playing ball with each other—having a good time.

ELDER: Ain't it a shame—How long, Jesus, how long?

WILLIAMS: It's enough to make a man doubt there is a God.

ELDER *(chidingly)*: Don't say that son. It seems dark, I know, but God reigns. Right's going to triumph.

(noise of laughter and mingled voices from within)

WILLIAMS *(to reporter)*: What's going on now?

REPORTER *(wearily):* Same thing—same old thing, filibustering—just stalling and stalling.

WILLIAMS *(doubling up his fist with restrained emotions):* What will I wire the folks back home? God! This awful strain.

(Telegraph boy comes hurriedly down the hall and shows telegraph to guard, who lets him pass. Unnoticed to the guard, the telegraph boy leaves the door partly open and the reporter presses forward curiously to see what it is about.)

(Excited voices can be heard more distinctly now. The rapping of the gavel restores quiet, then a voice issues loud and clear.)

"Mr. Speaker, *(pause)* may I have the floor?"

SENATOR: I have just received a telegraph that I feel affects us all—while we have been idly arguing here, in meaningless delay, another atrocious lynching has occurred down in Mississippi. Gentlemen—this sin is upon our heads! This blood upon our hands! We can hesitate no longer. This bill *must be passed!*

(At close of speech, reporter dashes from stage. Williams stands for a moment stunned—breaks down, then covers his face with his hands. Elder puts arm around Williams's shoulder patting him on the back paternally as the two walk slowly off the stage while the curtain descends.)

(Finis)

[Alternate ending:]

WILLIAMS (*stands for a moment as if stunned. Then he squares his shoulders, clamps his teeth together. To Elder*): "Must be passed" he said, "must be passed"—good, and I answer back with every beat of my pounding heart, yes, yes, fight on and we will leave no stone unturned; the battle is on, it will be passed?[!][*]

(Finis)

---

* Note: In a 25 January 1938 letter to Miss Juanita Jackson (NAACP staff) Johnson wrote: "I notice the last punctuation mark in the play is a question mark. Of course that should not be. . . . So please change that and look it over carefully for any other foolish error." Although Johnson did not specify a new punctuation mark it is reasonable to assume she meant an exclamation point.

Johnson supplied the words to the songs "Sisters Don't Get Weary," "Walls of Jericho," and "Go Down Moses," all of which appear in this volume at the end of *A Bill To Be Passed.*

A Bill to Be Passed

A ONE-ACT PLAY IN FOUR SCENES

(1938)

Characters:

REVEREND TIMOTHY JACKSON
DEACON BROWN
FIRST SISTER
JOE DANIELS, *Victim*
BOY
HENRY WILLIAMS, *Delegate*
ELDER, *Jasper Greene*
REPORTER
GUARD
TELEGRAPH BOY
SENATOR
ENSEMBLE—CHURCH GROUP—SENATE GROUP

SCENE 1

Time:
Early afternoon

Place:
Mississippi

Setting:
Interior of small, unpretentious church. Pulpit stage left, Bible open on altar. Three windows stage up. Double door stage right. Benches lined to within six feet of pulpit. Oil chandelier hanging from center of church. Deacon's chair left stage front. Scene opens with Reverend Jackson and Deacon Brown busying themselves about the preliminaries of the meeting.

Note: Scenes 2 and 4 can be arranged in one minute by simply dropping a curtain or sheet down in front of church scene which will make the long hall scene for Congress with door at one end and open hall corridor from other end.

REVEREND JACKSON *(looking at his watch):* 'Most time for the meeting to start by my watch. Folks ought to be here by now—Eh Deacon?

DEACON BROWN: Oh you know how 'tis with our folks—they're always late.

REVEREND JACKSON: But this ain't no time for foolin' around.

DEACON BROWN: Ain't it de truth—Rev?

REVEREND JACKSON: I'm sure glad we sent us a delegate on up to Washington to hear them Senators pass that bill.

DEACON BROWN: And we couldn't of picked out no better young feller than Henry Williams. He's got plenty of schoolin'. He'll get the news.

REVEREND JACKSON: Yes, Praise the Lawd! And it's none too soon. We sure need it.

(Sisters and Brothers start to come in. Business of greeting between them. Reverend Jackson goes to pulpit, clears his throat.)

REVEREND JACKSON: Let's begin this meeting singing that rousing song "Walls of Jericho." Sing it like you mean it. Because we sure are trying to pull down that wall of hatred that's got us all shut away from our rights.

(Chorus of Amen, Amen. Congregation sings Jericho. *Few more brothers and sisters straggle in, as they seat themselves, a sister stands.)*

SISTER 1: Reverend Jackson, I think it's my duty to report what I just heard. Something that just happened downtown. Since we're here praying for the bill that's gonna stop all this lynchin'.

REVEREND JACKSON: Speak on Sister.

SISTER 1: You know that young Joe Daniels that they beat and drove out of town for bootlegging?

(VOICE: Yes, sister, we knows him.)

SISTER 2: He oughta knowed they don't 'low no colored folks do no bootleggin' down here. That's white folks' business.

(VOICE IN MEETING FROM CORNER: *Dat's so Sister.*)

SISTER 1: Well, it 'pears like de white store keeper on the hill was killed last night and dey took up Joe Daniels on suspect.

REVEREND JACKSON: You don't say.

BROTHER 1: He sure ought'ner come back. He might'a knowned these white folks would pin sumpn' on him.

SISTER 2: Yes, and the white folks already started to collect 'round the corners now. Putting their heads together and actin' 'spicious. I thought you ought know.

BROTHER 2 *(another late comer):* Yes Reverend Jackson, that's so and what's more, they're gone to round up the store keeper's kin-folks. Looks mighty bad!

(low murmurs among the members)

(Reverend Jackson lifts his arms to quiet the members)

REVEREND JACKSON: Brothers and Sisters, let us be calm. Don't you know these white folks won't make no move to stir up trouble while Congress is sittin' right now, trying to put a stop to this very thing! What we's got to do is to pray that these men see the light and have strength to do their duty and pass this just law that will lead us out "of our Egyptland." Let us pray.

(With bowed heads, the members begin to softly hum "Go Down Moses" throughout the Reverend's prayer)

REVEREND JACKSON: Oh Lawd, you know our hearts, you know our hopes—you know our down-sitting and our uprising. Like stumbling pilgrims trying to make our way through these dark shadows on and up to the precious light of day. You know Lawd, how long we've been in these low vales of sorrow. Dear Father, let the glory of your infinite love shine into the hearts of the men that make the laws and guide them to lift the heavy yoke that bows their brothers to the dust!

(Curtain)

SCENE 2

Time:
Mid-afternoon

Setting:
Outside the door of Congress. White guard stands beside double door stage left. Behind the closed doors, the murmurs of voices are occasionally heard. A curtain rises, three colored men walk on stage and approach guard at door.

(Note: Throughout scenes Two and Four, Williams and Elder are tense as they await the word passed on to them by the Reporter, who catches the bits of speeches and repeats them quickly and brokenly to them)

GUARD: You can't go in, the gallery is packed.
WILLIAMS: We can listen here, can't we?
GUARD: Sure, that's all right—it's not permitted, but I guess you can this time. You can't block the door though. Two of you better stand to one side.
REPORTER: Maybe I can hear it best and tell you two.

(Other two nod in agreement and wave him to go ahead. The two men move away from the door and reporter stands with ear at door listening. After a short pause during which loud noises of discussions is heard)

REPORTER *(to other two)*: They're arguing about the Fourteenth Amendment.

(then after another pause)

REPORTER: Now they're callin' the roll. *(pause)* Now they're saying they ain't got a quorum.
WILLIAMS: But you know they have. They've been here day after day and keep on saying they ain't got a quorum. You know they're playing for time.
ELDER: Of course, stallin'—debating—just debating—nothing!

(continued uproar from behind doors)

WILLIAMS: What are they doing now?
REPORTER: Just the same handful of crackers holding out so's the bill

can't be passed. They know what side their bread is buttered on. They want to come back to Congress—they know what they're doing!

WILLIAMS: It's enough to make a man's blood boil—having to stand here helpless while other men fight your battles.

ELDER: No truer words were ever spoken. I know I get so tired of waiting outside of doors, always outside waiting, but waiting is our part to play now—then we mustn't forget the good men who long ago fought our battles behind closed doors too—Lincoln and Brown and many more fought, bled and died for this very hour, so have patience my son.

WILLIAMS: But I'm tired, tired of just waiting.

REPORTER *(Turning to the other two)*: They've just finished reading the Bill . . . *(turns back, listens again)* One said it was unconstitutional . . . *(listens again)* They said, lynching is already decreasing and it would be a bad thing to pass a bill that's so unjust to the South . . . it would just make matters worse!

WILLIAMS: Worse! It couldn't be!

ELDER: *(shakes his head in assent)*

REPORTER: They're praising Thomas Jefferson's stand on justice when he said "I tremble for the future of my country when I remember that God is just!"

ELDER: God is just, and God is powerful!

REPORTER: Listen to this: Every time a colored man or woman is lynched or burned at stake, THE EMANCIPATION PROCLAMATION HAS BEEN SUSPENDED.

WILLIAMS: True.

ELDER: My Lord, how long . . .

REPORTER: Five-sixths of the men lynched were not even charged with rape . . .

WILLIAMS: Of course they weren't . . . the whole world knows that.

REPORTER: Let us provide for the protection of innocent women, children and men even tho they be black . . .

WILLIAMS: Good! Now they're going to it!

REPORTER: I'm not a prophet nor the son of a prophet . . . this bill MAY pass the House, BUT IT WON'T PASS THE SENATE! The Administration is FOOLING the colored people . . .

ELDER: That's a terrible charge.

REPORTER: The President feels safer in the South at Warm Springs, Georgia, than at any other place in the Nation . . .

WILLIAMS: Fool talk! . . . Is the President a black man?

REPORTER: If this bill becomes a law, there will be ten times as many lynchings. The Negroes will be unmanageable and I only pray that for the protection of the South, the Ku Klux shall not be forced to ride again!

ELDER: What a prospect . . .

(commotion heard from within of rising and walking)

REPORTER: They're adjourning for a recess.

WILLIAMS: Let's walk outside and get a breath of God's free, pure air.

REPORTER: You two go ahead. I'll hang around here and pick up some more news.

ELDER: Yes, let us walk and pray my son . . .

(End of Scene)

SCENE 3

Time:

Dusk

Setting:

Same as Scene 1.

REVEREND JACKSON: Better light the lamp, Deacon—it's getting dark and we are going to stay right here like "Wrestling Jacob" until the good word comes from Washington City that this Lynching Bill is passed.

(shouts of "Amen," "Praise the Lawd"—etc. from the members)

(Deacon rises and lights the oil chandelier hanging in the center of church.)

DEACON: Yes, Reverend, it sho is getting dark fast, clouding up like rain too.

REVEREND JACKSON: It surely is, but let us keep in good spirits and don't get weary—

(starts singing as he walks up and down the platform, waving his arms)

(Deacon sings and Members join in)

Sisters don't get weary
Sisters don't get weary
Sisters don't get weary
For the work is 'most done.

REVEREND JACKSON: Come on, sing like you feel it.
(singing continues)

Brothers don't get weary
Brothers don't get weary
Brothers don't get weary
For the work is 'most done.

(The last line of song is interrupted by the sudden entrance of a young boy who pauses breathlessly inside of doorway and pants.)

BOY: They got Joe Daniels! *(He rushes to pulpit gesticulating as a few members rise to their feet in panic.)* They put him in a school bus and they's coming this way. A great big crowd is coming along with it. They goin' to lynch him!

(a sister's voice heard hysterically "Jesus God!")

(Reverend stands with face uplifted and lips moving in silent prayer. The boy dashes to nearest window and gasps.)

BOY: They're coming! I see the torches 'round the bend!

(Member's voice shouts "Put out the lights." In the meanwhile, a few members have moved over and huddled about the windows and peering surreptitiously out. A deathly silence pervades the church. Through the stillness, a faint sound of the approaching mob is heard which gradually grows louder and louder until it seems abreast of the church and then it becomes a roar. From outside, loud and angry voices piercing the hush of the church. "Kill him! Kill the Nigger," "the black so and so" among other epithets and then, "I didn't do it, I ain't guilty! God knows I ain't guilty!" They go on past. The noise becomes less distinct as the mob ascends the hill a short distance be-

yond the church. Subdued murmurs in the church for a short while as they listen.)

BOY: Look, they's on top of Lynchin' Hill now!

SISTER: They's dragging him! They must be chaining him to that old pine tree!

(members grunt agonizingly)

BROTHER: They're tearin' his clothes off of him! They're kicking him! They're beating him!

(voices of members—"Merciful Lawd—Poor boy!")

SISTER: What's that flame they got in their hands? Ain't no torch!

BOY *(frantically exclaims)*: My God! It's a blow torch!

(An agonizing scream from outside. The members in church answer with a moan. A second scream, louder than the first is heard. Members begin to rock and moan.)

BOY: They're blowin' holes in him!

(Voice of member "Oh Lawd, how long?" A sudden red glow of fire illuminates the windows. Another wild scream from outside. Hilarious rejoicing of mob on hill outside, pierces the night.)

OLD BROTHER: They's through. They's burning him up. They sot fire to him.

(A low chant of sorrow broken by occasional sound of feminine weeping. Clap of thunder is heard. Woman's voice plaintively raised, "Lawd, take him in your arms." A second clap of thunder followed by the sound of quick, sudden rain. Woman's voice from near window, "It rains!" Reverend Jackson who has been standing in the same spot throughout the lynching episode, speaks.)

REVEREND JACKSON: The angels weep. *(pause . . . He begins praying)* Oh Merciful Lawd, forgive me if I sin in thy sight, but Father, I humbly pray that you sear the heart and conscience of these white people as they have seared the flesh of our brother, and Lawd, help us all to walk humbly and justly before Thee, Amen.)

(End of Scene)

SCENE 4

Time:

Night (stage lighted from above)

Setting:

Same as Scene 2

Congress has resumed session. Reporter again at door listening—Elder and Williams to one side as before)

WILLIAMS *(to Elder)*: Think they're going to pass it tonight?
ELDER: God knows we can just hope and pray.

(sounds of uproar and a gavel rapping is heard from inside of door)

REPORTER *(turning to the two waiting men)*: They're at it again—playing ball with each other—having a good time.
ELDER: Ain't it a shame—How long, Jesus?
WILLIAMS: It's enough to make a man doubt there is a God.
ELDER *(chidingly)*: Don't say that son. It seems dark, I know, but God reigns. Right's going to triumph.

(noise of laughter and mingled voices from within)

WILLIAMS *(doubling up his fist with restrained emotions)*: What will I wire the folks back home? God! This awful strain.

(Telegraph boy comes hurriedly down the hall and shows telegram to guard, who lets him pass. Unnoticed to the guard, the telegraph boy leaves the door partly open and the reporter presses forward curiously to see what it is about.)

(Excited voices can be heard more distinctly now. The rapping of the gavel restores quiet, then a voice issues loud and clear.)

CONGRESSMAN: Mr. Speaker. *(pause)* May I have the floor? I have just received a telegram that I feel affects us all. While we have been idly arguing here in meaningless delay, another atrocious lynching has occurred down in Mississippi. Gentlemen, this sin is upon our heads! This blood upon our hands! We can hesitate no longer. This bill MUST BE PASSED!

GUARD: Just one of you at the door, please.

(Williams and Elder stand to one side and the Reporter resumes his watch at the door)

WILLIAMS: I'd give anything to be in there now.
ELDER: Things are going to happen, I feel it in my bones.
WILLIAMS: It's time . . . Another lynching . . . while they talk, talk, talk!

(sounds of wild applause from within)

REPORTER: A Southerner said "every drop of my blood revolts against lynching. *You* sold the slaves to us! *You* stole them out of Africa and sold them to us, and *we're* paying the price!
ELDER: We're paying one too . . .
REPORTER: One said "The bill is constitutional and OUGHT to be passed by Congress . . .
WILLIAMS: That's talking . . .
REPORTER: A man from Alabama said: "I'm going to vote for it!"
ELDER: Hear that . . .
REPORTER: I'm Irish . . . Next to the love of God, we believe in law and order, with EQUAL JUSTICE TO ALL . . .
WILLIAMS: Don't miss any of that . . .
REPORTER *(listening, then loud applause is heard):* I PROPHESY that 275 votes will show that the Seventy-Fifth Congress answers this challenge—showing that we love Democracy and that we will protect every man, woman and child REGARDLESS OF CREED OR COLOR BY PASSING THIS ANTI-LYNCHING BILL!
WILLIAMS: A Daniel at last . . .
ELDER: The pure in heart . . .
REPORTER *(turns from door with look of disapproval on his face):* One says this bill is meant to break the spirit of the white South—fosters social equality—mongrelizes them.
WILLIAMS: That's silly. Who's worrying about social equality? We're battling for the right to live . . .
ELDER: They always hide behind that smoke screen . . .
REPORTER: Says, this bill will encourage Negroes to commit rape . . .
WILLIAMS: Crazy . . .
REPORTER: Listen to this. No matter where the poor Negro goes, he

is not given a fair deal by any class of people in the United States! If clergymen would preach the BROTHERHOOD OF MAN INSTEAD OF HATRED, ALL WOULD BE WELL BOTH WITH OUR SOULS AND WITH OUR COUNTRY!

ELDER: That's the doctrine . . . LOVE!

WILLIAMS: Preachers could help the world so. If they would . . .

(loud applause sounds from behind doors)

REPORTER *(looking pleased):* I don't think this is the most perfect bill, nor the best bill, but it is a definite and truthful expression of this Congress against mob rule, and FOR THAT REASON, I intend to vote for it.

WILLIAMS: Seems like things are breaking for us.

ELDER: It's a long lane . . .

REPORTER: One said, "the bill was conceived in prejudice and born in demagogy" then he started about the State's rights . . .

WILLIAMS: Don't miss it . . .

ELDER: Yes, get it all . . .

REPORTER: I don't regard lynching as a racial problem, it's an American problem and should be passed on that light . . . then he talked about lynching so many innocent men . . .

(loud applause is heard from behind doors)

REPORTER: Let's vote according to our conscience, as we were led to see the right from our mother's knee . . . I NEVER HATED TO VOTE FOR A BILL AS FOR THIS ONE, because of the bitterness it has caused, BUT, I'LL VOTE FOR IT . . . I MUST!!

WILLIAMS: Wonderful, That was a truly great soul . . .

ELDER: Sounds like they're voting now.

WILLIAMS: I believe so.

(Both men are very tense) (Wild applause is heard)

REPORTER *(turns a beaming face to them):* It's passed! It's Passed!!

ELDER: Glory hallelujah . . .

WILLIAMS: Thank God . . . let me send that telegram to the church back home. Then ON TO THE SENATE!!!

(End)

Songs

Chorus

Sisters don't get weary
Sisters don't get weary
Sisters don't get weary
For the work is 'most done

First Verse

The Lord has promised good to me
The work is 'most done
I'll wait right here for victory
The work is 'most done

Chorus

Brothers don't get weary
Brothers don't get weary
Brothers don't get weary
For the work is 'most done

Second Verse

My troubles all will soon be o'er
The work is 'most done
I'll wait for victory is sure
The work is 'most done

Joshua fought the battle of Jericho
Joshua fought the battle of Jericho   Jericho   Jericho
And the walls came tumblin' down
Oh
Joshua fought the battle of Jericho
Joshua fought the battle of Jericho   Jericho   Jericho
And the walls came tumblin' down

Ole Moses went down in Egyptland
Let my people go
Oppressed so hard they could not stand
Let my people go
Go down Moses
Way down in Egyptland
Tell ole pharaoh
To let my people go

Envoy

So ended the activities on the Anti-Lynching Bill. TIME MARCHES ON!! And with it, the Bill has moved along its hindered way through the toils of the Senate, to this avail:

[In the NAACP Papers, Library of Congress, Johnson's script for A BILL TO BE PASSED was attached to the following skit, KILL THAT BILL, written by Robert E. Williams of the NAACP, Cleveland Ohio chapter. Since Johnson added the above speech for the ENVOY, knowing full well her play could be used in conjunction with other anti-lynching scripts, KILL THAT BILL is included in this collection.]

Kill That Bill!

A DRAMATIC SKIT PORTRAYING THE SIX-WEEK FILIBUSTER OF SOUTHERN SENATORS AGAINST THE WAGNER-VAN NUYS ANTI-LYNCHING BILL

(1938)

Robert E. Williams

Scene:

Two or more rows of chairs arranged on the platform in a semi-circle facing a large chair raised on a dais, somewhat in the manner of the Senate chamber. Any number may be used. This represents a portion of the United States Senate in session. Two women should be included in the group.

To the extreme left of the group, facing them, stands a man who represents Walter White, executive secretary of the N.A.A.C.P. At all times he seems extremely interested and affected by the actions and speeches in the Senate. Just in back of him, and closer to the Senate group, a man reclines in a chair, his head resting on his hand, his arm propped on the arm of the chair. He represents Senator Wagner, who is ill during the filibuster.

To the extreme right of the group, half facing both senators and audience, sits a man at a small table on which may be a microphone. He is a news commentator. He reads from notes lying on the table in front of him. He paints a word picture of the Senate filibuster while the senators stand (alternately) and make dramatic gestures during the entire presentation, especially whenever the commentator refers directly to the filibuster. Always exaggerate facial expressions and attempt to portray vividly everything related by the commentator.

When spoken lines are uttered, make them extremely loud and clear and emphatic.

Note: Someone may sit in front of senators with a large calendar of 1938 and gradually lift off sheet after sheet—calendar facing audience—through January and February to the 11th month.

COMMENTATOR: Good evening, ladies and gentlemen! The Youth Council of the Cleveland Branch of the National Association for the Advancement of Colored People brings to you the truth behind the scenes of the great anti-lynching bill filibuster. Everyone knows of the Wagner-Van Nuys Anti-Lynching Bill. The Congressional Record refers to it as "a bill for the prevention of and punishment for lynching," a bill to assure persons within the jurisdiction of every state, the equal protection of the laws, and to punish the crime of lynching.

That's the purpose of the bill, pure and simple. Anything wrong with it? It sounds all right to me. It sounded all right to millions of law-abiding, peace-loving citizens. It sounded all right to scores and scores of organizations of intelligent and progressive Americans, for Congress has been literally flooded with telegrams, resolutions, petitions, letters and post cards, not only requesting, but *demanding* passage of this bill by legislation without delay!

"But wait!" cried Senator Borah, way back in December—

(a senator representing Borah is now standing)

BORAH: Kill that bill! It's unconstitutional!

COMMENTATOR: Good old, big-hearted Borah, the gentleman from Idaho wants to do a favor to the U.S. Supreme Court by sparing them their right to pass on the constitutionality of the bill when it becomes a law. So it isn't the principle of the thing with Mr. Borah, who has never been lynched—*it's the constitutionality of the thing!*

(all senators get up alternately, gesticulate vehemently and sit down, repeating from time to time, looking at each other politely as they offer others the opportunity to rise and continue the debate)

COMMENTATOR: And so, ladies and gentlemen, the filibuster continued during December; during January (they start the New Year *right)* for Senator Ellender of Louisiana has proclaimed *(pardon his southern accent)* "Kill that Bill!"—

SENATOR ELLENDER: We don't need no anti-lynch bill! Only eight lynchings in 1937—that's a record low mark!

COMMENTATOR: *Only* eight human beings, *all* of whom might have been innocent, to die ghastly deaths, victims of vicious mobs, ladies and gentlemen, victims of rope and faggot—only eight! Were their lives worth saving? What if only *one* of them had been *you*, kind senator from Louisiana. Ah yes, what if it had! And so, time staggers on!

(senators express sleepiness and lack of attention, yawning, stretching, and rising as though speaking) Some say:

VARIOUS SENATORS: The south understands the Negro. We love the Negro! We are his best friends! *(they repeat these statements)*

COMMENTATOR: But eight Negroes died horribly in the south last year. The south that loves and understands them did not come to their rescue! It did not even give them a chance!

ELLENDER: This is more than the problem of lynching—it is a social problem!

COMMENTATOR: Indeed, the Senator from Louisiana said something—it *is* indeed a social problem! And that is why the south is fighting against the anti-lynching bill. They label it as coming from only a small group of Negro politicians. They fear it may bolster the morale of the southern Negro—make him feel like a human being instead of an animal.

ELLENDER: We keep the Negro in the south in his place. He is polite by instinct. He is taught from childhood to respect the whites.

ANY SENATOR JUMPS UP: Why the next thing you know they'll be asking for the right to vote!

WOMAN SENATOR *(indignantly)*: How perfectly ridiculous! You'd think they were human!

ELLENDER: We of the south believe in white supremacy—keep races separate!

ANOTHER SENATOR: Kill that bill! The Negro thinks he may gain recognition by the passage of that bill! The moment you give them an inch, they'll take a foot!

ANOTHER SENATOR: The next thing you know, they'll try to have the marriage laws passed by the various states nullified!

ANOTHER SENATOR: It's just a group of Negro politicians. Political equality leads to social equality, and social equality eventually will spell the decay and downfall of our American civilization!

COMMENTATOR: And so on, ladies and gentlemen, far into the days that come and go, they confuse a bill to protect lives against mob violence with an effort to obtain social equality or amalgamation of the races. Walter White has said, so aptly:

WALTER WHITE: I'm sick of all this poppycock about inter-marriage! It's beside the point. In one breath, they say the Negro is inferior and strut about Nordic superiority, and in the very next breath they express fear that the amalgamation of twelve million Negroes into a total population of more than *one hundred and twenty million* would cause a decay of their civilization! What powerful stuff those *inferior* Negroes must be made of!!

(Calendar pages turn occasionally)

SENATORS, ALL: The south is friendly to the colored race. We of the south realize that the colored people are our wards. The Negro is in the south to stay! We are kind to Negroes. This is a social problem. Kill that bill! Do not hurl an insult at the south. Kill that bill! I demand a roll call. I should like to have the floor again tomorrow morning. Gentlemen, may I read something to you? Where is everybody? I demand a roll call. I announce that Senator Wagner is ill. I should like to review some of my remarks.

COMMENTATOR: All because, as the Louisiana Senator says—

ELLENDER: They are trying to eventually give the Negro social and other rights equal to those now enjoyed by the white people of this nation.

WALTER WHITE: Eight persons met violent deaths due to mob violence last year!

COMMENTATOR: And so on, *endlessly,* ladies and gentlemen, these southern gentlemen have unlimited energy and have withstood every effort to dislodge them. It is not they who are tired, but the others, and there is an increasing fear that the American people may relax in their demands for the sponsors of the bill to stand by and fight for its passage.

BILBO, MISSISSIPPI SENATOR *(viciously):* Mr. President, this is a Negro conglomeration talking to the Senate. Kill that bill! In New York, in Chicago, even here in Washington, we will find nine out of ten of the mulattoes, the quadroons, the octoroons, and all the rest of the mongrel breed yelling for the passage of the anti-lynching bill.

OTHER SENATORS: Kill that bill! I move to adjourn! They'll want social equality next! I announce that Senator Wagner is ill.

BILBO: Mississippi has been good to the Negro.

COMMENTATOR: So, good, in fact, Mr. Bilbo, that at Duck Hill, Mississippi, last year two Negroes were tied to posts and their bodies *bored through* with a flaming blow torch, to record the most bestial murders of recent times!

BILBO: The Negro is not free, nor will he be free until several hundred years from now—oh, maybe, thousands from now.

WALTER WHITE: What about the anti-lynching bill?

BILBO: The Negroes want to be segregated. Why not send 'em back to Africa, or segregate 'em in some chosen territory where they can have their own everything?

OTHER SENATORS: Where is Wagner? I announce that the gentleman from New York is ill.

BILBO: We moved the Indians, tribe by tribe, from one part of the country to another. Why can't we move the Negro?

WALTER WHITE *(to audience):* And while the American people stand by, this handful of southern hell-raisers are burning up the taxpayers money at the rate of $8,000 *per day.* Hundreds of pages of the Congressional Record are filled with the kind of low-grade arguments you have just witnessed. Hundreds of pages at $55 per page, while they frustrate the ends of justice and other pending legislation of vital importance to this nation. Senator Wagner has been ill during much of the filibuster—only recently has he arisen from a sick bed to say . . .

(form of Wagner rises to firm sitting position, fist raised)

WAGNER: I will not deviate one inch! I am in the fight to stay!

COMMENTATOR: From a sick bed, Wagner responds to the call—the needs of the people he represents.

WAGNER: I will use every ounce of strength to prevent anything else displacing this bill.

WALTER WHITE *(to audience):* But what about you? You have helped—

you have done your part. But you must do more! You, too, must exert every ounce of strength—use every power at your command to help pass this bill. You can't do too much, nor too little. The overwhelming strength of numbers is vitally necessary!

COMMENTATOR: And remember, ladies and gentlemen, that eight persons died horrible deaths due to mob violence and we cannot relent—we must not relax until the barbaric crime of lynching in America is completely eradicated and this country can raise its head proudly among the civilized nations of the world!

(End)

Editor's Note: The United States Senate, on June 13, 2005 and in the presence of nearly 200 descendents of lynching victims, apologized for never having passed any anti-lynching legislation despite the hundreds of bills that were introduced. This historic apology coincides with the recent recognition of Georgia Douglas Johnson as the leading anti-lynching playwright. Johnson's plays attest to her timely and prolonged resistance to mob murder of Black Americans and her solidarity with all artists and activists who participated in the anti-lynching struggle.

Credits

"Brotherhood Marching Song" music and lyrics on page 40 reprinted from the Glenn Carrington Papers, Manuscripts, Archives, and Rare Books Division, Schomburg Center for Research in Black Culture, the New York Public Library, Astor, Lenox and Tilden Foundations.

Photos on pages 1, 2 and 3 of the photo gallery are reprinted with permission of the Moorland-Spingarn Research Center of Howard University.

Photo on the bottom of page 3 of the photo gallery is reprinted with permission of the Photographs and Prints Division, Schomburg Center for Research in Black Culture, the New York Public Library, Astor, Lenox and Tilden Foundations.

Photo of Johnson with President Clement on page 4 of the photo gallery is from the *Atlanta University Bulletin* (July 1963), p. 25. Reprinted by permission of the Atlanta University Center of the Robert W. Woodruff Library.

Photo of Johnson's home on page 4 of the photo gallery by Kathy A. Perkins, and reprinted by her permission.

GEORIA DOUGLAS JOHNSON (1877–1966) wrote a substantial number of plays, only a handful of which have been recovered, but was best known for her poetry. She opened her Washington D.C. home for Saturday night literary salons, where she hosted such influential Harlem Renaissance writers as Langston Hughes, Jean Toomer, Zora Neale Hurston, and Alain Locke. Throughout her writing career she also raised two sons and held various teaching and civil service positions.

JUDITH L. STEPHENS is Professor of Humanities and Theatre at Penn State University, Schuylkill campus. She is author of scholarly articles on American and African American theater and coeditor with Kathy Perkins of *Strange Fruit: Plays on Lynching by American Women.* She is a member of the Association for Theatre in Higher Education and the Black Theatre Network, whose executive board she served from 1992 to 1998.

The University of Illinois Press
is a founding member of the
Association of American University Presses.

Composed in 10/14 Fairfield
with Fairfield display
by Jim Proefrock
at the University of Illinois Press
Designed by Paula Newcomb
Manufactured by Sheridan Books, Inc.

University of Illinois Press
1325 South Oak Street
Champaign, IL 61820-6903
www.press.uillinois.edu